SERENDIPITY

...of life and love and taxicabs and finding God in a Muskoka murder

G.A. COOPER

Benchmark Publishing & Design
251 Fairview Boulevard, Windsor Ontario N8S 3C9

Canadian Cataloguing in Publication Data

Cooper, G.A. (Gary Arthur) 1940 - 1995
Serendipity: — of life and love and taxicabs and finding God in a Muskoka murder

ISBN 1-895305-41-1

I. Title.

PS8555.O59194S47 1997 C813'9.54 C97-901228-7
PR9199.3.C6436S47 1997

Given the impossibility of consulting with Mr. Cooper during the editing process, the publishers deeply appreciate the efforts of Mark Stewart in ensuring the book would remain true to Mr. Cooper's original story and philosophy.

Cover Design by Karen Veryle Monck

Benchmark Publishing & Design
251 Fairiview Boulevard
Windsor, Ontario N8S 3C9

Printed in Windsor Ontario Canada
by Wheeler's Printing & Copying Ltd.

Serendipity:

An aptitude for making desirable discoveries by accident.

Editor's note

My moments with Gary Cooper were too few and far between. I met Gary through my wife, Margo Dimmick, who helped me edit this book. Margo's father, Gerry, was one of Gary's best friends since college — back in their socialist years at the University of Western Ontario. My father-in-law describes Gary as a self-made man. You could see that in his eyes.

We lost Gary to cancer way too soon. He died only hours before my nephew Dylan was born. I sometimes look for Gary in his eyes.

Gary's original manuscript — loosely bound in a tattered orange binder — spent most of the last few years tucked in a desk drawer at home. Serendipity seemed destined for oblivion until earlier this year, when Benchmark Publishing & Design Inc. responded to positive reader surveys and decided to put the book into print.

Working on the book gave us a chance to reflect on Gary's life, his honesty and his positive impact. Gary's words and characters helped me to understand him a little better — helped me understand some truths about myself.

The story of Serendipity Lodge is a Muskoka detour to the truth — or what there is of it. Mike Kramer, a disgruntled half-owner of a Toronto cab company, looks north to Muskoka for some answers.

Through his journey, Kramer is admonished by the words of his Masters — Berkley, Whitehead, Wordsworth and Blake. He is beleaguered by the trappings of his North American Zoo — a cheating business partner, a self-serving banker, his wayward romance and a battered conscience. Kramer discovers Serendipity Lodge by happenstance. The Lodge becomes his dream, his ship, his hideout, his headache.

Through the cryptic prophets of cottage country, Kramer learns of "God's big toe," the battlezone of secret lives and proper thoughts.

Like Mike Kramer, Gary was bound by circumstances — like a fit vessel in fog.

"Pain in this world is not death — it is life," Gary writes. "It is the living that makes martyrs of us all."

Mark Stewart

Instead of a Dedication . . .

Our birth is but a sleep and a forgetting:
The Soul that rises with us, our life's Star,
        Hath had elsewhere its setting,
                And cometh from afar:
        Not in entire forgetfulness,
        And not in utter nakedness,
But trailing clouds of glory do we come
        From God, who is our home:
Heaven lies about us in our infancy!
Shades of the prison-house begin to close
        Upon the growing Boy,
                But He
Beholds the light, and whence it flows,
        He sees it in his joy;
The Youth, who daily farther from the east
        Must travel, still is Nature's Priest,
        And by the vision splendid
        Is on his way attended;
At length the Man perceives it die away,
And fade into the light of common day.

William Wordsworth
Ode - Stanza V - 1807

Part I

The North American Zoo

I

Something invisible clung to Mike Kramer as smoke to fabric, and he was sick of it. Whatever had shielded him from it in his youth was long gone. Now, out of frustration, he fidgeted like a harassed cat.

"... and I'd like to know why three of my cars sat on the lot last night!" He shook his fist at Jack Kirkpatrick, then slammed it on the desk in front of his partner for effect. "Your cabs were out! We've been alternating for ten years; now, all of the sudden, you change the rules — one for me, two for you... one for me, three for you. What the hell is going on around here?"

Kirkpatrick wasn't ruffled. He'd expected trouble, had prepared himself to deal with it. Confidently, he leaned back in his chair and bit into his cigar. Kirkpatrick loved a good cigar, was never without one. Though he hadn't smoked a puff in his life, he enjoyed chewing them to a pulpy nub that left brown stains at the corners of his mouth. "If you spent more time here, tending to business, you'd know."

Kramer told him to skip the bullshit.

"What bullshit? I haven't seen you for three days. Hell, I haven't even had a phone call!"

There was no excuse for that, Mike agreed. He could have called, and should have. But whatever had been pestering him travelled the phone lines too. "I've got to get away."

"You and a million other poor slobs."

"You owe me a month. I'm taking it."

The cigar was getting a real workout — from one corner of Kirkpatrick's mouth to the other. He had accomplished the art of rolling it along the tracks of his lips, occasionally setting it between his teeth to force a smile. "Thanks for the notice."

"You still haven't answered my question. Why do my cars sit while yours work?"

"Seventeen was overheating... the brakes are shot on 12... 25 was odd-man-out last night." Kirkpatrick blushed, accentuating the freckles that dominated his red-haired, polka-dot complexion. He knew what was coming.

"Why would 25 be odd-man-out if I already had two cars on the lot?"

That was right, of course. From the beginning, they had agreed to alternate drivers. If, for reasons mechanical or otherwise, one had more cars left after all their drivers were assigned, his units were the first to go, should someone arrive late wanting a shift.

It was just a little thing, a very tiny crack in the dike, but No. 25 should have gone out. Their partnership had always worked because they kept it equal — from the half-share in their first taxi, to the 15 vehicles each of them now owned. And they had been successful because they liked each other. Still did, but this was their most serious confrontation.

Brains and bodies had been enough in the early days. Now it was politics and big bucks — and the stress that accompanied them — that moved the machines. Money on wheels. While their business was growing, neither of them could appreciate its value, anymore than a farmer could estimate the worth of his cows with his head tucked under their tails day and night. Characteristically, Jack Kirkpatrick was first to suspect they were near the motherlode.

He spoke seriously: "Look, Mike. The cab business has been so good to both of us. I sure got no complaints — except when my ulcers act up. But times change. Maybe a guy like you should think about gettin' out."

"You'd like that!"

"Well… in a way I would. There's things I want to do on my own — things you wouldn't have the stomach for. Surely we can work something out."

"You're the one with the bad stomach," Mike reminded him.

The sounds of horns and sirens and squealing tires on King Street reached them through the walls of Kirkpatrick's dingy office.

Speed adds beauty to the deer came too, at a pitch that only Mike Kramer heard. He plucked it out of the air, though he knew not it's origin nor it's meaning.

Speed adds beauty to the deer.

"I've got to get out of this zoo! See you in a month, Kirk." He started for the door, then came back. "I can trust you for that long. Can't I?"

"Of course. But I am a businessman, not a saint. Don't expect me to put your interests ahead of mine. I'm telling you, there are things I want to do and nobody's going to stop me. Not even you."

"I thought our interests were the same,"

"Not anymore."

"Thirty days," Mike said flatly, walking away, not stopping this time. "Thirty days."

"By the way," Kirkpatrick shouted after him. "Linda called earlier. She hasn't heard from you for three days either."

From the hallway: "Screw Linda!"

Jack Kirkpatrick rocked in his swivel chair and rolled his cigar. He stretched out and looked up at the sooty office ceiling. Listening to the sounds of his partner leaving the building, he imagined what a pleasure that would be.

Kramer cut across the lot to the gasoline pumps, glancing at his watch — 6:15 p.m. Six cars parked — three each. That's better! They wouldn't all get out, but that wasn't unusual for Monday. The regular, full-time drivers showed up early for their cars, no matter what the day, but the fast-buck, part-timers stayed away Mondays and Tuesdays. They were the ones who, by 3:30 p.m. Friday and Saturday, would be clamouring for cars and those who got them would be gone until three or four the next morning.

As Mike approached the gas-pump island, the lot boy topped off a cab and sent it out. "Hi Andy. How goes it?"

"Good, Mr. Kramer."

"That'll be the last one out today, I guess."

"Nope. Tesky phoned that he'll be late. Mr. Kirkpatrick said to give him 17."

"Why was it overheating?"

"Thermostat. It's okay now."

"What about 12? The brakes?"

"Good as new."

Kramer let it go at that. He had a couple more questions for Andy, but decided against them. "I'll be at the hotel for about an hour."

The air stunk. Lakefront smokestacks had been farting all day. As Mike crossed King Street, he breathed like a bottled creature at the holes in the lid — short, desperate breaths. Before he turned the corner, he glanced back at the lot. Tesky had just arrived — one of his best drivers, an honest, good booker. Cash packages and double fares were recorded on his trip sheet. If a fare paid in advance, his flag went down and the trip was noted (not like the others, whose trip sheets would be in direct proportion to the number of tickets they had cashed at Greenwood Racetrack). There wouldn't be much on the streets for him tonight. Not a hint of rain. Unusual for April.

Speed adds beauty to the deer.

Mike used the last short block to the hotel to ponder the strange course his life has taken.

Thirteen years ago, he was in school, driving a taxi to help with expenses. He enjoyed the freedom of that work, the melange of characters that he met, and he maintained an eclectic recollection of the best of them. By graduation, he decided to pick up a taxi license that was being sold, car and all, by a retiring owner within the huge co-operative association for which he worked. There were no savings, but with the help of relatives, he scraped together half the asking price — $ 5,249.00. He went to another young driver, Jack Kirkpatrick, for the rest. Why not? They liked each other, played cards together, even covered for each other on occasion. Kirkpatrick was a few years older, admittedly more mature; but both were enthusiastic, hard workers. Together they kept old "No. 1" moving around the clock, seven days a week. Their business grew rapidly, yet they were always careful to split everything down the middle — work, cars, expenses, profits. Everything. Not a bad investment, old No. 1. Today, taxi licences were $10,000 — if you could find one for sale.

That was the spring of '63. Now, exactly 10 years later, the bond they had kept through all that time was beginning to break. Sad... and good, if sad can be good. No. 25 was the first of it.

It wouldn't be the last.

At the polished brass handle of the bar-room door, Mike winced, perceiving the far off sirens as a banshee wail.

Not his. Not quite.

The bar phone rang. Gus, a happy bartender, with fewer hairs on his head than dimples on his cheeks and chin, plunked the phone in front of Mike Kramer, then quickly returned to his work.

"I'm not here," Mike said, loudly enough for the caller to hear.

Gus came back and reached for the receiver, but as he did, Kramer waved him away.

"Yes?"

"I thought I'd know where to find you."

"Very well, Linda, you've found me." He thought she sounded angry, but restrained, considering he had disappeared for three days.

"What happens now?"

"Our session with father Kelly. Have you forgotten? We're waiting for you."

"No I didn't forget," he lied. He had forgotten that, at 6:30 p.m. Monday, he was to be at his fiancee's Jamison Ave. apartment for special counselling in the Roman Catholic faith — object, conversion. "You both can wait. I'll be there when I'm ready."

"Please Mike."

How he dreaded those sessions. He felt admonished for days before and after each session by the wraiths of Berkley, Whitehead, Wordsworth and Blake — no wonder he forgot. They were as easy to forget as dentist appointments.

The phone went dead when he didn't respond. "Another, Gus. I'll be right back," he said, pushing the phone away as though it was diseased. Gus smiled and nodded as Mike headed for the urinals.

That was the last time they saw each other.

Before he returned to the bar, Kramer stepped outside, the murmurings behind first muffled by the closing door, then lost to wheels and horns and sharp city smells. He couldn't take much of it. When he turned to go inside, he heard: "Evenin', Mr. Kramer," and looked down.

"Jimmy! where did you come from?"

Jimmy was half a man — only because his legs were gone. He lived upon a board that rolled on casters from an abandoned bed. Life on as slab in a world of concrete, cigarette butts, protruding upper lips and gaping nostrils. With a tin cup fastened firmly to his waist, he always waited for Mike Kramer to come out. They would speak, then off he'd go, zig-zagging his way to another man who always dropped a quarter in his cup.

He looked up from his board and Mike unconsciously let his shoulders sag and bent his neck to shorten his six-foot frame.

"You growin' a moustache?"

"Thought I'd try it, Jimmy. What do you think?"

"Looks good!"

Jimmy was one of the few who knew he had a scar under his chin, deep and long, between his jawbones.

"Don't grow a beard," he said "I'd never know you."

"How come you always seem to know when I'm inside?"

"I got ways. It's a business. Just like yours. Steady customers an' all."

"If I'm a customer, what do I get for my money?"

Jimmy scratched his head. "How 'bout a smile you don't have to think twice about."

Mike felt in his pocket for a quarter.

"You got troubles tonight, Mr. Kramer?"

Mike paused for a moment. "Nah," he scoffed, dropping a piece of silver in Jimmy's cup. "Get out of here if you've got business to do."

"Thanks a million! See ya 'round."

And off he went, making ski-poles of his arms. They gave him speed and balance; they guided board and body to another swinging door. As he watched Jimmy go, Mike consciously decided not to return for his drink.

There it was again. He felt it — not a mist that he was moving though, but an ominous aura attending him, an unpleasant extension of himself. He didn't expect to escape the warning of that night by hiding in a bar.

It was there, like flies around a carcass.

So, he took to walking.

At King Street, he could see the lot again.

Still five cars. It was dark now and he walked slowly, still taking in the tainted air with guarded breaths; still searching out the reason for his restlessness; still bottled like a frog.

Father Kelly wasn't Linda's fault, he conceded as he waited for the light at University Ave. From infancy, she had been taught to think certain thoughts, to believe specific things. Nothing wrong with that.

He supposed that was the predicament of every human. Naturally, she wanted their children to share her thoughts; it would be cozy if he did too. Personally, he had no objection to becoming a proselyte Catholic, for Linda's sake... to pretending to understand for Father Kelly's sake. But the masters — the Romantics and Idealists of his youth — were kicking up one heck of a fuss, making his life plain miserable, insisting that he had compromised long enough — with Kirkpatrick, with Linda, with himself. It was time to take a stand.

A taxi cut him off before he crossed Spadina. Tesky pushed the passenger door open: "Hi boss. Kinda bad place to be walkin', doncha think?"

"Yeah, I guess so," Kramer admitted as he jumped in the cab.

They followed the cobblestones that kept the trolley tracks apart to Jamison Ave., where 10,000 people shared a few short city blocks — Mike Kramer and Linda McDermott among them. "That's a bad spot to be walkin' alone," Tesky was saying. "A guy can get himself hurt down there after dark."

"I know."

Though Tesky worked at a conversation, he could not distract his passenger from brooding. Mike didn't speak again until the cab stopped in front of Linda's apartment building. He got out and threw five dollars on the seat.

Tesky protested. Mike closed the door and walked away.

II

A door opened slowly to him and Linda stood there in soft, fine sleeping clothes. Just-brushed blonde hair fell around her face. It set her deep blue eyes to glowing. Bedtime was the only time that Linda appeared to be what she was.

She left the door open to him and walked away.

Mike stepped in and closed it after him.

"Sleeping?" he asked.

"Reading."

At least he hadn't wakened her. It was going to be difficult enough without that.

"When did Kelly leave?"

"*Father* Kelly left right after I hung up the phone. Why would he stay?"

Mike knew the feelings behind her cold defiant stare. "Hmm... I'm surprised he gave up so easily."

"I told him to go. Did you expect him to wait all night?"

"No. I guess not. And I'm glad he didn't." Mike smiled with only one side of his face. "Did you have a nice, quiet talk about me?"

"About us."

"I'll bet the old boy hasn't changed a bit since last time."

"Not a bit. Why should he?"

"You haven't either?"

"No." Linda was thinking of something. There was nothing more dangerous than giving her some time to think. He knew he was in for it, like waiting for the dentist. "At least you could have talked with him again instead of acting like a child."

"I've listened too long — 'my dear boy this'... 'my dear boy that.' You don't give a damn what I am when we're in bed."

"I care what my children will be."

There was a silence both used well until Mike broke it. "The next man may be a long time coming."

"Maybe I'll marry Maxwell. He's proposed to me twice."

"I know. I know." He knew it well indeed, for she often reminded him of that distasteful fact.

"But a man says things to his secretary that he doesn't always mean."

"He's serious." And why not? Linda was pretty, attractive, intelligent. "Why not? He's always been good to me."

"Our company, which art in heaven, hallowed be thy name. Thy kingdom come; thy will be done on earth ... *AS IT IS!*"

"But, I'd rather have you, Mike."

"For thine is the kingdom and the power and the glory forever and ever."

There was more to the debate — old points of argument reviewed, new ones introduced — all leading to the accomplishment of nothing, save the finality of their conflicting opinions. Their harsh words were more the fruit of frustration than of anger.

The talking was finished. Linda thought it best that they shouldn't see each other again and Mike agreed. She informed him that his letters, if he wrote, would be destroyed with the seal unbroken; telephone calls would end immediately upon her recognition of his voice.

"It's finished between us, Mike," she said, leaving no doubt that talk was an annoyance. "I don't need this aggravation in my life."

When suggested that she keep the ring he had given her — for pawning, throwing-in-the-river, whatever — she took it off and threw it at him, then rose from her chair, went to the door and held it open. "It's late. Please go."

The lid is off!

Frozen by disbelief, confused, afraid, he stared at the ring on the carpet at his feet. Freedom was his. The keeper was urging him to go.

"Please, Mike. It's late."

He touched her hand at the door and the feel of her took his breath away. Unemotionally, she asked what he was going to do with himself.

"I'm going away for a month. I'm very tired of this North American Zoo."

"Where?"

"Maybe visit my sister in Vancouver. Maybe just go. I haven't thought about it."

"What about your business?"

"Kirk's taking care of it."

"I don't trust him."

"Why should you care?"

"I do care, Mike. This is your choosing, not mine."

"Give my regards to Kelly... and Maxwell Taylor."

The elevator swallowed him, then spit him out again into the lobby. The moment his feet touched the sidewalk, he started missing her. Damn it! Why was it not raining? It should have been raining — this a night most foul. Instead, the tilted quarter-moon was there to frown on him — or smile, according to his shifts in mood.

Linda was probably crying by now. No... not her! She was too demure to cry. She would be busy cleaning the cage for Maxwell Taylor.

Speed adds beauty to the deer.

There would be no rain tonight, no tears to fall unless they were his own.

Mike left his apartment in darkness after he entered it. Light was no solution to his problems. This time, Linda would not be his by day or night. The unrest he felt outside and within himself would not dissipate with the sun, nor would he gain peace of mind with the flicking of a switch.

He went to the window. The cold black water of Lake Ontario was parted by a dim reflection of the moon. It rolled into the bay like a giant wheel and the lights from cars on Lakeshore Boulevard were sparks beneath its grinding weight.

Somewhere in the middle of that lake, a line was pencilled-in to cut a continent in half — the same kind of line that had cut Jimmy in half. There were other lines too, doing the same to him.

There was the clash that came with thoughts of change and then the stench of guilt. His conscience was left to stand alone against a dangerous half-lie, the bite of it augmented by years gone by. And in his anguish, it came to him that a way of life — not Linda — had kept him caged. Everything for money — the first and 15th of each and every melancholy month. Content to sit and wait behind the bars that gave him food and made him less in need of dignity. He scratched at them from time to time, then settled back into his reserved space in the North American Zoo.

Speed adds beauty to the deer.

Where did *that* come from? Just to find a road with something like the speed of a deer at the end of it — commitment, purpose, peace. Just to be on it. That would be enough.

He saw Jimmy smiling up at him and felt the weight of coins in his pocket. Then his mind was still.

"I'll go away for a while. I'll drive. Just turn the magic key and start the magic wheels to rolling," he said aloud.

IIII

The magic wheels were rolling now — along an asphalt line between two unknowns.

His Thunderbird moved steadily into the night, past little rolling hills. Eventually, small patches of snow, caught by the moon, betrayed a hard winter past - heavier precipitation and much colder temperatures than in the city. Rocks, birches and pines began to crowd the highway as it narrowed and licked into the north like a long, black tounge at the inside of a cone.

Sleeping towns grew smaller and further apart. Narrow roads — erratic tribituaries — left the highway at irregular intervals. They led to the lakes and lodges, fishing camps and hamlets that, for the most part, laid dormant as the trees around them in the winter.

Mike turned off at Sidney Road to find the village by that name and a lake called Limberlost. For there, according to a faded sign at the corner, JAKE'S GARAGE would be of service motorists day or night, any time of the year.

The road met Limberlost and turned to follow it's shoreline into the village of Sidney. The town slept and JAKE'S GARAGE was in darkness. But he caught the figure of a man moving like a shadow at the side of the building. Mike turned abruptly and brought the car to a noisy halt at the gasoline pumps. The shadow came to the front of the building. There was a large mongrel dog at it's heels.

"Can I get some gas?"

The man moved toward him, grumbling about the boisterousness of city folk and their bad driving habits. The dog, sensing his master was disgusted, started a low growling. A head — middle-aged, perhaps more, with a three-day beard and missing several teeth — appeared at the window and stared blankly at Mike.

"Fill 'er up." Mike said, abruptly.

"Eh?"

"Gas! Fill 'er up."

"You from Tronna?"

"Yes."

"One of them city slickers, eh?"

"I suppose so."

"Goin' someplace."

"Just driving."

"Not on this road, Mister. Bridge's out at the lodge."

"How far?"

"Few miles."

"Put some gas in anyway." Mike persisted. "I'm almost dry."

"Nice car, Mister." He reached in to touch the leather dashboard, then shook his head either in envy or disgust.

"Are you Jake?"

"Yeah."

"Jake, I'd like to get some gas and be on my way."

"Ain't got none. Went dry a few days ago."

"Went dry?"

"Yep."

"Is there another place close that hasn't gone dry?"

"One 20 miles south o' here."

"It was closed when I passed it. But I'm not driving anymore tonight. I'll find something in the morning."

"Where ya gonna sleep, eh?"

"I thought you might tell me that."

"Two fishin' camps down the road. Ya can get a cabin. Talk to Doc Roger's... friend o' mine... but Doc ain't bin so good lately."

"I'll find the camps."

Jake scratched his head and slowly began to circle the car. He paused as his dog lifted a hind leg at each wheel.

"Nice car, Mister," he repeated. "Wait here."

Jake disappeared into the garage and Mike, seeing that his pet had followed, seized the opportunity to get out and exercise his legs. He left the door open though, in case the animal returned. But, he returned to the car without the canine's help. The night air had become uncomfortably cool.

There was a strange clattering coming from the garage and, within a few minutes, Jake emerged with a five-gallon container in his hand. He was mumbling something to the beast at his heels.

"Fown' some!" he called from behind the car.

"Come an' see. Last I got, eh?"

"No thanks. Just put it in."

"Scared o' Pal here?" Mike could hear Jake chuckling. "Ain't gonna hurt ya, less I tell 'im. Anyways, don' need me to tell 'im nothin'. He knows what to do. Doncha boy?" He scratched Pal's head for a moment, then poured the gasoline.

"How much did you put in?"

"Don' know fer sure." Jake leaned against the car and began rolling a cigarette.

"Well, what do I owe you then?"

" Ah... catch ya in th' mornin'. Safe's locked anyways. Ya hafta come back out this way. Stop in fer breakfas', eh."

"Okay. Are the fishing camps easy to find?"

"Can't miss 'em. Stay right on this road," he called out as the car moved off. "Welcome to Sidney, Mister."

Mike grumbled to himself. He thought it odd that Jake should trust a stranger and even more odd that he could come up with a few gallons of gasoline like that. It couldn't have been much. The gas gauge hadn't moved. Mike suspected that Jake had a row of partly-filled gas cans in his garage precisely for such emergencies. He made a mental note to stop by in the morning — Pal or no Pal.

In spite of all the miles he had driven, Mike Kramer had the eerie feeling that he was not yet far enough away from home.

The road beyond Sidney clung to Lake Limberlost. Strange sounds of water playing beneath trees along the shore came to Mike wrapped in the bland fragrance of an anxious forest — one as impatient as himself to be alive again. He watched for the fishing camps and thought ahead to a peaceful sleep, as though that would sanction his escape. They were not to be found. As Jake had warned, the bridge across a wide ravine was badly in need of repair. His headlights picked out a simple sign in black and white on the far side — GREENBERG.

Mike sought in vain to find a way to cross the crevice, a wrinkle in the earth filled with the sweat of a hard winter. Then, while looking for a place in the road wide enough to turn around, he came upon a second sign, this one hidden by the branches of a fallen tree — GREENBERG LODGE.

Other branches, carefully placed by human hands, concealed a road that wound through the trees toward the lake. Mike took his flashlight from the car and only walked a short distance before he came upon the lodge.

In a long building set apart from the others, he found a window that would open and shone his light into an empty room, except for the framework and springs of two beds which leaned against a wall. Having abandoned hope of finding the fishing camps, he returned to his car for a sleeping bag and blanket, took them to that room and there he slept.

The moments of his sleep, when they came, were disturbed by the turning of his mind, by the sound an empty stomach makes, by the pain of bedsprings digging into his body. Mike awakened many times that night — always to a throbbing headache from too much thought, to a stomach ache from too little food and to an aching heart for want of Linda's warm and gentle touch.

But near dawn, Mike slept well. By mid morning, when he heard the sound of the lake again, the air had warmed to a more comfortable degree — fair evidence of the brilliant sun in a clear blue sky. The day could not have been more beautiful to him if nature had prepared herself for his eyes alone.

Lake Limberlost was bluing between its tiny central islands where the ice had not broken. On the hills around it, the last of winter's snow lay in strange abstract patterns, like Holstein spots. Beauty was there for the turning of an eye.

On the way back to Sidney, Mike looked for the fishing camps again and, again, he could not find them.

It was quiet when he reached the village, as though most of it still slept. There was a woman hanging clothes and three children playing near the road. Two fishermen sat motionless at the end of a wooden wharf. At the filling station, Jake and Pal were in the same place Mike had first spotted them the night before.

The car stopped in front of the garage and sputtered as the engine died. Jake approached — still staring blankly, still unkept. Mike could hear him mumbling to Pal as he approached.

"How's th' car runnin', eh?"

"Not so good. Sounds sick to me. It's been missing since last night."

"I'll fix it."

"Never mind right now, Jake. I've got to eat." Mike pointed to the front window of the garage. There in uneven white letters was the word FOOD. "What's for breakfast?"

"Hungry, eh?" Jake grinned and shook his head.

"Ain't got nothin' you'd like, anyways."

"Try me."

"Jus' por'ge... oatmeal por'ge."

Ugh. Mike imagined his stomach full of the sticky stuff. He pictured it turning into hard cement. If his stomach was permanently full, he would never have to eat again.

"Do you sell coffee?"

"'Course."

"'Course... then I'll try a cup."

"C'mon inta the rest'rant."

Pal seemed to have mellowed somewhat with the daylight.

Nevertheless, Mike kept an eye an the animal as he followed Jake into the building.

The restaurant was as homey as a bus depot. It consisted of a card table — the legs of which met an oily concrete floor at four different angles, a hot plate on a stool and coffee, oatmeal, milk and sugar on a shelf beside it. There was an ugly coil of fly paper hanging from the ceiling, spotted black with dead flies.

"I couldn't find those fishing camps last night," Mike remarked when he was seated. "Where are they exactly?"

"Left han' side. Mile or so past the bridge."

"Then how the hell was I supposed to..." There was little point in pressing the matter further. Mike had no desire to become more confused than he already was. Jake appeared oblivious to his frustration.

The coffee came before him in a paper cup and it turned mud-brown when he added sugar and milk. Jake sat with him and the two of them silently stared at a 10-year-old automobile, the innards of which were spread at random on the floor around it.

"A guy left it here a while back. Wanna buy it?"

"No."

Jake farted.

"Too much por'ge."

They were quiet again. Something in Jake's eyes betrayed the fact that he was in deep thought. Then a perplexed expression showed itself just before he asked: "Where'd ya sleep?"

"In an empty room in the lodge."

"Ahh... of course. Where else?"

"The place seemed pretty desolate."

"What?"

"Run down. He'll have a hard time getting it ready this season."

"Greenbug ain't gonna open it this year."

"Who?"

"Greenbug — that's what I call 'im." Mike smiled, though Jake was obviously very serious. "Tol' me hisself. Close the g'rage ev'ry summer an' kinda look after the place for 'im."

That explained the lodge's condition, *and* the open window.

"Hafta keep this place open now."

"It must get lonely here in the winter."

"Sometimes. But if 'twere my choosin', I'd rather be alone. Them city folks scared o' somethin' — every last one of 'm."

"So are you."

"Nope. Not me."

"Maybe you *should* have a look at my car before I go."

"Know the trouble!" Jake jumped up, found a cardboard box with some cans in it and was at the door. Pal was sleeping in the corner. "Leave Pal in here, eh. Don' let 'im out. Betcha a dollar it's fixed 'fore ya finish your coffee."

For a brief time, Mike was sitting quietly — too hungry and tired to think. Without apparent reason, Pal stirred and, missing his master, whined at the door. Then the dog began to circle the room. The creature was free to take a nip at him without fear of reprimand. So Mike sat motionless, afraid to follow him with more than his eyes, which strained to turn in his head when the dog was behind him and flashed quickly the opposite way as Pal came into view on the other side. But, as though Jake's presence had been the cause of unrest between the two, Pal eventually came to the table, sniffed for food and, finding none, settled at Mike's feet.

The coffee was cold. Mike tore away the upper half of the Cup and placed it before the mongrel.

Pal sniffed, tasted, tipped the cup over and finished the brew with a few healthy, noisy laps. Then, out of appreciation, he muzzled his way between Mike's legs and stayed there — eyes half closed — to have his head stroked.

"I know how you feel, Pal. I can't understand him either."

This growing friendship ended with a resounding roar that seemed to shake the table. Mike looked out through the "Os" in "FOOD" to see his car rocking on its wheels, pushing a cloud of bluish-black smoke from the exhaust. Jake crouched over the steering wheel like a race-car driver. The sound from the engine was unsteady at first, with a noticeable sputtering, but gradually it evened and softened, than ceased altogether just before Jake returned.

"Fixed!" he announced proudly.

"What was wrong?"

"Water... water in th' gas. Boun' to happen this time o' year, eh. Took three cans o' stuff to fix it."

"There was no water in my tank before last night, Jake."

"'Tain't my fault you let your tank run dry."

"How much I owe you?"

"Twenny-five should do it."

"Three gallons of gas! One cup of coffee! Three cans of stuff! How much?"

"Twenny-five."

"You're joking!"

Jake wasn't. He farted again, took the money and went straight to the safe with it. He had obviously trained Pal to be on guard when the safe was open. The dog moved between him and Mike and started a low growl.

"Ya still owe me a dollar, eh."

"What for?"

"I betcha I could fix your car before you drank your coffee."

"Not a chance, Jake! Never! I've been robbed already. You got nerve, I'll give you that."

"You city folks is all alike. You owe me."

"I'd rather owe you a dollar than beat you out of it."

They talked for some time after that, because Mike was loathing to take up the challenge ahead. For at the junction of Sidney Road and the main highway, his future — the rest of his life — hung upon the turn of a wheel, a direction. South: a darkened sky, where black chimneys rose to mark the graves of men. North: a crazy-quilt dream, stitched with loneliness.

Some choice!

Later, at the junction, Mike sat and waited for phantom vehicles to pass. The trees were tall and straight, with strong limbs to support the budding foliage, unlike the one outside his apartment window — twisted and torn to facilitate the passage of trucks, stunted by the same foul air the people breathed around their monstrous buildings. He thought of Linda. He was not surprised that he felt her presence, that he could imagine her sitting beside him.

What choice? There was nothing North for him. He would go back to Toronto and try — really try this time — with Linda, with Kirk, with Father Kelly.

What choice, if humans have themselves rooted in a place as deeply as any helpless tree?

What choice?

IV

You have come here too early in the year." The voice came from behind Mike, so he turned to see an aging, balding, rotund man approach. "It is much nicer later on." The sun made his bald head shine. He reminded Mike of an over-the-hill Pillsbury Doughboy.

"I can see that it would be."

"You are on my property."

Mike ignored the remark. "You're Mr.Greenberg, then."

"Samuel Greenberg... I am very strict about trespassing." The squat man clasped his hands behind his back and rocked slightly from heel to toe. "Have to be, these days."

"My name's Mike Kramer."

Greenberg didn't offer his hand. "Why are you here?"

"I'm on vacation. I'm merely passing by."

"The bridge is out." He removed his spectacles and held them up in the sun to inspect them for dust. "There is no passing by this place."

Mike pointed to a narrow, wooden footbridge crossing the ravine near a cluster of small cabins, leading to the Greenberg house. He noticed that the house itself, unlike the lodge, was freshly painted and the grounds were well kept. "Had I been able to find your foot-bridge last night, I would have troubled you for accommodation. As it turns out, I slept in one of your buildings."

"How did that happen?"

"Jake."

"Oh-oh."

"Last night, he sold me some gas with water in it, then charged me 25 bucks to fix it. I got to the highway before I remembered there was something at his garage that I wanted to check. Do you know he sells watered gas out of a row of jerry cans in the back of his shop? Quite a scam!"

"You from Toronto?"

"Yes."

"He'd get you for that."

"I figured as long as I was in Sidney, I might as well come back here for one more look at Limberlost."

Sam asked if he had eaten lunch.

"No..." It was hard, trying to sound unconcerned about food.

"Come with me," he said patting his stomach. "My Anna is the finest of cooks. She'll be pleased to see that your belly is as round as mine before you leave."

They sat on a screen-covered porch, looking out to the lake, while Anna Greenberg — a beautiful woman despite her years — pampered them with food and drink. Anna was good at first glance.

"Jake and I have had words on occasion regarding the price of his questionable services," Sam was saying.

"He mentioned a friend named Doc Rogers."

"A hermit who Jake supports. Rogers saved the life of that mongrel of his and has lived off the act ever since. Doc Rogers lives in a cabin on Jake's land — back in the bush. To my knowledge, Jake is the only one who has seen him for some time."

"If you ask me, Jake is a few bricks short of a load."

Sam Greenberg peered at Mike over the rim of his wire glasses. "Don't make *that* mistake, my friend." His smile was couched in an ample triple chin. "You wouldn't be the first. Jake knows what he's about. I could give a few examples, but they would embarrass me."

"I don't know. I still think his mother must have eaten some funny mushrooms. Jake fascinates me. If he has taken it upon himself to support this Rogers fellow, no wonder his prices are so high."

"You can be sure his prices were high long before Rogers became Doc; they're merely a thing of habit. In fact, Jake used to own hundreds of acres of land around here. He's sold most of it. I would guess that if we had his money, we could burn ours."

Mike shook his head. He was obviously perplexed. Sam continued: "You have to understand that Jake is obsessed with oneupmanship. He has to feel he's come out on top, no matter what — especially with a stranger like yourself. He has worked for me as a handyman each season. But if it weren't for my wife, I would have stopped having anything to do with him years ago."

As she came onto the porch with more coffee, Anna overheard her husband. "Papa!" she interrupted, "Jake has your heart and a better nose for profits... perhaps you envy him."

"You see?" Sam looked to Mike for sympathy. "A man has little chance with such a woman."

"Jake told me you were closing the lodge."

"Ahh..." Sam sighed, yet appeared satisfied that the subject had been raised. He sat silently, as though in thought, for a considerable time. "You know, Michael, on this earth we have the time to think a million lives and time to live just one. I believe we all — or at least most of us — try to put together some kind of eclectic pattern and purpose to our lives; some kind of substance, gleaned from all the thoughts, ideas, experiences that bombard us every day."

Sam's eyes began to moisten. The flesh beneath them was pouched and wrinkled. To Mike, they hinted of pain and disappointment.

"I'm sorry, my friend. You asked a simple question, and I... "

"No. No. Go on! I appreciate your honesty."

And, he thought, isn't it a pleasure to think of something besides dollar bills.

"At one point, when I was stronger and my dreams were fresh, I came to an understanding of God. I knew that he was an actual, physical being and that I (along with every tiny atom in the universe) was a part of his real body. His shape didn't matter and I didn't concern myself with the identity of my very insignificant function. It was enough to be a part of a greater scheme. In those days, I could at times feel a power running through me — an electricity, if you like. An endless current of thoughts and ideas, plans and dreams that was mine and God's at once. It's gone. So is the lodge. I don't know how it happened. I can't give you a day and a date. But when something makes an old man see that after all his thinking and living, his existence has been useless, he is better off to be rid of it."

Mike admired Anna — her appearance, her serenity as she stood silently beside her husband. She knew the pain he felt like no other human could, yet seemed not to be hurting. Anna was strong; no question of that. Her hand was on Sam's shoulder as though to drain some of the anguish from his body into hers. She had things under control, including her husband, who wiped his brow and eyes with a handkerchief, then blew his nose.

"So I must close the lodge and be content to eat and sleep with Anna until I die."

"Do you have any children?"

Sam touched his wife's hand and she moved closer to him. "We have a son," he answered.

"Then give the lodge to him. Perhaps you could help him gain from what you think were your mistakes. It isn't too late for that."

"Not Ronnie! No, sir!"

Anna moved away. "Who knows why any of us act the way we do?" She spoke softly but firmly, the set of her face indicating that Sam was in for another lecture. "He is alive and well. He is doing his best in his own way. That is enough to be thankful for." She turned and went quickly into the house.

"I'm sorry," Mike apologised, realising his good intentions had floundered.

"No, no," Sam said. "Anna is right. We are both to blame for Ronnie's actions. And I am to blame more than anyone." There was a cautious silence before Sam decided to continue. "Ronnie wanted very much to be a lawyer. We sent him to the best school we could afford. He left in the middle of his first term and we haven't seen him since. That was four years ago now."

"Maybe his teachers… "

"I have been to the school. They could tell me nothing. We haven't completely lost touch with him though. He often sends postcards from this place and that. Anna writes back but most of her letters are returned."

"She seems to handle it well, to have herself under control, I mean. I like that."

"That's Anna, all right. She lives in a world of angels, spirits and demons. She's not fanatic about it, but she's convinced that Ronnie is well looked after."

"I hope she's right. Things will work out eventually. They usually do."

Sam struggled to his feet. "You'll have to excuse me my friend. I have to pick up some groceries and supplies in town."

"I've been wondering how you get there with the bridge out."

"By boat. It's only three miles across the bay. They are going to start on the bridge next week… You should come in and rest. As you can see, there is plenty of room. We will have dinner when I get back. Do you play chess?"

"I play at it. But, no Sam, I have to go. If I can trouble you for a shave, I'll be on my way. I have to get rid of this new moustache, it's driving me nuts." Mike scratched his head and ran his fingers through his short, curly black hair. "Maybe I should have a shower, too."

"There should be no reason for you to hurry away my friend. Spend the afternoon with us; stay for dinner; sleep here tonight if you wish. At least you will resume your vacation refreshed in the morning."

Mike hesitated.

"Come, I'll show you where you can get freshened up."

Sam Greenberg opened the door for him and as they entered the living room, Mike's weary eyes picked out a painting above the fireplace — Lake Limberlost and the halo of hills around it immediately. Beneath the painting, on the fireplace mantle, there was a baseball. Mike picked it up and held it in his hand. It had been autographed by players unfamiliar to him.

"You play?" Mike asked, jokingly.

"My son." Sam was proud and it showed. "Ronnie loved baseball. I'm saving it for him."

There were stacks of books and magazines everywhere in that room. Sam had to clear a chair so Mike could sit down. "Why do you like that painting?" he asked.

"Because it's real in every detail and yet the whole is more than real — in the sense that truth is more than fact." Mike went to examine it closely and replaced the baseball. "It seems to have the power of an honest mind."

The speed of the deer. Something like it.

"Everyone mentions it as soon as they see it."

"Except Jake."

"Of course. But even he said it was 'better 'n most' as he left."

"Fran Greenberg." Mike read aloud the signature on the painting. "A relative?"

"My daughter." Again Sam was visibly suffering. "She is dead now."

Mike dropped his chin to his chest and stared at the floor. "I'm sorry."

"There is a story there too, my friend, but I'm not up to it this afternoon. It will have to wait."

"Sam, I... "

"Please stay the night, Michael. We can enjoy one of Anna's special meals. Then we'll have a go at chess and chat by the fire until we begin to bore each other. You will sleep well, I guarantee it."

After a polite hesitation, Mike said that he would.

"I thought so. Clear the branches from the entrance and bring your car up to the lodge."

It had driving back to Toronto beat all to hell.

Maxwell Taylor looked, but didn't act, 48. The grey in his hair and moustache, the slightly sagging features of his face, the lines of time in his

Bermuda-tanned skin. His same youthful eyes had once looked covetously out of his father's shop window to the store next door. His father was gone now; so was his grocery store. A block of office buildings hid his passing — footstools of fortune.

Those eyes now coveted Linda, through the curling smoke of his pipe, and she, realising herself to be the object of his admiration — his inspection — turned bashfully away, aware of her beauty; proud of it. But she had no intention of becoming another one of Maxwell Taylor's acquisitions.

"Did you enjoy this evening, Linda?"

"Thoroughly! I was very proud of you."

"Proud? Because the banquet was in my honour? Because I received an award? What do you mean?"

"Proud to be working for you."

Maxwell sighed deeply and went to Linda's liquor cabinet for a drink.

"Have one?"

"Not now."

He sat close to her and sighed again. "I wish your affections were as easy to come by as those of the people at the banquet tonight."

Linda went to the mirror and began fussing with her hair. "I'm not for sale, if that's what you mean."

"That may have been true a couple of days ago. But now, I'm not so sure. Darling Mike has seen to that. You won't go to the highest bidder or God knows I would have had you long ago. But you'll go to the strongest." He paused to think a moment, then added: "Mike certainly isn't what I'd call strong."

"Something about him seems to bother you."

"Not anymore."

Linda came near him and touched his hand.

"Maxwell... You're the kind of man who replaces his shoelaces before the old ones break. You've always lived your life years in advance. You know exactly where you're going, what you want and how to get there. Those qualities are very attractive to someone like me and I'm flattered that you want me. I really am. You've been so good to me that I'll always owe you. But I love Mike. In spite of his foolishness, his shortsightedness, his nonsense, I love him. It may sound strange, but he offers me more security than you do." She moved to the window and looked out. "Right now, I wonder where he is and what he's doing; why he would leave the business he's worked so hard to build. That Jack Kirkpatrick! He'll destroy Mike if he get's the chance."

"How could you ever be secure after the way he's behaved?" He showed bewilderment by the way he handled his pipe. He was visibly annoyed.

"I can't explain it. It has to do with caring, needing someone and being needed. You wouldn't have time for me. How would you fit me into your life? By appointment?"

"Linda, I always get what I want." His voice was low and determined. She was his chance to reclaim 20 years. "One way or another."

"And you want me?"

"That's right."

"But it's not because you love me, is it?"

"Don't talk to me about love. Is love so good if you want to waste your life because of it?"

"Is money?"

Maxwell Taylor went to her. "Linda... "

"Please Maxwell, not now."

"Not now, but very soon."

"I'll know for sure in a month. If I love him enough to wait that long... You'd better go."

"I'll go. But promise to let me know if you hear from him — and *what* you her from him."

"Why?"

"Never mind why... just make me that promise."

"I will."

V

The night became a week for Mike. His presence seemed to please the Greenbergs, and he in turn was satisfied to be there. Why not? What better place to pause before returning to the North American Zoo? Sort of a few things out, regain some strength, then go back. There were no bottlenecks here. Just quiet moments near Limberlost, hours spent before a blazing fireplace.

Each never-never-land day, after the evening meal and before the two men settled into cards or chess, they invariably chatted while Anna went to her needlework or knitting — a click-click-clicking metronome to their patter. She rocked endlessly by the fire and no matter how Mike tried, he couldn't determine the impetus that moved her chair. For she appeared to sit motionless, except for her busy fingers. Occasionally, she would stop, letting her knitting fall to her lap, lean back and stare at her daughter's picture above the fireplace, then rock again, as though that was the improbable source of her movement.

Anna Greenberg was a strong one all right! Not tough, but strong and Mike knew it. So did Sam.

Seldom was Mike left alone, nor did he wish to be. Solitary moments in the woodland near the lodge, meditations at the water's edge were dangerous; they made a temptress of Muskoka. It would be good to snuggle in her warm bed forever.

The masters came after him there, by Limberlost, not with a vengeance but with a coaxing, a simmering… bringing him to a boil — like Linda, beautiful Linda, had coaxed him to climax so many times. She was beautiful Linda here; she sat with him; he talked to her and she talked back.

A road with the speed of a deer at the end of it. Sidney Road?

Nah! Not likely.

Almost persuaded, drugged by the sirens of Limberlost, he would return to the Greenberg house with a nebulous understanding of that which he sought and a dim comprehension of how to find it. Then, Sam would coddle him and fetch his chessboard and make him sit and play, while Anna knitted him back to reality.

"You have a good day?" Sam would ask.

And Mike would assure him that he had.

"This is a perfect place for one to regenerate one's self," he would suggest, always careful to speak impersonally so not to offend.

"Is that what I need, Sam, regeneration?"

"I don't know."

They broke their pattern on the eve of Mike's departure. Instead of staying in the house after dinner, they went walking along Sidney Road — not north toward town, but south of the lodge where the pavement ended and the road became a dusty car trail. They passed the clusters of tiny one-room cabins that were the fishing camps.

"I still can't figure out how Jake expected me to get here when the bridge was out." Mike smiled but got no response from Sam, who had become sullen. The older man was obviously winded, so Mike shortened his step. "I suppose he figured the walk would do me good."

"Who knows with that fellow?"

At the southern end of the lake, the road veered sharply to avoid a huge conifer and headed east — away from Limberlost and into the forest. There was a steady sound coming through the trees — like a monster breathing.

"What's that?" Mike asked.

"Thunder Falls. There's a path leading up to the top. You can see the entire length of the lake from up there, It's a popular hiking spot in the summer." As they passed the giant cedar, Mike saw that the bark had been skinned from the base and chunks of wood had been gouged from it's trunk.

"Boy! Someone sure smacked into this baby!"

Sam had become morose — a troubled silence was followed by an abrupt recrudesense. "I'll tell you about my Fran," he said. "She showed remarkable artist ability, even as a little girl. I saw beauty coming from her that, all my life, I had wished for myself. By the time she went away to college, many important people had become interested in her painting. Anna and I were so proud. It was a dream come true for me. Fran came here to spend the summers with us. But even then, when she needed rest and relaxation, I drove her to her studies — as though I possessed the talent, not her. During her last summer with us, she befriended one of the guests — the son of a very wealthy couple who never stayed at the lodge before — a fop if there ever was one. I detested the shallowness and I foolishly interfered because, for the first time, I could see Fran abandoning her gift in order to feed his selfishness. How can someone like that know or care about such a gift? Fran openly resented my interference. I'm not so sure, looking back, that she didn't know exactly what she was doing. No wonder her resentment became so strong!

One evening, after all the guests had left the beach, I noticed a bonfire down close to the boathouse. I knew it was Fran and her friend. Anna stood in the doorway and forbade me to interfere. God help me! I cursed at her and pushed her aside. When I reached the beach, I found them using Fran's paintings to kindle their bonfire. In fact, the landscape above our fireplace is the only survivor. I struck the young man and ordered him to leave and take mommy and daddy with him. He ran off, but, to my amazement Fran followed. I chased them to the road, but his car sped away towards the fishing camps. I sat by the side of the road, bewildered. I was waiting there when I heard the crash. Fran died; the young man walked away with a few bruises and cuts; the cedar back there still stands to bear the mark of my folly. All I have to do to be reminded of the price of my own selfishness is take a walk along a dusty road."

Mike knew instinctively that his response to Sam's anguish was relatively important — not necessarily vital, for surely the earth did not turn on the acts of one man. But nonetheless, the scab had been picked from an old sore; the poison had to be drawn and the wound dressed if it was to be properly healed. The two men walked silently for a time as Mike Kramer attempted to work his way through the maze of his friend's torment.

"Sam, you said that Fran probably knew exactly what she was doing. I don't think so. She wouldn't have destroyed her paintings if she had been thinking clearly. Don't blame yourself for what happened. You were right to try and stop her."

"I don't know. We all destroy things we love if it suits us. She was young. She had a whole lifetime of painting ahead of her. Maybe she was unhappy with her work. I know for a fact that Fran didn't like the picture that was saved. We were very close. Maybe it upset her to see her art causing trouble between us. Oh no, my friend, she knew."

"Still, you're not responsible for her actions or reactions — whether she wanted to hurt you or not."

"Michael… it's not a question of blame or guilt." Sam Greenberg paused for a moment to gather his thoughts. "Do you know who helped me to realize that?"

"Anna."

"Yes. Even after the way I hurt her that evening — the things I said and did — she came to the road to get me. She told me that Frances was dead. She knows things like that. She said I wasn't to worry; Fran was going to be all right. It was Anna who called the police — *before* the crash. She took me back to the house and talked with me until they came. I'll never forget how calm she was. She has helped me to accept what happened to Fran."

"Then what is it, Sam? Why are you hurting? Why are you so deeply troubled?"

"I can at least try to talk about it. Here. Now. With you. I haven't been able to do that for some time."

This wasn't the same Sam Greenberg who calmly and rationally solved the world's problems from his front porch, not the man who could predict the morning weather and declare checkmate at the same time. He struggled to walk and his voice trembled.

"I thought I would go to my grave believing all existence is a part of the actual, physical body of God. Things were going well then and I was complacent in my belief. But Fran's death triggered a reaction that has slowly eroded my faith *and* my reason.

"I don't understand."

"Neither do I! In seven short years I have lost my daughter, my son, my business *and* my conviction. God! My faith is almost gone. I can feel it oozing out through the holes in my life. Anna does her best to patch them up, but in vain."

How could a man of Sam's age and intelligence become spiritually destitute? Mike wondered the same inexorable process that dragged some humans to the bowels of the bowery could also work to deprive others of their intrinsic glory — even this man, surrounded by natural growth and beauty, couched in material stability. Mike Kramer considered himself 30 years hence. It was impossible to imagine such a fate. Impossible! So much time to think and plan, so much time to work... to do... it could never happen to him. He would not permit it!

"You said that you were over Fran's death," Mike remarked.

"Personally, I am. But generally, in terms of my belief, Fran's death triggered a reaction that... "

He shook his head and sighed deeply. Mike sensed that he was brooding. Sam was breathing heavily; there was a gurgling, raspy sound coming from his chest as he struggled for air.

"We'll rest here," Sam said, squatting on a low-cut stump and drying his face. "My ticker." He put his hand over his heart. "One of these days."

"Take your time," Mike said. "I'll just walk on a bit alone."

"The road ends just around the next bend."

Mike promised he'd be back in a few minutes.

There may have been deer in the forest around Mike Kramer, but none of them were at the end of Sidney Road; whatever he was seeking wasn't there. As Sam said, it ended abruptly, soon after the bend, looping symmetrically around a darkened ranger station.

Momentarily, Mike stood statue still, listening for sounds of movement from the umbral recesses of the forest — nothing, save the settling of birds. Then, remembering Sam, he left that place thinking that, if he didn't have to leave in the morning, it would have been nice to return alone — to pack a lunch and stop at Thunder Falls, to make a day of it.

"It's almost dark," Sam called when he saw Mike come round the bend. "I'm fine now. Let's go back."

As they walked, Mike didn't press his friend to resume their conversation. If Sam had lost the power to think through his despair, further discussion would only deepen it. There wasn't time to close the open wound.

It was dark when they passed the fishing camps. There was no moon, but the stars appeared. Sam gazed at them as he ambled down the road.

"What is the speed of light?" he asked.

"Very fast."

"Exactly, I mean."

Mike confessed that he didn't know.

"One hundred eighty-six thousand two hundred and eighty feet per second — give or take a few feet. Know how long it takes for light from Quasars, at the edge of the universe we know, to reach us?"

"No."

"Ten billion years, give or take a year, ten billion years at 186,280 feet per second." Sam answered. Do you know how many planets — like the one we're walking on — there are in our Milky Way galaxy?"

"No."

"Trillions. There are over 200 million stars in our galaxy as well, including the sun. Can you guess how many galaxies we've found?"

"No."

"At least a billion, give or take a galaxy. The numbers and the distances pertaining to the particles of matter that form our planets are relatively the same. If the energy that keeps them apart and in motion stopped, if the earth imploded at this moment, it would simply reduce the size of the rubber ball. The weight would remain the same, just a neater package. What does all that I've said mean to you, Michael?"

"I don't know, exactly."

"I knew once. Exactly! You may call my ideas primitive, if you wish. But they made sense to me, for I could see no logical reason why *my* God should not have a physical body, just as I do — perhaps not the same shape as me, heaven forbid, although shape is not important. Any one of my body cells is unmistakably human, whether it be part of my leg, my arm or my ear. So far as I was concerned, I didn't have to know which part of God's body I belonged to, realized that I was one tiny individual particle of his physical being — probably billions upon billions of light years away from his brain, from the truth. Because I had a mind, that did not necessarily mean that God had one; because I walked and talked, God did not have to do the same. It meant to me only that I could be certain that thought and motion and sound were functions in the body of God. That was at the very core of my philosophy... that, generally speaking, the function of God's body was similar to mine. If you have the patience, I will give you an example."

"I think you'll have to."

"As we walk, if your shoes are comfortable, you are not aware of your big toe. It is the most distant part of your body from your brain and though you may not be conscious of it at all times, there are obviously certain processes that keep your toe functioning as it should. Stub it and you become aware of it instantly. In fact, you become one big throbbing toe! The brain sends help, but as far as your toe is concerned, it takes ten billion light years to get there. But eventually, the damage is isolated and repaired. I used to think that our relationship to God was just like that! That we were probably cells in a remote part of his body, depending upon his brain to arrange healing and comfort when we were injured and hurting. That his approach to us, as part of his body, was similar to our concern for our toe. You may extend the example as far as you wish. For all we know, maybe God has stubbed his toe."

Mike chuckled audibly at that. "What happened when Fran died?"

"Well... have you ever heard or read of a tragedy — a plane crash, an earthquake — and wondered why, when there was so much pain and suffering you didn't feel a thing? At times, I even feel guilty that I am so insensitive. Right now there is hurt and death. Don't you think we should be feeling something?"

"I suppose so. I don't know."

"Fran and I were very close. Surely, if we were both a part of the body of God, I should have felt some pain when she died — her pain I mean. I heard the crash. I knew. I should have felt something more than grief and self-pity. And why can't I feel Ronnie this instant — his loneliness, his fear? Why doesn't he know how much I need him to come home? God doesn't have a body. He doesn't hurt like we do."

"The more questions we answer," Mike offered, "the fewer answers we have; the more we learn, the less we know. We can solve the riddles of the universe one moment and be blown away like dust the next. That's the human predicament, Sam. We all have to learn to live with it. I guess most of us ignore it and carry on. We don't know, can't know, but surely someone has guessed right. Maybe it's you. You've lost your perspective, that's all. You've worked yourself into a maze and you don't know how to get out. I can't tell you why we don't feel the pain of others. A few *do,* I think. By your own admission, the distances between even the closest entities are staggering. Bite the end of your finger. Do the fingers beside it hurt? Is there any reason why they should? If we could feel the pain of others, we would be hurting constantly."

"We should at least know about it," Sam insisted. His pace had slowed again. It was too dark for Mike to see his face, but he was obviously struggling to breath. Mike asked him if he wanted to stop and he refused. They reached the scarred cedar. Sam passed it without looking back. "Boom!" he said. "Gone... my life has imploded to the size of a pea."

Sam Greenberg may have been physically overweight, but in his mind he was lean and nimble. There was no mental obesity here, no laziness or rustiness. He was simply bound by circumstance — like a fit vessel in fog.

"Anna knew about Fran's death," Mike reminded him. "*Before* it happened. You've forgotten Anna. Her losses are the same as yours."

"No they aren't. She hasn't lost Fran or Ronnie at all. I can't comprehend it, but she seems to have them with her in a very real sense. If anything, she has gained in strength. As I told you, she tries to help. But it's no use. Sometimes I think even she is giving up on me." Sam grimaced. "I've lost it, my friend. Thank you for trying to help me, but it's gone."

"You may have lost it, Sam. But it isn't gone. You'll recover."

"Believe me, it's gone!" His voice quivered as he pointed to the stars. "Could you understand what that meant to me? Could you possibly?"

There was little use to press the matter. Mike Kramer knew it and let it go. They walked on, past the fishing camps, before Sam Greenberg spoke again.

"Have you enjoyed your week here, Michael?"

"Very much." Mike's reply was sincere. He was relieved to change the subject. "I've been able to relax."

"And learn a little chess?"

"A little. I would have liked to win one game, though.

"Maybe tomorrow, before... "

"I'm leaving early. I've decided not to go to Vancouver. I'm going back to Toronto. I can see it's time to straighten out my business, to settle things with Linda one way or the other. I'm not going to run."

"But you're searching; Michael — the reason you came here — what about that?

"It will have to wait."

"There's no need for you to go. You can stay on here," Sam pleaded. He was offering help and asking for it at the same time. "This place — the lodge — could bring your searching to an end."

"The lodge is closed."

"It need not be! There's a challenge for you here. I think that's what you need."

"I haven't enough money to buy your lodge."

"Ahh... money! You dream of something, then restrict your dream to a price you can afford."

"Who's dreaming? My life is in Toronto, not here. Even if I somehow found the money to buy your lodge. I'd only be locking my problems out — not solving them."

"Nonsense, my friend. They will find you here more quickly than anywhere else. Take my word for it."

"I only came here to think. Nothing more."

"Think! I'm an expert on thinking! Ten minutes of honest thought would burn a human brain. You didn't come here to think. You came here hoping something would happen to you."

"No more Sam! I don't want to hear about the lodge, the matter is closed."

"Very well," Sam concluded, "but I think you're being foolish."

A fool perhaps, Mike thought, but a determined one — too determined to believe an old man who, by his own admission, had wasted his life on a bunch of silly buildings.

"You'll waste your life on a few silly taxicabs," Sam Greenberg complained.

Mental emphysema... psychic myopia... rickets of the soul — imaginary ailments all, with real symptoms which Mike Kramer had suffered for longer than he could remember. Leaving Toronto had at least alerted him to the fact that he had problems beyond Linda McDermott and Jack Kirkpatrick. He began to realize that he had always been to busy to attend to them.

And now he was hurting.

Maybe Sam was right! Maybe man *was* part of the actual physical body of God and all existence known to humans was merely a small portion of the most minute of his cells. Maybe God was stirring and that's what he felt.

Mike Kramer knew that in his last quiet hour by the lake, he needed not to question, but ingest the power that surrounded him; not to doubt, but to accept the insignificance of his existence and so understand its importance.

It had grown dark and chilly by the time the two men returned from their walk. Mike didn't go inside. Instead, he said a helpless good night to his dejected friend, them crossed the footbridge and descended the terraced lawn to the beach. Although it was uncomfortably cool, he removed his shoes and socks and stood barefoot in the sand... motionless... staring... listening to the loons. The coming colours of middle spring would simmer beneath the thin cover of cloud that was moving in over Muskoka. Mike could feel them quickening, like the stir of blood in his veins. The stars were still visible. He played join-the-dots with them like he had as a child. Sam could measure stars in light years and billions of miles if he wished, but Mike's eyes could see that they weren't very far apart. Regardless if distance, if one stubs a toe, his head bows; if he stubs it a second and third time — like Sam — the heavens are lost. Philosophy and distance just don't matter anymore.

Kramer's body was electric. He could feel the snap of his thoughts as they leapt from his brain. Some of them shot like bullets, to the farthest stars; some skipped across the water to the tiny central islands; others fell to the sand at his feet, where he inadvertently scribbled the words SPEED and DEER, then erased them in disgust.

He thought of Jimmy.

Speeds adds beauty to the deer.

Mike Kramer sighed. His chance of finding those words tomorrow on Toronto sidewalks was as remote as the likelihood of Jimmy finding them along the shores of Limberlost.

A breeze was coming with the clouds and the water made a droning, hypnotic sound where it fused with the sand. As Mike drifted, a soft, persistent voice came to him with the waves. "Michael... Michael." Anna spoke quietly... so quietly that she had to speak his name again. "Michael."

His body remained motionless, yet a strange part of him danced to the thought of being alone with her. Anna paused behind him: "Forgive me if I've bothered you."

Without turning, Mike said politely that she had not. Anna moved to his side and he looked at her. She was the kind of person that could stand inspection; there was a beauty in her that the age of her skin, the grey of her hair, even the deterioration of her slim figure could not hide. And, as she stood there, he made love to that quality in her. He wondered if she knew it.

"Would you rather be alone?"

"No."

"Michael... I've come to explain about Papa."

"Explain?"

" I know he spoke to you about the lodge tonight."

"Yes, he did. But there's nothing wrong with Sam being honest."

"He's convinced you are going to buy the lodge. He would do anything to have it open again — except open it himself. Papa has lost his spirit, but not his nose for business."

Mike listened, remembering: "Ah... spirit," Sam had once said to him. "That's Anna's department. Myself, I've never understood this spirit stuff."

"You must trust your judgment," Anna said.

"I'd trust yours, Anna."

"Trust mine least of all! My concern is for Papa. No man should have to endure his kind of suffering. Everyday he lives with the pain of uncertainty and self doubt. Twice he has reached out to touch life and twice he has received a shock. I don't know if he will ever reach out again."

"What about you? Didn't you reach out too?"

"My shoes have rubber soles." She hesitated. "If you stayed a little longer, I think you could help Papa."

"I'd like to stay. I'd like to be able to stay. But I have problems of my own and I'm going back to deal with them."

Anna was embarrassed and turned her head slightly to hide it. "You are right... if you have decided." She picked up his shoes and socks and handed them to him. "I'll leave you now," she said as she watched him put them on.

"Before you go..." Anna turned and looked into his eyes. "Can you tell me about Fran?"

"Yes." She stood erect and Mike thought he saw her shoulders tighten. "I know about Fran. I can tell you."

"Well... Sam told me what happened; he's still suffering."

"You don't have children."

"No. I've been married but there were no children. That shouldn't matter. You don't have to be an egg to understand one."

"You are partly right. But it's not Fran that is tearing Papa apart. He has learned to accept her death. It's Ronnie. He can understand what happened to Fran. He knows she cannot come back and why. Ronnie disappeared too — just like Fran. But Papa cannot see the reason he left or the reason he stays away. Can you imagine losing two children so suddenly?"

"Tell me Anna... do you know the reason Ronnie left?"

"Yes. Jealousy. Ronnie was never able to compete with Fran. She was more gifted in most of the obvious areas — music, art, even sports. Her school grades were always better. Ronnie tried, but he could never quite match her. It was one thing for him to compete when she was living because she actually helped Ronnie feel at ease. But after she died… How does one compete with a saint? Believe me, Fran was no saint! But she *was* in Papa's eyes. When Ronnie reached college, I'm sure he realized no matter what he did or who he became, he would always be in Fran's shadow. So I suppose he must have felt that it didn't matter how he lived his life."

Mike shrugged. "You don't seem to be bitter."

"Bitter?"

"Towards Sam, that is. After all… "

"Oh, no! Papa did a fine job raising our children. There are too many factors to consider to blame one individual when things go wrong."

"Will you tell me how it is that Fran's death, Ronnie's leaving school, Sam's pain seem to have strengthened you? Sam is devastated. He has lost his will to live. You appear to enjoy your life."

Anna reached for his hand and held it between hers. She looked directly at him, but he was not uncomfortable. She spoke without hesitation: "Pain in this world is not in death; it is in life. It is the living that makes martyrs of us all. Death is good — the bug is devoured by the frog, the rabbit dies in the eagle's claws, the lovely girl whose life is snuffed out in a crash against a tree. All death is good."

"I don't believe you Anna. It can't be."

"Dear Michael," she said solemnly. "I wish we had the time to talk. Now we are only scrambling to exchange a few words before you leave. I will only say to you that birth and death are the front and back gates to the battleground of good and evil. They are both the prerogative of God; both add beauty and dignity to life, no more to be feared than the budding and falling of the leaves." Anna stopped abruptly. "My, my," she said, "I haven't rambled on like this for a long time. Not since Fran was alive." She shivered. "I should have dressed more warmly. It's chilly."

Mike put his sweater over her shoulders.

Anna continued: "I have seen Fran and spoken with her since her death. I am not concerned." She startled Mike with her frankness. "But don't say anything to Papa. It would upset him to hear me talking like this. He has no time for such things."

"And Ronnie? What about your son?"

"He is on the battleground with the rest of us."

"Is there nothing you can do to help Sam? Can't you talk to him the way you have me?"

"No. Papa and I proceed in harmony along two separate roads that will never meet. We can communicate but never touch. He is searching in a different place."

"He's confused."

Anna smiled at that. "Papa reminds me of the man who went out ice fishing and came home with two hundred pounds of ice. If I fry it for him to spare his feelings, we will both drown. I love him, but I don't know him. I cannot."

"How do you think I could help him?"

"I'm sorry. I must go in now. It's very cool. It's going to rain."

He walked with her to the house. They took the foot path, for the grass was already damp. Sam had gone to bed; their walk had done him in. A gentle, half-whispered "good night" was all that was passed between them as Mike Kramer tiptoed the creaking stairs to his room.

There, patterned cotton curtains fanned cool night air over his bed. He fell upon it fully clothed and drifted into a half-conscious contemplation of his conversations with the Greenbergs. They were on separate roads all right.

Downstairs, he could hear the tinkling of dishes and cutlery. It wasn't noise, but melted music that was putting him to sleep. He didn't struggle. There was much to consider, but drowsiness didn't concern him then, as though he knew his mind would keep on working when his body fell asleep. There was a gentle, feminine knock upon his door.

"Michael... Michael."

"Come in," he half-whispered. "The door's unlocked."

Anna opened the door, hesitant to leave the lighted hallway for the darkness of his room.

"I'm still dressed," he assured her.

"Here's a drink of cocoa to warm you a little."

He thanked her, sitting up on the edge of his bed as she approached. She left the cup and turned to go. "Anna..." His voice stopped her. "Stay a while. Sit here while I drink my cocoa."

With some bashfulness, she obliged.

The door was open; there was just enough light from the hall for them to see each other. "For about a month now, I have been obsessed with the phrase 'speed adds beauty to the deer.' It came to me suddenly and at the most unlikely of times." He sipped his cocoa. "I dismissed it as silly at first, but lately — especially since I've been here — it comes more frequently and I dwell upon it for longer periods of time. It must be connected to my college years as well, because the poets and philosophers who shaped my early life swarm around me whenever those words come to mind. And it is connected to sinister forces as well, for they are there too and I quickly become depressed. But it goes back much further than that: while I was resting, just before you came in, I remembered something that happened to me as a child. I'd like to tell you about it. I know it's late, but maybe you know what it means."

Anna told him she wasn't tired, and that she would listen even if she was.

"When we were on a family vacation in Algonquin Park, I spotted a deer grazing undisturbed at the edge of a wide meadow by the side of the road. My father stopped the car and we watched it for the longest time — all the while, my younger sister crying that she had to go 'No. 1 real bad'. Something in the trees must have spooked the deer, because it suddenly began to run across the open meadow, bounding with such grace that I was awe struck. Never had I seen such beauty in my young life before. The deer crossed the road in front of us, and with a mighty leap, cleared the fence on the other side and disappeared into the forest.

"I wanted to talk to my parents about what we had seen, but my sister kept crying that she had to go 'pee-pee' until I slapped her. The squabble that ensued was enough of a diversion to lose the dream… until tonight. When you knocked, I was thinking how the deer's running adds beauty to it's life, whether we are there to see it or not; how flight must do the same for birds. Surely, Anna, there must be something that comes as simply and as naturally to man that lends his existence grace and dignity. It must be connected to the speed of a deer, but I don't know what it is. It must also be in the battle-zone that you spoke of earlier — between the influences that want me to find the answer and those that don't. And I know that you and Sam and Linda have been drawn to one side of the battleground with me; that my partner in Toronto, Linda's boss — Maxwell Taylor — and a priest named Father Kelly have aligned with the other side. But, for the life of me, I can't sort it all out. Can you help me, Anna? Will you? Here? Now?"

"I can. I will. We can make a start at least."

Her forthrightness constantly caught him by surprise, like the deer. Maybe that was it! Perhaps honesty was the beauty that embellished a human life. God, she was good — not hoity-toity good — good at whatever she was about… knitting, cooking, gardening, coaxing him to stand his ground on the battlefield. Truth is beauty… beauty, truth!

"I don't have what you are looking for, Michael. I know what it is, and I can help you find it, but I don't have it myself and I don't expect to have it. I'm too selfish; I don't have the strength for it."

Now, Mike confessed, he was more confused than before.

"Let us begin at the beginning," she began. "Let us set the battleground before we start. I told you that birth and death are the front and back gates to that ground; the only difference is that when we enter, we have no idea of the struggle that is before us, and when we leave, we pray to be shed of it. As the bible has told us, out battle is not with flesh and blood, but spirits and principalities. Try to think of those warring, earthbound spirits as electricity, then imagine them vying for your attention from birth. Bertrand Russell said that electricity is not a thing; it is a way in which things behave. When we have told how things behave when they are electrified, and under what circumstances they are electrified, we have told all there is to tell. So it is that, when we leave this world, if we can tell how the warring spirits have affected us, we have told all.

"You see, Michael, there are many earthbound spirits, bereft of their physical bodies and obsessed with the desire to return to earth, which roam about, seeking opportunities to attach themselves to living mortals. They are the babies still-born, the young taken by sickness before their time, those whose lives are snuffed out by accident — they are the Frans. There are others whose lives have been spent on criminal, violent endeavours; they are required to suffer the self-punishing experience of dwelling upon their unsavoury past — a state not unlike the Catholic concept of purgaroty or the Christian concept of Hell."

Mike finished his cold cocoa. There was nothing uglier, he thought, than the inside of an empty cocoa cup.

"These then are the warring forces," she pressed. "They mill about the battlefield — earthbound spirits good and bad — wanting a piece of us from the moment of our conception, seeking possession of us so they may return to a physical existence. The good ones gain entrance to our lives through love, kindness and positive thinking, leading us to peace and joy; the bad through violence and over indulgence, leading to sickness, nervous breakdowns and even suicide.

"The Ouija board, palmistry, Tarot cards, automatic writing, things of that sort, leave us open to the fancies of the spirits. It is like playing Russian roulette. You have opened the door to them, Michael, and you must accept the consequence. If you continue to dwell upon your deer, upon the good and positive, you will survive the battle; if you allow self-doubt and negative, harmful thoughts, you will not. A word of caution: it sounds simple; but it is not. Time will tell."

"I think I understand for myself," Mike said rejuvenated. "Where do you and Sam fit in?"

"Well, I am inextricably attached to the earthbound spirits." Anna explained. "In fact, I have a personal 'spirit guide' named Ariel, which keeps me in contact with Fran and Ronnie. Because of Ariel, I am sensitive to things that happen at considerable distances, that I can to some degree divine the future."

"Do you mean that you can actually see your daughter, that you can be with Fran whenever you want?"

"No... it doesn't work that way. I can be with Ronnie — though we do not touch or actually see each other — because he has a physical body, something to touch and see. With Fran, it's different. We have been given an obvious clue. Remember what Bertrand Russel said? Stare into a lamp for a few seconds, then close your eyes and the image of that lamp will stay with you, fading gradually, the strongest impressions going last. So, I don't see Fran... just her hand, with a brush in it, repeating the swift, sure strokes that created the masterpiece above the fireplace. Ariel assures me that all is well with her and I believe it! Ronnie? I can see for myself that all is not well with him; but nothing can be done about that, unless he comes home."

"What about Sam? Where is he in this world of yours?"

"Papa and I are diametrically opposed. There is a third group of spirit beings: Those who have, by their earth thoughts and acts, completely bypassed lower, earthbound spiritual reigons, who have lept clear of the battlefield. I am told that Papa will be one of those. You see, he rejects my spirit world; he scoffs at the things I have told you tonight. I presume you have had the 'body of God' speech." Mike nodded. "The 'big toe' speech?" He nodded again and they both smiled. While Fran's death and Ronnie's disappearance have bound me to this earth, they have sprung Papa free of it, although he doesn't know it yet... and probably wont until he dies. But Ariel has promised that there will soon be a sign, showing that what I say is true."

Abruptly, Anna stood, picked up the cocoa cup and started to leave. "That is enough for both of us tonight."

"You forgot to explain the speed of the deer," he begged.

"I thought I had. As your deer directed its speed in such a way as to leap the fence and free itself from danger, so we must try to direct our thoughts away from the dangers of the battlefield. Thought is the quality you seek, Michael; it's proper thought that enhances our existence."

He turned on the bedside light and went with her to the door.

"About the lodge... tell Sam I'll stay another day to discuss it."

"He'll be very pleased," she said.

Mike closed the door behind her and fell back on the bed, complaining to the ceiling: "Damn it! What am I doing here?" He stared into the light before turning it out, then rolled into the wall, contemplating the light's fading image, remembering what Anna had said — yellow... to red... fade to black, like a dying star imploding... an imploding man.

Once during the night, he roused to the sound of thunder and rain on the roof. He was not long disturbed by it, for lovely Linda painted his thoughts until dawn and left about the time she would have been getting up for work.

VI

Indecisively toying with the telephone, Mike lifted the receiver a few times, then cradled it. No, he wouldn't phone ahead. A surprise might do Kirkpatrick a world of good. Instead, he called his bank, making an appointment with the manager, Newton Bass, for the next afternoon. He called his lawyer too, and after a heated argument with the secretary, secured an appointment for 4:30 p.m. the same day, leaving the lady in some distress because poor Curtis would have to miss handball.

His mischievous mood faded as he dialled again, wondering what to say if there was an answer, relieved when the phone rang six... seven times Just as he started to replace the receiver, he heard her voice.

"Linda?"

"Mike!"

At least she didn't sound angry. Almost pleased.

"Yes. You were a long time answering."

"I'm just in from work."

They had found enough warmth in their first few words to overcome the strangeness that disagreement and separation had brought.

"Are you in Toronto?" Linda asked.

"No, I'm calling from Muskoka."

"Oh..." she paused. "I thought perhaps..." and paused again.

"Thought what?"

"It doesn't matter," Linda answered sadly.

"I've been staying with Sam and Anna Greenberg, Linda. They own a lodge here. It's for sale and I'm coming back early to see if I can put an offer together."

There was silence, but Mike could feel the tension through the telephone.

"Relax," he added. "Nothing will come of it, but I'm going to try anyway."

"Good luck!" She said half-heartedly.

"Your work. How is it?"

"Good. I've had lots of time for work lately."

"And Maxwell?"

"He's fine."

"I'll be in town tomorrow afternoon."

They were momentarily silent. Mike could hear her swallow — as though she wanted to cry and couldn't.

"Do you want to see me then?"

"Yes. If you don't object. I'll come over tomorrow evening."

"Just to talk."

"Of course. What else?"

"I know you."

"Just to talk, then."

Maxwell Taylor tamped his pipe and stared knowingly at Linda as she struggled to regain her composure after the call. He knew two things: she loved Mike Kramer and only Mike Kramer could change that. It was to his advantage to be patient.

"What's he up to now?" he asked.

"If I told you, you wouldn't believe me. He'll be back tomorrow."

"I think we should bring Sylvia in and you can start training her. I have the feeling I'm going to need a new secretary."

"Don't be silly, Maxwell."

"Come on, my dear. We'll be late for dinner."

"We aren't talking about the House-at-Pooh-Corner here you know."

"I know."

"This is a sizable investment. Too sizable for you to handle alone."

"Probably."

"Why would Greenberg want to sell to you?"

"He wants to retire."

"But there must be dozens of buyers. Why you?"

"I don't know."

"Well the price certainly is right, no doubt about that..." the young banker commented. "I wish there was something I could do to help you Mike." He was visibly uncomfortable and it wasn't because of his starched shirt and stove-pipe vest.

"There is! Lend me some money."

"I can't." His head jerked up and down, back and forth as he spoke. "I... the bank would never touch a thing like this. Never!" It was strange for him to be so nervous. Mike had done business with Newton Bass for seven years. They had become friends during that time. Mike had never seen him so jittery.

"What's wrong, Newt?"

"Nothing," he insisted. "Believe me, if there was any way that I... the bank, could help you... but, God, look at the thing realistically — from the bank's point of view, I mean, you have no experience. You have very little cash to put into it. It's already the middle of April and you expect to be — hell! you *have* to be — in full swing by July first."

"I've shown you Greenberg records. The place makes a profit."

"1967? What about 1967?"

"The weather was bad. And everyone went to Expo '67 in Montreal."

"And 1973, Mike? What happens if the weather's bad this summer? A bad year would ruin you before you started. Hell, an average year would ruin you! You're playing Russian roulette, for God's sake!"

"Forget it, then."

"Even if you had more cash. You're taking a flier on this one and you know God damn well the bank doesn't gamble. We'll lend you an umbrella on a sunny day, but we'll want it back when it starts to rain. Sell a few of your cabs and at least you'd have a workable down payment. Jack was in the other day talking about expanding. He'll buy."

"Forget it, I said."

That should have been the end of it. As Mike Kramer rose to leave, he was not disappointed. Rather, he was relieved. That was that! He had tried.

"Uhmm, by the way... "

Here it comes, Mike thought: The 'by the way' that tells me what's bothering him; the 'uhmm' that says my account must be overdrawn.

"I shouldn't tell you this, because I think you're making a serious mistake. But just this morning a man came to see me — a representative from Gem-Star

Mortgages. I checked them out. They're owned by Malor Holdings, a *very* reputable company. He claims his company intends to become more aggressive. They're going after deals like yours."

"No thanks. Those guys are too expensive."

"Not according to him. Their terms sounded pretty reasonable to me."

Mike knew suddenly why Mr. Bass was ill-at-ease.

"He offered you a commission. Right? Ordinarily, you'd tear his card up and throw it in the trash. Right? But… "

Newton Bass smiled. His nervousness disappeared. "I'm putting in a swimming pool," he said dryly. "I need the money."

"Set up an appointment. No harm to talk."

"When?"

"Tonight." *No, not tonight. Can't.* He had forgotten about Linda. "Tonight." He took two steps toward the door, turned and looked at Newton Bass. "You know Newton, in a sense this lodge is my swimming pool."

"Sure. I hope you don't drown in it."

"See you tonight."

Mike made two phone calls after he left the bank. He waited until 4:45, then rang the lawyer's office to cancel his appointment. Curtis grabbed the phone from his receptionist.

"Kramer!" he yelled. Curtis had been yelling at him since high school. It was their ritual. "You know I play handball every afternoon. Not today, though! Thanks to you!"

"You always loose, anyway."

"That's my problem. What did you want?"

"I don't know yet. I'll see you tomorrow."

"What time?"

"4:35, of course."

Curtis hung up.

Mike called Linda to explain that their meeting would have to be delayed 24 hours. She said she understood and that it would be all right.

It was 7:00 a.m. All of Mike Kramer's cars were out — for the first time in more than a week — and Jack Kirkpatrick was having breakfast in the hotel coffee shop, no doubt sulking because four of his cars were sitting on the lot. Jack was never bashful when it came to money, but he had left without complaint. Mike hoped he would choke on his ham and eggs. Scoundrel!

Mike's desk was covered with paper — trip sheets, bank slips, bills. Used paper hung from his adding machine and curled in a pile on the floor. He finished tallying the score for the past 10 days: trip sheets 293 to 254; bank deposits $7,474.00 to $6,180.00 — both in Kirkpatrick's favour. Mike dropped his pencil on the desk, pushed his chair back and stretched his legs. He picked at one of his fingers as he thought. When Newton Bass mentioned that his partner had been looking for money to expand, he knew there would be trouble. That was a flagrant violation of the terms of their partnership. There was to be no expansion unless both agreed. Kirk shouldn't even have been thinking of expansion without consulting him.

"Talk about cool," Mike thought. "This guy's the champ! Gone 10 days and he's found every way there is to cheat me. The man doesn't expect me back for three weeks. I walk in and catch him with his hand in the cookie jar. He shakes my hand. slaps me on the back and says how good it is to see me."

Mike stared at the mess on his desk. Nothing remotely like the speed of the deer there. Not for him, at least.

"Hard at it, eh?"

"Come in, Jack. How was breakfast?"

"Great!" Kirkpatrick unwrapped a fresh cigar and sank his teeth into it. "The Seymour brothers just came in," he said with satisfaction. "Two to go."

"Good."

"Those other two cars could stand some fixin' anyway," he rationalised. "Whatcha doin'?"

"I'm figuring out how much I've lost in the last 10 days."

Jack didn't flinch. "Whatcha talkin' about?"

Mike had summarised the totals. He handed the paper to his partner and watched him read it.

"So?"

"So! What the hell do you mean? So! I'm out of pocket $1,300 and that's all you can say. What are you trying to do?"

"I'm not doin' nothin'"

"Some partnership! Fifty-fifty." With one sweep of his arm, Mike cleared his desk.

Jack removed his cigar from his mouth and looked in disbelief at the adding machine. It was belly-up on the floor.

"Yeh," he said indifferently, "some partnership."

He left the room.

It was noon before they spoke again. Friendship mends faster than love. A bare, fuzzy arm appeared in the doorway. There was a white paper bag dangling from the end of it.

"Buy you lunch?"

Mike smiled. "Shoe yourself, you hairy brute."

A red-haired, grinning face peeked around the frame. There was a cigar stump stuck in the middle of it. One thing hadn't changed. They still liked each other.

"You know we have an agreement — no more than a couple hours a day behind the desk." Jack pulled burgers, fries and all the plastic condiments from the paper bag and set them on the desk. "Take your pick," he offered. He blew into the bag and popped it. "What have you been doing here all morning?"

"Straightening out the stuff I knocked off my desk."

"Does the adding machine still work?"

"No."

"Don't get ketchup on those trip-sheets." They laughed together. Jack set his cigar on the edge of the desk and stuffed some French fries in his mouth. They seemed to relax him. "What have you really been doing here?" he said with a mouthful.

"Thinking. Trying to think. About us. About what I'm going to say to you."

"Fire away! No. Never mind. I already know what's happening. I'm getting bigger. You're getting different."

"Bigger?"

"Growing! Like a balloon."

"Like that bag you popped."

"Whatever."

"We both expand together. You know that."

"Not this time. I'm ready to make a big move. You ain't."

"I'm moving, Kirk. But not with you. I'm thinking of buying a lodge in Muskoka. That's why I've come back early."

They finished their lunch without further conversation. Jack scraped the remains of their lunch into the waste basket. He put the cigar back in his mouth. His eyes were shining. "You want me to buy you out? How much?"

"No, I don't. I need the income."

"Where you goin' to get that kind of money?"

"I have a mortgage company looking at it right now. Pending a good appraisal, they've assured me of the money. It was easier than I though it would be."

Jack shook his head. "I knew it," he said. "For sure, I knew it."

"What concerns me," Mike continued, "is that I will have to be away from here until mid-September. You've been taking a hundred dollars a day extra for yourself. From now to September, that's a lot of money."

"I can keep your cars on the road. If that's what's bothering you."

"Sure. But I noticed on these sheets that the best drivers were taking *your* cars."

"You can't have it both ways. You can fly to the moon, for all I care. Buy your lodge. I don't give a shit what you do. But I told you before you left that I'm looking out for number one. You do the same. You want good drivers in your cars? Sit your ass down here every day and put them in. I'm goin' up Mike. And I ain't waitin' around for you."

Kirkpatrick's cigar was a mess. It was getting a good working over. Mike Kramer stared at him and purposely didn't speak. He waited for his hot-headed partner to cool out.

"Look." Jack's tone became conciliatory. "I'll make you a deal." He even smiled. "You need me. I need you. Even Steven."

"I'm listening."

"I want to buy Comet Cabs. Gord's sick. He has to sell. You go ahead. I'll look after your end the best I can. In return, you put in a good word for me with Mr. Bass. You're good friends. Convince him that nothing's changed as far as we're concerned. It's business as usual. Know what I mean? Give me your blessing, so to speak."

Mike knew what Kirk meant! He remembered that this was a battlefield — where deals would be struck, backs would be slapped, palms would be oiled, knives would be stuck. "It's a deal," he said without shaking hands. "You take care of my business. I'll take care of Newton Bass."

"Good!"

"But I'll still be down here once a week. I don't trust you."

"I can't blame you, Sometimes, I don't even trust myself!"

Convincing Linda that he had changed, that he wanted her to be part of that change, would be as tacky as the floor in Jake's restaurant. How could she understand Sam's ossification? Why should she accept that he was having a Platonic affair with Anna Greenberg?

Speed adds beauty to the deer.

Occam's Razor: The simplest solution is usually the best.

Straight out, Mike told her that he wanted to buy a lodge, that he still loved her, that he wanted her with him. "... and, if the deal goes through, which it probably won't, I'd like you to ask Maxwell Taylor for a two-month leave of absence and come up and help me this summer."

"Don't be ridiculous!"

She didn't trust Jack Kirkpatrick, she said. He didn't trust Maxwell Taylor.

"Mike! Stop it! We can work things out without running. I know we can."

"It isn't running, damn it. Two days ago I was prepared to face my problems here... to 'work things out'... to say I'm sorry and carry on. But I've realized that we could never straighten our lives out here. My business is a living — not a life. It's not what I want to do with my life... I mean, it's not what I want to do with *all* of my life."

"You'll lose everything!"

"Everything?" Mike knew if he persisted, Linda would begin to cry. He could see the hurt of the past several months rising... wanting out. He looked away, embarrassed because he had caused that pain, sad because there would be more before this thing was resolved. "I'm going back," he whispered. "To Muskoka. I have to."

Linda cried. Openly and unashamed. She didn't move or speak. Just wept quietly because she couldn't understand.

"Look... Maybe I should have waited a while before coming here. If I can't raise the cash I need and put a reasonable mortgage on the place, then we're arguing over nothing."

"If not the lodge," she sighed, "then something else."

"You're right. I've come to realize that if I stay here, marry you and look after my business, I *will* lose everything. I'm at the point in my life where I have to dig a little deeper than the bottom of my pocket; I have to look a little further than my company's year-end; I have to find the speed of a deer for myself. If I don't, all is lost."

The food, the wine, the music, Occam's Razor hadn't helped. Linda made no attempt to answer, appeared not to care about what he was saying.

He reached for her hand across the table and she let him touch it. Maybe not everything in life was electricity, but some things were.

"We are all confronted with this at some time in out lives. You will be, too.

Maybe tomorrow... maybe 20 years from now. It started for me — the showdown, my Armageddon — when we used the Ouija board a couple of months ago. My time to face it is now, and I'm not going to turn from it. I'm not running away; I'm running *to* ! Whether I buy Greenberg Lodge or not, I'm asking you to run with me."

"I can't leave Maxwell! He's been to good to me. It wouldn't be fair."

"If we have the summer together, who knows what will happen?"

"No... I can't."

He would be in town for at least another week. Would she reconsider? He would call before he left, just in case. "Please come. I need you there with me."

She wasn't sure.

The taxi left them on the sidewalk outside her apartment on Jamison Avenue.

Occam's Razor: in the elevator, on the way up to his own apartment, Mike lamented that he hadn't asked to see Linda to her door.

VII

Sam Greenberg sat on his porch and waited. All morning, he had been following Anna — her sounds in the house, her play in the garden. She had gone in and out so many times that he had propped the screen door open with his book to keep it from clattering. She had hummed Bridge Over Troubled Water so often that he began humming it to himself.

He waited.

They had received a post card from Ronnie in the morning mail. There was a return address in New York. Anna had already written her reply. With Ronnie, she had to be quick. For the first time, she had brought her letter to her husband and had asked him to write something at the bottom. He read her words: "Thank God you are well... Papa is fine... We think the lodge is sold... a nice young man from Toronto... he's coming today... we'll know for sure." And Sam wrote: "I love you, son. Come home" with a shaking hand.

He waited.

"He should be here," Sam fussed, "if he left early."

"Stop fretting Papa! Michael's world does not revolve around us. He'll get here in good time."

"Don't you think the lodge is important?"

"To you, Papa. And therefore to me. No more than that."

It was past noon when the Thunderbird rolled into the large parking lot behind the lodge. The sun flashed off it's chrome. From his higher vantage point Sam watched the car ease to a stop near the kitchen. Mike emerged from the vehicle, looked over toward the house and waved with his arm held high above his head. Sam was not absolutely certain, because of the distance but he thought Mike had formed a 'V' with his fingers. He returned the greeting from the steps and watched Mike Kramer disappear in the shadows between the office and lounge.

Sam Greenberg hobbled down the stairs to join his wife in the garden. He knelt down beside her and they dug in the soil together.

For the first time, they shook hands. There was steady strength in the old man's grip. Greenberg's lodge had been his life. He was saddened to lose it, relieved to be free of it, resigned to living the remaining fraction of his existence without it.

He smiled and still held tighter, as though to wish success without a word. There was a need to pass on something more than a group of buildings and the ground they sat upon.

"I was once where you are now, my friend," Sam offered and he finally released Mike's hand.

"I've given the biggest gamble of my life the least amount of thought. It was so much easier than I figured it would be."

"You'll likely lose money this year," Sam warned. "Maybe next. I'll hold onto the hundred acres around the lodge. Just in case."

"Just in case what?"

"In case you want to expand."

"Expand! Hell, the goal is to survive."

"You seem happy, though."

"Why not? It hides my anxiety. The rep from Gem-Star will be here tomorrow. There's no turning back after that."

"We'll help. We promised we would and we'll keep our word. Anna has looked after everything since our first year. Her knowledge will be invaluable. Most of last year's staff will come back if we contact them right away. None of the guests know I was closing nor that the place has been sold. In fact, I have a few reservation requests that came in last week."

"I'll let them know what's happened."

"Why?" Sam questioned. Already he was operating on cylinders that hadn't fired for years. "Why bother? I've kept a record of everyone who has ever stayed here. I have two thousand brochures left over from last year. Send them out and let your guests find out about the sale when they arrive at... Do you have a name?"

"Not yet," he admitted. There hadn't been time to think about names, the way everything fell into place so quickly. He'd have to have one for Gem-Star, he supposed.

"There is one little detail I should mention," Sam said. "My guests have mostly been Jewish. Perhaps that makes a difference."

"Not to me. Bring 'em on, Sam."

"Then I'll send out those brochures at my expense. Call it my good luck gift to you," he beamed. "You'll need help in the office, you know. Anna can get you organised, but she can't... "

"Linda is coming! July first. Her employer has given her leave until Labour Day."

"How did you manage that?"

"Damned if I know! Like everything else so far — Kirkpatrick, Gem-Star — it just slid into place, as though that's the way it's supposed to be," he bragged, thinking that possibly he had a spirit guide of his own, knowing very will he hadn't.

"Then things are straightened between you?"

"No, not really. We're going to make a fresh start. We're hoping that being together this summer, away from the city, will make a difference."

"A difference?" Sam challenged. "I see... well, perhaps it will. But first you must concentrate on opening day. There are so many things and so little time. You have May and June to prepare."

"I'll be prepared."

"In *every* way, I trust."

"Like the best boy scout."

"If you are, my friend, you'll make a hundred new discoveries here. There's a word for that. Do you know it?"

"Serendipity."

VIII

First and most important on the list of things to do was the general rejuvenation of Serendipity Lodge. To that end, Mike had asked Jake to come and see him — against Sam Greenberg's advice. He waited at his desk. The bell at the main door rang once to indicate that someone had opened it, but failed to ring again in a lower tone as it should have when the door closed. There was a small window, with sliding glass, in the wall between Mike's office and the reception area. He looked through it.

Jake was standing in the doorway and Pal was behind, peering at him through his master's wish-bone legs. The shape was evident in spite of the baggy pants he wore.

"Pretty picher, eh boy?"

"I'll be a minute, Jake. Come in and sit down." Jake didn't move. "Okay. The dog too."

Mike closed the window. He wrote the figure $25.00 on a scratch pad and doodled around it for five minutes. He could hear Jake talking to the dog: "Pal! Sit... atta boy!" "Pal! Sit! Good boy." "C'mere Pal! Now sit!"

"How are you, Jake?"

"Good."

"How's business?"

"Bought this place, eh?"

"Yes. Though sometimes I wish I hadn't."

"Me too."

"You too what?"

"Wisht I hadn't."

"Is your business that bad?"

"Ain't no money in it. Nothin' but complaints. People's always wantin' somethin' fer nothin'."

"Too bad." Mike would have tried to sound concerned if Jake had seemed to be that way. There was a silence that bothered him, but he sat through it.

"Bought this place, eh?"

"Yes, Jake."

"Funny name ya give it though. Pal! Sit! That ain't your las' name."

"No. Serendipity has a special meaning."

"I'd of called it Sidney Lodge."

"I know."

"Need a hand, eh?"

"No. I'll have plenty of help."

"School kids! Play all night. Sleep all day. Ask ol' Greenbug. He knows."

"I'll manage."

"Ya bought yourself a bushel o' headaches. Fella come fer gas. Tol' me Big Pin Inn's gonna close. Biggest lodge in Muskoka. Fella's gotta know what he's doin', Ask Greenbug. Pal! Sit! Nobody knows this place like me. I was the boss over everythin!"

"Are you asking me for a job, Jake?"

"Nope! Ain't never done that in m' life. Jus' tellin' ya, eh."

"You had some trouble with Mr. Greenberg. He told me you charged too much for the work you did."

"Never got a cent fer all th' bossin' I done. Tol' 'im hunnerts a' times. Jus' like all the res' — wantin' somethin' fer nothin'."

"There isn't any *bossing* to do this year. I intend to be the boss."

"Ya askin' me t' help ya out, eh?"

Mike glared at him. He was inclined to put Jake in his place, but an involuntary sigh relaxed him.

"Yes," Mike conceded. "But only as a repairman and handyman — nothing more. If I hire extra help to do some of the repairs, you can be in charge of them and that's all!"

"Com' ere Pal! Sit!"

"Each morning you will come to me and I'll have a list of things for you to do. Each item on the list will have the amount you are to be paid next to it. That way, I won't have to worry about how long you take to cut the grass or fix a window and *you* won't have to worry about how much to charge me."

"Pal!"

"When the work has been done to *my* satisfaction, you'll be paid for it. Then you can go on to other things. I'll put it on paper and we'll both sign it. There will be no misunderstandings between us, the way there was with Mr. Greenberg."

"Ain't signing no papers! Don't put no trust in 'em."

"Well *I* do — and *I'm* the boss."

"Ain't signin' no papers."

"Then forget about working for me. No papers. No job."

Jake extended his arm a little and Pal slipped his body under it. They looked at each other, obviously disgusted. "I'll sign 'em then, if ya need me that bad. Never like t' see any man stuck. But them papers gotta say that I got metal rights."

"What on earth are metal rights?"

Jake chuckled and ruffled the fur between Pal's ears. "See! Lotsa things ya don't know 'bout runnin' a lodge."

"Skip the lecture. What are metal rights?"

"Got a machine that finds metal. Use it on the beach. I find it. Pal here digs it." At the word dig, the dog became a panting bundle of wiggles and wags. "Not now boy," Jake said to settle him.

"You fill in the holes, of course."

"'Course."

"I don't want the beach looking like gopher heaven."

"Put it in them papers."

"Fine. I'll get them ready. And Jake... this is a place of business. From now on, if you have to break wind, do it outside. I came here to get away from pollution."

Jake thought. "It's th' dog. He's gettin' old."

They went outside and talked while Pal relieved himself against the nearest tree.

"By the way, Jake, how is Doc Rogers."

"Ain't good." Jake shook his head slowly. "Ain't good at all. Bin takin' medicine to him fer a week. No good though. Seems he kin help other folks easy. But can't help hisself. He'll get better."

"When he does, have him come see me."

"Be 'round. Friendly sort, Doc. Likes t' meet people."

"Maybe I should visit, him. After all, we're neighbours and of he's sick..."

"Too sick to see ya. Be 'roun' soon enough."

"Okay. Can you get some help? I want every inch of this place repaired and painted."

"Sure."

"They're going to finish putting up the sign tomorrow. You can help with that. Stop in and see me first. I'll have the papers."

"Papers," Jake grunted. "C'mon Pal."

Mike watched Jake dawdle along the narrow path behind the games hall and entertainment building. He stopped for a minute at the tennis courts, then disappeared into the trees. Strange that Jake should be walking. Mike wondered if he should have listened to Sam Greenberg. He had the feeling that Jake might be more a hindrance than a help. Still it would be better to have him puttering around the lodge than sitting in Sidney telling every visitor horror stories about Serendipity.

There were so many things to do. Sam had graciously offered to help him fill the staff positions: a maitre d'hotel, a hostess, waitresses and busboys for the dining room; a chef, first and second cooks, a foreman and student help for the kitchen; a head chambermaid and her assistants for the rooms and laundry; desk clerks, night and day, for the office; someone to lease the coffee and tuck shops beneath the lounge; a local boy to take charge of the boathouse; bellhops; counsellors for the children; an athletic director and a dance team to instruct the adults; a master of ceremonies, a resident band and a variety of weekly entertainment for the dance hall. At this point, Sam's assurance that everything would fall into place didn't help.

There were a dozen small cabins tossed like dice among the trees by the ravine. According to Sam, they would be filled first and stay filled for the summer because they each had a fireplace and offered considerably more seclusion than the rooms in the three, two-storey buildings that formed the main lodge. They, to Mike, were the logical area for him to begin his attack. That's where Jake would start.

Hopefully, in two months, he would have worked his way back to the office... Hopefully.

On his way to the cabins, Mike stopped at the shuffleboard courts. He noticed cracks in the cement and made a note to have Jake pave and repaint them. From the highest terrace of the lawn, he glanced at the main lodge buildings behind; they needed paint too.

Limberlost was blue and shining now; the ice between the islands had broken and melted under a sun that forced him to remove his jacket. Gentle waves nagged at the beach and boathouse. Far off shore, a solitary, paddling loon moaned. Mike watched it dive and surface 50 feet away, just to paddle some more and dive again. Funny thing about the loon, you could never predict where it was going to come up. Stupid loon, he thought. From the land around the lake, sprang a mystic, salamander voice, telling Mike "pay attention" and he would begin to see the fabric of Muskoka — springtime's sylvan, gossamer net.

Amidst these sights and sounds, below him, the terraced lawn and beach lay like an amphitheatre with an empty stage. He looked forward to the time when the stage would be busy with playful, wet, browning bodies. His immediate chore — make sure the stage was properly set. He would offer his guests more than room and board and would expect more than profit from them in return. That would be the concept, he decided, which would shape Serendipity Lodge.

He would be about it immediately. Then, he would come to grips with the speed of the deer.

As Mike worked his way toward the cabin to prepare a preliminary maintenance list for Jake, he thought he heard the wind and waves and birches applaud. It could have been his Romantic imagination. He wasn't sure.

There were so many things to do.

IX

To Mike Kramer, the burden of those first few weeks would have been intolerable, if not for Sam Greenberg. The old fellow stayed with him much of the time. Sam was openly apologetic for his presence, yet eager to assist in any way he could. He had a fresh vitality but the loss of an integral part of his life was still evident to Mike. Once financial matters were out of the way, their friendship deepened, even to the point that when Mike was in Toronto, he consciously missed Sam's companionship.

Frequent trips to the city were necessary, but Mike made them with reluctance. His interest never left Serendipity. He would leave early in the morning, settle matters at hand by late afternoon — hire a chef, secure supplies, line up entertainment, whatever — surprise good old Jack Kirkpatrick, dine with Linda and return to Serendipity the next morning.

It was too early to know for sure, but initial indications were that Kirkpatrick intended to continue his "after me comes you" approach to Mike's affairs. Converted to dollars and cents, that would be his baby-sitting fee for the summer. "Yes, Jack. I stopped in to see Newton Bass. Yes, Jack, I put in a good word. Yes, Jack, I've reserved a weekend for you and a full week for Rachael and the kids." Let me out of here, Jack.

When he dined with Linda, he spoke incessantly of Serendipity and of the time when she would join him. He carefully outlined the progress that had been made since their last dinner and she listened dutifully. They touched... kissed... did most of the things they had done before. He took Linda back to her apartment. Since Mike had sublet his apartment to two university students who were staying in town for summer courses, he slept in a hotel room and called her the next morning before leaving the city.

"You understand, Mike?" she would ask. "We can't. I won't. Not until we see if we can work things out."

"I understand."

He didn't mind the city — liked it, actually. As long as the lid was off. But when he turned at Sidney Road, he was home — as much home as Jake could ever be. And when he found Sam waiting for him, he knew the "why" of his being there and what to do with it.

There were two storeys of suites attached to the main office and reception area. They were larger and more expensively appointed than the others and were to be reserved for special guests. Mike still took his meals with the Greenbergs, but he had taken a double suite on the second floor. Beyond that, the application of the label "special" was solely at his discretion. Linda, for sure. He had already picked out a room for her.

As Mike lugged his suitcase up the back stairway to his suite, Sam followed. Ordinarily, because of his weight, he would have stayed behind and waited for Mike to come down.

He was excited. "Ray Mildenhal was here yesterday," he puffed. "You know, the fellow I lost track of. An excellent master of ceremonies. Lots of connections."

When they reached Mike's room, Sam took out his handerchief and wiped his face and the top of his bald head.

"He wants to come here this summer," Sam continued. "I took his number and told him that you'd look him up next week."

"Great! Thanks, Sam."

"How about you?"

"Me?"

"How did you make out?"

"Fine. The chef is coming back this year, too. He's sending a cook up next week to feed the staff that arrives early."

And on they went. Mostly Sam, while Mike patiently unpacked his things.

He listened.

"What is it Sam? Why are you so excited? Not Ray Mildenhal. Not the chef. You caught Jake sleeping on the job. So what. Something else happened while I was away."

"Yes!" Sam Greenberg look straight at Mike. His clear, sparkling eyes were dancing. "Ronnie called. He's coming home. My son is coming home!"

Mike grasped Sam's hand and pulled the old man to him. He held him by the shoulders and Sam took a firm grip on Mike's wrists. "My friend." They didn't release each other until their eyes began to moisten.

"When?"

"Soon. We sent his fare to New York this morning." Sam hesitated. Michael... would it be alright if Ronnie worked with us... with you, this summer?"

"You mean a job. Just a regular job."

"Yes. That will give us enough time to get to know him again. Maybe he'll stay on with us. Go back to school in the fall, even."

"Of course. He's got a job."

"You're good for this place, my friend. See how things are working out. Anna said from the beginnig that you would be good for this place."

"I had sort of hoped it would be the other way around."

They had a happy meal that night. But as Mike returned to his suite, he remembered the broken man who walked with him to the forestry station and back, who talked of hurt and loss and disappointment. He *could* help Sam. He knew it — by being rational, objective, realistic. Ronnie's return would be the wedge in a door that opened to as much heartache as happiness. Sam still had to come to grips with a loss of confidence in himself and in his God. He *would* help Sam. He *would* . In exchange, Sam would turn out to be a very important piece to his puzzle: what happens to a human being from the cradle to the grave? How can he spring from star to star one day and be mired in muck the next. What sinister forces and benevolent powers have conspired to volly humans in their frivolous contests of give and take? How could humans be expected to endure such a pounding?

As Mike quickened his pace to escape the night air's chill, he was oblivious to the pointless complaining of the loons on Limberlost.

X

She sat there like carved marble, waiting for him. And Jake, waiting for him with her, was visibly uncomfortable in her presence, obviously relieved when Mike entered the reception office with a morning cup of coffee in his hand. As was his ritual, Jake shook the work-list that had been left on the counter, argued less than usual about the amount beside each item, then shuffled off in a wake of mild profanity.

At least he hadn't broken wind.

Mike turned to the young lady with a look of apology. Her eyes were deep brown — black enough to discourage him from looking into them. She had hearse-black hair, evenly and closely cropped so that it sharpened her delicately featured face. She was slim — not thin but lean and supple. Mike instinctively knew that she did not want to be at Serendipity. In spite of the vague categories his mind had fixed to her, his attraction to Toni Warden — to something about Toni Warden — was instant.

"The employment agency sent me."

"As?"

"A waitress."

Their introduction included a few pleasantries that took them to Mike's office. Her attractiveness and neatness were enough to convince Mike that she was adequate for the position. Yet, whenever he looked at her — not into her eyes — he began to suspect her motives and it piqued his interest.

"How old are you, Toni?"

She hesitated. He watched her slender fingers work at old nail polish.

"Lie if you want."

"Twenty-two."

He couldn't tell. But that was approximately correct. "Are you from Toronto?"

Toni nodded her head.

"Are you married?"

"No."

"I suppose you've been a waitress before."

She nodded.

"And why do you want to work here?"

"A change."

"Nothing more? Just a change?"

"No... nothing."

There *was* something more. He was sure of it.

"At least I have to know your working background before I can hire you. That's really all I have to know, I guess. If you tell me, it will save filling out an application."

"I left school when I was 16. I've worked in restaurants since then." She remembered the names of her employers and didn't hesitate to mention them or the reasons for leaving their employ.

"You've changed jobs because of wages and working conditions. But why have you come to Serendipity? Not for a change. The hours are long and the wages are terrible. My guests won't be any easier to serve. You can count on it."

"If you're not going to hire me, say so." She struck out at him unexpectedly.

Mike wasn't bothered by her abrupt change in manner, though he thought it a fault in a waitress. He could see a hint of regret on her face. "She's here for a good reason," he thought. "But then, Kramer, so are you. That's what you want Serendipity to be all about."

It seemed to him that she needed help and he was the only one there.

"If you had your choice of being something other than a waitress here," he tested, "what would you choose?"

"I don't know." She was timid again.

"Don't you want to get ahead?"

"I don't care if I do."

"How did you get here?"

"By bus to Sidney Road, I walked in from there."

Ten miles.

"Did you see the two long buildings by the road," he asked.

"Yes."

"Those are the staff living quarters. There are two cleaning ladies here already. I'll send one over. Bertha's about your age. I'll have her meet you there now. The rest of the day is yours to relax a bit and arrange your things. Tomorrow morning you'll begin helping with the mattresses and bedding. That will be your job until we open." She went for her suitcase.

"I'll have Jake bring up your suitcase." he said. "You're welcome to use all facilities until July first. Your maitre d' will let you know the rules regarding conduct when we have guests. You'll have very few expenses, so the money you earn will be money saved."

Toni Warden left without speaking and in the stillness which followed, there was a simultaneous warning of his thoughts and increasing awareness of a scratching sound outside his office window. He looked through the screen. Jake was raking a patch of barren ground beneath a birch tree. Pal was gaurding a bag of grass seed at his feet.

Mike spoke through the screen. "Have you finished all the jobs on your list, Jake? That wasn't one of them."

"Ain't had time."

"Ain't had time?" I ain't surprised you ain't had time! Too busy eavesdropping."

"Too busy carryin' suitcases 'round for healthy people. Ain't on the list."

"Neither is sleeping in the cabins when you're supposed to be working. Take the suitcase and go tell Bertha about the new woman."

"Women," Jake snorted. "Phuh."

XI

Ordinarily a meal, a quiet game of chess, a bit of busines with Sam and a final, peaceful hour by the fireplace in the lounge; this particular evening was different. Sam and Anna both wanted to talk. The subject didn't matter, as long as it took their minds off Ronnie. They hadn't heard a word from him and Mike understood their concern. Ronnie had probably spent his plane fare by now and was running again. He wondered if Sam's frail spirit could handle another major disappointment.

"Thank you Anna." Mike pushed himself away from the table. "You are the best cook I know, bar none."

"Come now. Stop it."

Mike pointed to Sam. "Your husband is living proof."

"I often tell Papa he is twice and half the man he used to be at the same time," she teased. "I'm to blame for both I guess."

"Three more reservations came in today," Mike said, mentioning one in particular. "A Mrs. Cohen wrote, Sam. She seemed to be a friend of yours. She reserved a cabin for the entire season. Ninety-nine more letters like that and I can relax."

Sam offered a smile but he was not enthused. "I had hoped she wouldn't come this year. I wrote to her only because we'll... you'll need the money."

"What's the matter? Does she have leprosy?"

"If this year is like the others, my friend, there will be the odd bad incident. But guests come and go and troubles are quickly forgotten. Not so when Mrs. Cohen is around. By her nature and the duration of her stay, she will become the conscience and the memory of your lodge."

"Someone said that conscience is a triangle in our temples," Mike remarked. "Each time we do something wrong, the triangle turns. The sharp corners prick us and cause pain. If we turn the triangle often enough, it wears down to a smooth circle and the turning doesn't hurt anymore."

"You'll never wear down Mrs. Cohen. Believe me. She'll pile your sins on top of you and each new guest will learn of them before their bags are unpacked."

"Well, I'll be happy to have her here... her and any others like her."

"That's why I wrote to her, my friend. But during Serendipity's first year, I think it could do without a conscience. Incidentally, Mrs. Cohen's husband comes to visit her almost every weekend. He takes a separate room."

"Good!" Mike thought of the extra money first and then of the peculiar arrangement. "A separate room?"

"Don't ask me." Sam shrugged and showed amusement. "Except when the lodge is full. Then he stays at Bighorn." Sam tried to mask a devilish smile. "Last summer, one of the bellhops cornered him and, not realizing who he was, proceeded to curse his wife. Did I get a blast from Cohen! Believe me, if he hadn't known the bellhops complaints were justified, I never would have seen either of them again."

Anna joined them. She was through with the dishes by the time they finished talking. Mike stood as she entered and reached for her hand. "I'm going to borrow your wife for a while," he said to Sam. "I'm afraid to walk by myself in the dark."

"Go ahead," Sam chuckled. "Take my word for it. She's on personal terms with the bogeyman."

With a sweater over her shoulders, Anna walked him to the footbridge. Mike leaned on the precarious railing, thinking that was another thing for Jake's list. Spring run-off polished the boulders in the ravine below.

"Your son should have been home by now. Are you concerned?" Mike asked.

"Ronnie is doing what he has to do. Papa and I have tried to influence him. We can do no more."

"Actually... "

"Actually, you wanted to talk about something else. We have some unfinished business."

She knew. She always knew.

"Where did we leave off?" Testing, as if she didn't know. Anna leaned on the railing beside him, moving close so that their arms touched from shoulder to elbow.

"You were telling me that thought is to humans as speed is to the deer, that a deer's speed is paled by comparison. You said that by proper thought we can prepare ourselves to leap clear of the dangers of the battlefield."

"Do you have a problem with that?"

"In theory, no. In practice, nothing but trouble. There are so many diversions, so many excuses — trying to get Serendipity ready — maybe this isn't a good time to be thinking noble thoughts."

"Procrastination! Welcome to the battleground, Michael. You permitted your taxicab business to distract you for 10 years. Now it will be the lodge."

"I'll try, but it isn't easy. That's all I'm saying."

"Fair enough. I'll help you if I can. Where would you like to start?"

He asked her to explain again Fran's predicament as an earthbound spirit. "How is it that she cannot free herself of earthly ties?"

"Most young people, whose lives are snuffed out suddenly, are trapped like Fran. She was so vibrant when she was here, there was so much of her talent not spent, so much of her life not lived, that her spirit refuses to accept somatic death. So she's trying to live her earthly life through us. As I said before, with the help of Ariel, she has reached me through her art. Who knows? Maybe she has reached someone else in another way. Something is holding her here. Maybe it is the unfinished love of the lad she ran away with. Whatever it is, until it is resolved, Fran will not be free."

Nor would Anna, he reminded her.

Anna admitted that. There was Ronnie, too.

It all seemed so complicated. He wondered if there was nothing she could do to simplify it for him.

"Imagine being able to visit and talk with a fetus in the womb," she tried. "'How are you doing?' you might ask, it might reply 'Excellent! My hands and feet are developing nicely. I expect to be able to open my eyes soon.' 'Are you warm enough?' 'Perfect!' 'Are you getting enough to eat?' 'Plenty! All the food I need comes to me through this tube. In fact, my every requirement is provided before I have to ask for it.' 'Then you are content here?' 'Not content exactly. I want to grow some more. And what good are hands and feet if I can't use them? But on the whole, I am content.' 'How is your mother, by the way'

Mother? What is a mother?

"Not until that fetus has been born and put some distance between itself and the womb, will it begin to comprehend the concept of motherhood. Our spiritual lives run an identical pattern, except that "mother" becomes God. Personally, I have no understanding of God, because I am still in a spiritual womb. Now Papa is a different story: he has been born; he grows steadily, whether he wants to or not, and his understanding grows with him. He certainly has a concept of God, strange as it may sound to us."

"Where am I, Anna?" Mike wanted to know. Oh God! Where am I?

"You, sir, are just this moment being conceived!"

Suddenly, Anna became alarmed. "Who is that?" she asked, pointing to the beach, just beyond the boathouse, directing his attention to a frail silhouette, barely visible in the darkness.

"A new waitress I hired," he said, unconcerned. "She's helping Bertha with the rooms."

Anna complained about the cold and the lateness of the hour — apologised, but she had to go in. "We'll make time to talk again," she promised. Before leaving, she pressed Mike's hand and said: "There is nothing evil spirits like better than to catch us with our pants down. Our body, for its own sake, has many ways to deceive the mind… and *vice versa.*"

As she reached the porch-light perimeter on the Greenberg lawn, Anna's shadow fell over him, then shortened as she neared the house, leaving him standing not in the light, but on the penumbral edge of it.

On the dark side of the bridge, Mike spoke from a distance to avoid alarming the woman. But she didn't speak, even when he asked if she was comfortably settled in the staff quarters. Not until he came close to her — near enough to be attracted by the aroma of her perfume — could he tell that she had been crying. Klutz that he was, when it came to such matters, he wanted to know if he could help.

"No. I'm just lonely."

"Is it Bertha?"

"Bertha's okay. Can't I just be lonely?"

There was an awkward silence, during which she looked at him, so that the whites of her eyes revealed a mournful, searching look — like a frightened animal, expecting punishment.

"I want to help you as much as I can while you're here, I intend Serendipity to be a happy place — for staff as well as guests. A girl… a woman your age, should be living each moment…" That wasn't it. "It's late. Long day tomorrow." That wasn't it either. Damn!

"I don't need to be put to bed. I want to be left alone!"

Up the grass terraces she ran, slipping and sliding, needing help.

Conscious of a warmth in his loins, a gentle stirring between his legs, he let her go.

Speed adds beauty to the deer.

Such potential for good was here.

As he made his way up the cement steps, Mike promised himself that would be the last of his involvement with Toni Warden.

XII

Serendipity, caught in the transition from a peaceful paradise to a bustling communtiy, appealed in a different way to Mike Kramer. He did not begrudge missing morning coffee at the fireplace in the lounge — where a myraid of influences crossed his mind without the slightest panic. Then, more than any time of day, he realized that he was free of the North American Zoo.

Lately, there had always been someone in the lounge by seven. When that someone happened to be Toni Warden, he scurried out, slopping his coffee and vowing to find an alternative.

He took to retiring earlier and being at the shuffleboard courts by six, where he would yawn and stretch and look out over Limberlost, knowing that he was standing on the very spot where Fran had set up to create her landscape masterpiece. Then he would work his way down to the lake, hoping not to slip on the dew-damp grass. Funny... there were three terraces to the lawn, and if he stopped at each of them and looked out across the countryside, he saw three different scenes.

Once by the lake, he spent an hour listening to the stupid loons and the creatures in the woods, squeaking and squawking of matters above or below his human understanding. With workers coming, Mike eventually lost that hour too. Eventually, he had to lay wide-eyed in bed, letting Anna and the masters have their way with him — for he knew that the moment he oponed his apartment door, someone would be at hand to greet him with a problem.

Occasionally, Mike allowed himself a treat — as one might take a liquorice to stray from a diet — a minute off to watch Toni Warden sun herself. A few extra steps to catch her moving from one building to another did no harm. The two sides of him were always there, with equal power to attract... waiting for one to prevail, not caring which at times, wondering how long his conscience could hold the reins of self-resistant, how long his body — piss on Anna, Ariel too — would tolerate indifference to his need.

His answer came with Rick Gerrard. He was a blond, young, handsome, physical education major from Queens, athletic director for Serendipity, perfect inspiration for men to lose the pots that hung like hammocks over their belts, incentive for the ladies to haul themselves out of bed in the morning to watch his genitals move beneath his workout suit during jumping-jacks.

Rick was reserved and polite by nature, though his appearance and scholastic record afforded reason to be otherwise. He seemed anxious to get on with his work, intent upon clearing his head of schoolwork and earning a pittance as well. He was an accomplished golfer, so Mike decided to offer management of the driving-range to him as well — instead of hiring an expensive pro — a responsibility Rick was eager to accept. No different than running a cab company.

Of all the people he had hired, Rick Gerrard would be the last to give him trouble.

Not surprising then that he should be the first.

Ronnie came, in his good time, his doting parents receiving their prodigal son with great joy. For his first evening home, Anna prepared a special meal of his favourite meat and vegetables, to which Mike was invited — an invitation he wouldn't have missed for a chance to see the Pope. Besides, he had been taking his meals at the lodge, since one of the cooks had arrived, so he not only looked forward to the reunion, but he anticipated one of Anna's incomparable dinners as well.

As an outsider, Mike watched as Sam drew up his belly into his chest to make room for the pride he felt. Repeatedly, he put his arm around Ronnie, gave him a shake and said to Mike: "This is my son! He's home!" Giving an extra squeeze at the end.

Mike saw beyond the pride, the flashing eyes, to something more than was being said: "Unless you have had a son, you would not understand that the past is erased. All is forgiven."

And Anna, beautiful Anna, kissed the top of Ronnie's head every time she passed his chair.

There were things hidden which would have to surface sooner or later. As the night passed, Mike sat quietly when Ronnie — knowingly, he assumed — encouraged his parents to be at ease, then quickly made them uncomfortable with an intimidating remark.

"If he was my kid," Mike thought, "I'd cuff him — homecoming or not.

Kid hell! He's 24 years old!" It bothered Mike that Ronnie behaved like such a child. It disappointed him that the Greenbergs treated him — almost worshipped him — as such. "If I had an only son," he thought, "I would..." The thought ended there.

When he had waited a polite length of time, Mike was able to excuse himself without appearing anxious to leave. He certainly didn't like Ronnie and it was a relief to be out of the house, another relief to cross the footbridge from the Greenberg property to his own. Mike was well past the ravine and breathing easily when he heard the sound of footsteps on the wooden bridge. He looked behind, turned and waited for Ronnie to catch up.

"What is it?" he asked, assuming trouble of some kind.

"Nothing." Ronnie shifted his feet and tried to catch his breath. He was medium height and slim, like his mother. His eyes darted from side to side when he spoke. They seemed to be uncomfortable with the gentle, features of his baby-face. "I wanted to thank you for coming to dinner tonight."

"Forget it..." He almost said kid. "I'm glad you came back. Your mother and father have missed you." Mike waited for a response but there was none. "How long are you staying?"

"I've been moving around a lot. I don't have much money. I'll hang around here until I'm broke. Then take off."

"How long will that be?"

Ronnie grinned a little-boy grin. "No more than a week."

Mike had to say it. All his reason, intuition and instincts told him not to, but there was no way that he could let Sam and Anna be disappointed because of his own feelings. "There's a job open on the reception desk — days or nights — if you really want to stay. Doesn't pay much, but I can give you a bit extra, since you'll be eating and sleeping with your parents."

Ronnie shifted his feet and his eyes again. "How can I thank you?" he asked.

"No thanks needed. I'd like to see you stay... for your parents sake."

"Oh no, Mr. Kramer. I don't mean it *that* way. I mean how can I thank you for giving me a two-bit, schoolboy job at a lodge that rightfully belongs to me?"

Mike made fists of his hands. Now the weasel was coming out of his hole. Mike had been waiting all night to get a shot at him.

Ronnie giggled. "Now, now, Mr. Kramer. Really! Would you cause a commotion on the night of my homecoming? Sam would never forgive you."

Mike's fingers slowly relaxed. "You gave up your inheritance when you ran away. Your father has it in cash. Talk to him about what you think is yours, not me. You left of your own free will."

"My own free will? You aren't as close to Sam and Anna as I thought."

"I knew about your sister if that's what you mean."

"I've had to live in her shadow." Ronnie put a hand in his jacket pocket. He was fingering an object nervously as he spoke. "All my life."

"You're in Fran's shadow only if you wish to be and, from what I've seen and heard of you tonight, that's exactly where you belong."

"Kramer," he grinned. "You don't bother me. I know a good opportunity when I see one."

"Most children do."

"I'll bet you're up to your eyeballs in debt with a place like this — a little man with big ideas. And I'll bet if too many things go wrong, you'll lose in a big, big way. I'll even bet that you can't make it without Sam's help and I'll bet you know you can't. If anything happens to drive Sam's only son away from him again, he'd be very peeved — very, very upset. You see, *my friend,* I don't want money. I wouldn't touch a stinking cent of Sam's! I want what's mine. I intend to act as though this place is Greenberg Lodge. Not your... Serendipity!"

Mike reached for the tie that hung loosely from Ronnie's neck, at the same time keeping an eye on the hand in his jacket pocket. He pulled him closer. "Come out of it, kid! The job's still yours because of your parents. But, if you hurt them or me, I'll break your wiry little neck." He tightened his grip when Ronnie laughed at him.

"You're on a hook, Kramer. If you make one stupid move, it'll sink so deep you'll never get off. The only thing breaking will be your financial back."

The tie tightened until Ronnie couldn't breathe. He choked even after Mike let him go.

Ronnie was still defiant.

"For starters," he said, "I'm working nights." The object in his pocket was the baseball that his father had saved for him. He threw it hard toward the lake and it landed with a splash that hurt.

"I don't need Sam," Mike thought. "I'll just give this dink one good sock in the chops. Just one"

"Very well," Mike said aloud.

"Just the way I want it."

"You're too small to do any harm. Do your job and you'll stay out of trouble. Screw it up and it's good-bye Ronnie."

"I'll be at the reception desk every night, *my friend* ."

The screen door snapped shut on the Greenberg porch. Sam called for his son from the steps.

"Get out of here before I knock your little head off."

"Ah-ah," Ronnie scolded with his finger. "Mustn't do." He went away, calling back: "Good night Mr. Kramer. Thanks again for coming to dinner," so that his father could hear.

Mike watched Ronnie go and waited until the porch light went out. As he retreated to the solitude of his apartment, he felt a sadness that the Greenbergs were to be so deceived by the son they loved so much. The night air was so foul with that deceit that Mike spat the taste out of his mouth.

It would have been good to talk to Linda then.

Mike Kramer stood at the window of his darkened bedroom. He relaxed somewhat with a hot drink and two aspirin. The sound of laughing, two people on the cement steps below his window, took his thoughts away from Ronnie Greenberg. He watched Toni Warden descend to the beach with Rick Gerrard. He could hear the sound of their voices but the conversation was muffled and unintelligible. Rick held her hand as they walked the entire length of the beach, stopping occasionally to throw pebbles in the water. Before they reached the harsh night light on the boathouse door, they scuffled like playful pips, then fell laughing to the sand. Mike lost sight of them, but he heard their voices for a while, gradually fading. Then, they were still.

Disgusted, Mike closed the window, drew the curtains and went to bed.

Six o'clock… he roused to Bertha's shuffling, sandpaper walk in the hallway, but kept his eyes closed. Ronnie Greenburg and Toni Warden were at him instantly, like hornets. They were there when he went to sleep; they must have been there all night, nesting in his brain… stinging now.

Bertha's commotion ended with the opening and closing of a door at the end of the hall. In the emptiness that followed, Kramer quickly decided how to deal with the "Rick and Toni Show," how to cup the candle before it got too hot. Ronnie, the earwigger was a different story. How to deal with him without hurting Anna and Sam? How to blot last night's performance from his mind? How to pretend, for his good friend's sake, that he liked the asshole? He wondered if the scenario Ronnie had created was realistic, if Sam would withdraw his support if he suspected his only son was being maligned, if he could survive without Sam.

By the time he had dressed and slipped quietly down the backstairs, Mike had decided it would be business as usual. The Ronnie incident, likely caused by the emotional upheaval of his return, had never happened. Without doubt, time and calm reason would work to solve his dilemma. Still, he wondered if all *would* be lost without Sam's help. It would be much more difficult — no doubt about that! But lost?

Mike had learned to avoid the office before breakfast. Even at this early hour there would be problems. Waiting. Over his final cup of coffee, he struggled with his feelings for Toni Warden, tried to tuck them away where he would not have to deal with them. His struggle ended at the office door. Larry Parkinson — the red-headed, freckled boat-boy — was waiting. Larry came early to do his work before school. He would be late this morning.

"Jake won't leave me alone," Larry complained. "He pulled one of the canoes out of the water. He said the caulking wasn't set."

"Well?"

"It doesn't have to set. My father and I use it all the time. I was checking it for leaks before I painted it. And he said I don't lock the boat house door when I leave. I always do. He must be making that up."

"You go ahead. I'll take care of Jake. Don't let him worry you. If he bothers you again, let me know."

"It won't do any good. Dad says he's getting meaner. He used to be real nice, especially to us kids."

"Never mind. I'll have a word with him. Are the signs finished for the boat rental rates?"

"Next Monday."

"Bring the bill to me," Mike said walking the boy to the door. And if you see Rick Gerrard, ask him to come to the office."

The head chambermaid was waiting too. All through the conversation, Olga Oliefson had sat stoically in her chair. Her business was laundry and rooms, not boats. She showed no interest in the young lad's plight. But God help Jake if he tried to tell *her* how to make a bed.

She reported that Toni Warden had encountered a porcupine near the trash cans beside the kitchen door. The result was a sprained ankle. She had gone to her room to rest.

⁂

Mike went after Jake first. He found him cursing a squeaky hinge in the entertainment building. Pal kept his distance. The noise obviously hurt his ears.

"Just a kid, eh," Jake explained. "Don't know nothin' 'bout boats."

"Larry was born in a boat. Leave him alone. Or you can have his job and I'll give him yours."

"One of 'em 'll sink with some fancy president in it or somethin' — then you'll talk diff'rent."

"Leave the kid alone, Jake."

"Ahh..." Jake went back to opening and closing the door. He oiled it and the whining ceased. Pal joined his master and they inspected the hinge together.

"There are porcupines hanging around the kitchen."

"Ain't hurtin' nobody. Pal! Sit! Atta boy."

"Toni Warden sprained her ankle. They frightened her, I guess."

"Phh... "

"Get rid of them." Jake stood up and looked at him. He reached in his shirt pocket, but Mike raised his hands in the air in a motion of surrender. "Okay, Jake. Okay. I'll put it on tomorrow's list."

⁂

He should have sent someone else to check on Toni Warden, but he didn't. Her ankle was swollen a bit, though it needed no medical attention. It was more an excuse for a day off than the catastrophe she pretended. Mike spoke kindly to her, over compensating for the attaction that was always there.

"Would you like some ice for it?" he asked.

"No. Bert can bring some up if I need it."

"Bert?"

"Bertha."

"I told Jake to take care of the porcupines. He'll catch them and take them back into the bush."

"They scared me. I've never seen a live porcupine before. Ugly things."

She seemed more relaxed and receptive than usual. It would not be wise for him to stay in her room too long, but he lingered anyway.

"Toni, do you remember I asked you about getting ahead?"

"Yes."

"The hostess position is open. I've kept it open. I'd like you to take it."

She showed no surprise. "I can't."

"Why not? You have the appearance for it. All you have to do is meet people and show them to their tables." There was more, of course, and he could see she knew it.

"Why are you doing this?"

"Partly because I want to be near you. But I also want you to know that you don't have to be a waitress for the rest of your life. Starting July first, you can wear fine clothes, earn twice as much, stay in a room at the lodge, eat steak with the guests instead of sausages with the staff."

"I can't become obligated to anyone."

"No strings attached."

"Is there time for me to think about it?"

"Of course. I'm driving to Algonquin Park this Sunday. Come with me. You can let me know then."

"No strings."

"None." He had been too close to her for too long. "Sunday?"

"I don't know. I'm not sure."

"Sunday." He insisted, leaving without waiting for an answer.

"I'm no prize," were the last words he heard.

"Neither am I," he said to himself. "None of us are."

By the time Kramer returned to his office, Rick Gerrard was waiting.

"Larry said you wanted to see me, Mr. Kramer. Is something wrong?"

"No... of course not." Mike respected the young man's gentleness. "If you have a minute, I'd like to know how you're getting on."

"Slow but sure."

"Opening is only three weeks away. We can't leave things until the night before."

"We'll make it sir."

"Sure we will. The equipment you'll need — do you have it all?"

"Not the tennis stuff. It's on order, though."

"Good. You know how important it is to be careful with the equipment, don't you? It's very expensive to replace."

"Yes, sir." Rick fidgited in his chair. "The tennis courts need quite a bit of work."

"Jake is getting there. But the handle fell off his gearbox. He's stuck in low."

Rick smiled and relaxed somewhat. "I like Jake," he ventured. "I've never seen a man and dog so attached to each other."

"Do you have a schedule of activities made up yet?"

"I have in my mind."

"Put it on paper. Everyday has to be different. Because we're expensive, very few reservations will be for more than two weeks. If you repeat every 15 days, no one will complain. Mrs. Cohen will stay the whole summer, but I don't think she's the outdoor type."

"Do you want to see the schedule?"

"Yes. Let's work together for the first while."

"I'll start on it right away."

Rick rose from his chair but Mike motioned him back. "Um... before you go, there's something else we should talk about."

"Yes, sir?"

"This is Serendipity's first time around, and naturally, I'm very anxious for it to be a good one. I know you are too."

"I'll help as much as I can."

"If a guest wants to learn to swim at two in the morning, you'll have to teach him. If a group wants to go on a hike at four, you'll have to get up and take them."

"I'll be glad to do things like that. They might mean extra tips for me too."

Tips — he and Kirkpatrick bought their second car on tips, saved in a jar. The good old days. Hustlers on four wheels. No doubts. No questions. Hard work and singleness of purpose. Where were they? Gone. How lost?

"I hope they do, Rick." He wanted to let him go. The triangle turning in his head pricked him and told him that he should. "In short, because we are an isolated group here, as long as your eyes are open, you are working for me. There will be certain rules that apply to all, but particularly to you and others who have direct contact with the guests. Anything that has an adverse effect on Serendipity is my concern."

"Yes, sir."

"So you see, there should be no social contact with the guests. There is no need for my regulations regarding staff to be as strict. But again, I don't want my high-profile employees to become involved with the regular staff. As a rule of thumb, there is a line between those who eat with the guests and those who eat in the staff mess hall — the office people, the maitre d' and hostess, for example."

"I understand."

"Good. Have you met any girls yet?"

"Toni Warden. We're just friends. She really needs a friend right now. Someone she can depend on."

"Discretion, Rick. That's all I ask. Come see me when you have the schedule put together."

"Yes, sir."

Rick was through the door before Mike could leave his chair. He drummed his fingers on the desk briefly, then set to work — confirming the Serendipity advertisement in the C.A.A. Travellers Manual. There would be time to think things through properly on his way to Toronto.

XIII

Two months ago, Newton Bass would never have considered it. The nerve of Jack Kirkpatrick to offer him a personal under-the-desk bonus to come up with the financing for the purchase of Comet Cabs. He would have shown him the door; but that bonus was already earned and spent. There were dozens of ways to line his pockets — easily, like gathering eggs. In fact, Kirkpatrick had left him with a standing offer of generous rewards for any similar deals he could put together — fair recompense for the long hours Mr. Bass had spent on programs, reports and analyses without so much as a thank you from his superiors.

Now that Mike Kramer was sitting across the desk from him, it gradually came to Newtom Bass that there was money — his money — to be made from the misadventures of his friend Mr. Kramer. Jack Kirkpatrick would reward generously to get his hands on a portion of his partner's business.

"No, Mike. I'm sorry. No more money."

"Newt! Twenty thousand wasn't enough. I need at least ten more. Probably fifteen."

"Ten or fifteen today! How much tomorrow? I'm sorry. You know I told you not to get involved in the lodge deal."

"But I *am* involved! There's a payroll coming up that I can't meet unless I use my own personal savings. You know I've always made it a rule never to do that. You can take collateral out of the cab business, if that's what you're worried about."

"There's nothing I can do. No more money, Mike. What about your partner? Maybe he could help."

"Please, Newton, spare me."

"Things are probably tight for him, too, I guess. After taking over Comet, I mean."

Mike remembered his agreement with Jack Kirkpatrick and the time had come to honour it.

"Jack's okay," he said sternly. "Don't you worry about him. He knows exactly what he's doing." The visage of Newton Bass brightened considerably. "We're talking about *me* ."

"Why don't you sell off a few of your cabs." The banker moved up to the edge of his seat. He had taken up the scent of another bonus. "Kirkpatrick would snap them up — at a good price, too."

Deja vu! That aerosol greed!

The reproduction of a crisp landscape above the banker's head, by contrast, called up an image of Fran Greenberg's painting and the people attached to it. For Kramer, it was a cogent illustration of the manner in which his life had changed. He glared at Bass, watched him mangle a paper clip and drop it in the ashtray.

"Newton," he said deliberately, careful not to sound angry. "I've known you a long time. We've been friends a long time. That's the worst piece of advice you've ever given me."

"Just trying to help."

"Some help. If I listen to you, Kirk will have his hooks into both of us."

Kramer's disposition soured after that. He purposely stayed away from his partner, promising himself a full day with Smilin' Jack the following week. He browsed the shops on Younge Street and picked up a book for Linda — *the Other Side of Death.* She like things like that.

They dined together as usual. "As for Ronnie Geenberg," Linda advised, "the next time he gives you trouble, get him by the ear and march him straight back to the house." He almost convinced her they should spend the night together. "No, the girl who is staying in my apartment this summer is already there. No, I don't think we should. Wait until we get a few things sorted out."

Almost.

Later that night, nearly to dawn, he wrestled with his financial woes. He slept until nine, skipped breakfast and stopped at his bank on the way out of town. Newton Bass wasn't in yet, but it didn't matter. He made arrangements for the bank to cash the paper in his safety deposit box, to close his personal savings account and transfer the proceeds to the Serendipity account at the Huntsville branch.

Mike hoped the band-aid would stick until the lodge began to make a profit.

No. He hoped it would hold until he and Linda had their chance to get a few things sorted out; to see Maxwell Taylor squirm; until Sam could put the pieces of his life back together; until Anna took Ronnie in tow; until he figured out what planet Jake came from; until his infatuation with Toni Warden resolved itself; until he began to understand the speed of the deer.

After that, he didn't give a shit.

XIV

Hufstader probably had it all figured out; time *was* nature's way of keep ing everything from happening at once. Amen to that! Yet even so, things changed too quickly. Sam Greenberg wasn't there to welcome him back from the city as usual. Instead, Mike was headed for the Greenberg house to seek Sam out. He stopped at the footbridge and stared in amazement. The loose railing had been repaired, two bad planks had been replaced and the bridge had been painted postcard white.

Jake couldn't have done it, *wouldn't* have done it — not in a day. Besides, it wasn't on his list.

"Hope you like the colour," Sam called from his porch. "Half of it's yours."

"Looks great!" Mike shouted back, as Sam struggled down the steps. Mike waited for him. They stood and talked across the ravine.

"Ronnie did that yesterday," he said proudly. "He's an excellent carpenter. He's down in the basement now working on the cabin signs.

"What signs?"

"He wants to change the numbers to names — like the main lodge. If you don't want your cabins named after trees, you had better speak up."

"The names will be fine," Mike said. He scratched his head. It was a strange, unexpected apology, but he intended to accept it and sighed with relief. No questions. "Have him do the Tuck Shop sign as well. Tell him I'll straighten up with him."

"No." Sam crossed the bridge. Don't pay him. It won't hurt him to help out. It will keep him out of mischief."

They started walking, drifting toward the road. Rick Gerrard was practising at the driving range as they passed.

"You've found a good one there, my friend." Sam remarked. "That lad never stops working. He was helping Jake yesterday."

"I despise anyone who can hit a golf ball straight," Mike joked. "Hit a golf ball, period."

"Shirley Boychuk was here this morning. She wants to lease the Tuck Shop again this summer. She and her husband own the grocery store in Sidney. Beverly, their daughter, is old enough to help out."

"What do you think?"

"I've never had a problem with them."

"I'll stop off and see them. That'll be one less thing to worry about."

"Michael, have you done anything about a hostess for the dining room? The girl we had last year can't leave her work in Montreal. It's a very important position. Impressions, you know?"

"Leave it with me. I have someone in mind. I'll know by this weekend."

They still drifted. Now they were walking toward the fishing camps. Mike recalled their first walk along that road. So much had happened to change them both since then.

"Sam, how are you doing?" he asked, but didn't give time for an answer. "We've both been preoccupied lately. We haven't been able to talk the way we used to. That doesn't mean I've forgotten."

"Ronnie's return has made quite a difference. This time around, I can see what a wonderful boy he is. I don't know about before. I don't know what happened. I've thought about it, but it doesn't make sense. Things seemed to be fine. Boom! Same as Fran. For all our egotism, all our misguided self-esteem, who of us can look back at the events of our lives and truthfully declare that we made them happen?"

"We help make them happen. They wouldn't happen without us."

"Obviously! But it is a tremendous leap from there to insisting that we are in command, that because we act in a certain way, predictable results will follow. I'm going to make a fresh start. Ronnie will be the cornerstone of a structure that builds itself. No more fancy stuff."

"Then you really are a part of the body of God. Don't you see? You still believe that! You don't act, you react. He moves. You move."

"I don't know. I can't get my head up high enough to sort it all out. But I do know that this time, Ronnie is going to know how much I love him, how much he means to me. This time, Anna can be the strict one. I am going to enjoy my son and all he has to offer. Somehow, he is going to know that I love him beyond... beyond life itself. Nothing else matters now, really."

"He knows that already, I think."

"Whether or not I am a part of God's body — large or small, important or insignificant — I am going to drift with the current from here on and take in some scenery along the way. I'm tired of paddling for nothing. We'll see what comes of it."

"You'll end up back where you started."

"So be it, my friend. Anna says there's nothing wrong with that. She's usually right, you know."

"I wonder."

"Enough about me," Sam insisted. "What about you, Michael? I haven't forgotten either, you know."

"What about me?"

"Don't be coy. You said earlier that we have both been preoccupied with other things. That preoccupation can only increase. We won't have time for many more chats like this. You came here searching for something. Have you found it?"

"I don't even know what I'm looking for."

They could see Limberlost through the break in the trees as they approached the fishing camps. When their conversation lulled, they could hear a small motorboat puttering in the water by the shore. Beyond it there was the distant, sacrilegious whine of a powerboat.

"No, I *do* know what I'm looking for. That is the one thing I've accomplished in the past two months. I just don't know where to find it. There are so many sign posts — you, Anna, Serendipity, this Eden and so many more. I'm gambling that they'll point me in the right direction. I can think back to how comfortable I was and yet how miserable; I can compare it to how uncomfortable I am now and yet how eager. When I make the comparison, I feel I have progressed. But if my partner, Jack Kirkpatrick, was here now, he'd laugh at me, that's for sure."

"You say you're uncomfortable. Do you mean financially?"

Mike nodded.

"I was afraid of that. Perhaps I should have said something. You try to do too much at once. Take the same approach you did with the taxi business — slowly, steadily."

"Too late now."

"Michael... I would like to be able to help you." Sam was obviously more concerned than Mike. "But, my family. I am obligated. What I have belongs to Anna and Ronnie. It's a matter of principal with me. I can't... "

"Please, Sam. It doesn't matter. You've done enough already."

"You are on your own, my friend — sink or swim."

"I know."

Sam insisted that they return to the house before they reached the scarred cedar that had taken his daughter.

XV

Sunday morning, Mike Kramer wakened early, when the sun rose above the hills that cupped the far shore of Limberlost. The thin curtains on his bedroom window were not impervious to its light.

This day was his. There would be no business today. As he lay quietly, streams of thought met and flowed gently through his consciousness. For the first time in years, those thoughts spawned a feeling of well-being. Serendipity was almost ready to go, would be for certain by July first; Sam was finally fighting back; Ronnie had repented; Toni...

No business today.

A splashing in the lake enticed Mike to the window. He pulled the curtains back and squinted into the white sunlight. Toni Warden was in the water to her waist, washing her hair. Before she finished, Mike was beside her.

Toni pointed to the bar of soap. "Lifebouy," she remarked lightly. "It floats."

"Did you remember that we have a date today?"

"That's why I'm up. I didn't know what time you wanted to leave."

"I've decided not to go to Algonquin Park today."

"Oh."

He was pleased to hear disappointment in her voice. She ducked beneath the surface, leaving a ring of soap, then began to swim. Mike swam with her until she stopped.

"It's too far," he continued. "Too much driving. I don't want to spend my one free day in a car."

"Oh." She swam back to get her soap and again he swam beside her. She was an excellent swimmer. He had difficulty keeping up.

"Have you been to Thunder Falls yet?"

"Yes. I go there to be alone sometimes."

"Will you meet me there at noon. I'll have the cook make up a lunch. We can spend the day together."

"Meet you?"

"I don't think we should leave the lodge together. I think we should be discreet."

"Discreet?"

"Please... will you come?"

"I don't know."

He watched as she left the water and climbed the steps to the crest of the lawn.

There is noise that affords peace, chaos that smacks of order, commotion that conjures rest. Mike Kramer thought it strange that the constant din of Thunder Falls didn't bother him; it was not much different than the aggravating moan of powerboats that screamed from one end of the lake to the other on weekends.

He could see almost the whole of Limberlost from the falls, trace the western shore that joined the fishing camps to Serendipity to Sidney like baubles on a string, count the coves and button islands. He coveted the few remaining peaceful days before the summer storm of boisterous people.

The white, shining buildings of Serendipity were different from two miles away, as a painting near and far. They weren't real from Thunder Falls, just sunbeams pausing on a distant shore. Kramer couldn't see the cabins nestled in the trees behind the boathouse, but they were there with the others — ready, waiting.

And it was the waiting that bothered him. Always waiting for something.

July first... Toni Warden.

It had been more than an hour now, almost two. The path was partially open for a quarter-mile down the hill and he watched, off and on, for a glimpse of her. Disgruntled, he folded the blanket, tucked it under his arm and picked up the cooler. It was a dumb idea in the first place.

As he reached the top of the path, she came into view, her head bowed because of the steep climb, so that she couldn't have seen him. Quickly, he respread the blanket and opened a book, pretending to read as Toni reached the top.

She apologised for being so late.

"No problem," he fibbed, unable to regain his composure.

They talked for a while, then worked their way upstream to a level clearing, where the rivulets between the rocks quit struggling. They drank the crystal water, scooping it with their hands into each other's mouths — touching, testing. They sat close on a fallen cedar and dangled their toes in the running water.

"You weren't going to come today, were you?" Mike asked.

"No." Though she had lost some of her bashfulness, she was still nervous — particularly when he wanted to talk.

When he asked her why not, Toni didn't answer until they were back at the falls. On the blanket, his head in her lap, he asked her again while she played with the curls in his hair: "Why wouldn't you want to be with me today?"

"I hadn't decided about the hostess job," she explained. "I couldn't come here until I did."

"Are you going to take it?"

"Yes. If I had decided not to, I wouldn't be here."

"Hardly complimentary."

"Call it looking after number one."

"I don't understand."

"I had to believe there was a chance."

"A chance? What chance?"

"For me... with you. There must be someone else in your life."

"There is."

"I've asked myself a hundred times what you want," she continued, as though he hadn't answered. "Why me?"

Kramer kissed her pursed lips. Even closed tightly, they were warm, exciting. Toni didn't resist, nor did she respond. "No questions. There can be no questions."

"From the first day in your office, there has been something between us. I wonder what it is. Do you feel sorry for me? Is there something about me you respect? I'm not naive. I've been around... too many times. I know why we're here. Yet, I wonder if you *do* see something that can bring me back."

"Of course I do. Now that you've taken the first step, your life will begin to open up for you. I know it. I want to help if I can."

"When I left Toronto, I was so badly hurt. I promised myself not to get involved with anyone for a long, long time. And here I am, with you. I can't be hurt again, Mike.

"I won't hurt you. Just don't expect too much. Go slowly. You'll be all right."

"You're different. You see, to care about me. Really care."

"Like Rick Gerrard?"

"He's just a boy. A friend. I'm so lonely."

"You're trembling. Why are you shaking, Toni?"

"I'm afraid."

"Not of me, I hope."

"Of myself."

"You are beautiful."

"Not inside, I'm not."

"No questions, I promise."

This time, Toni Warden's lips were apart to respond when Mike kissed her. She struggled to be free, but he held her firmly. Then suddenly something changed. She yeilded and fell back, taking Mike with her. "You're different," she whispered. "Oh Mike, this time there has to be a chance for me. There just has to be."

Thunder Falls stopped groaning, momentarily stood still. They heard no noise. A tiny drop of water fell into a shaded, limpid pool. It rippled there at first, then stirred and drifted slowly... slowly... to join the current of the stream... quickening it's flight between tha banks of deep foliage... toward the rocks and then against them... hurled high and back... faster now... faster... swirling around in space... falling a hundred million miles... a frightened cry of joy to reach the seething vortex below... finally peace, as it followed the rest into the shining, halcyon waters of Lake Limberlost... home.

"You're different," she said. "There *is* a chance. I know there is."

"Shhh." He touched her lips. "Be still. Listen to the water."

XVI

"You've got to be kidding! Tell me you're kidding, Kirk."

Kirkpatrick stared at him. "I'm not."

"Impossible!"

"Newton Bass was fired — Friday." He picked up the telephone receiver. "Phone the bank," he said rhetorically.

Mike Kramer slumped in his chair. "How come?"

"Greedy. He was lining his pockets, diverting bank customers to private investors for a fee."

"I'm not sure I understand."

"Simple, if you think about it. Some poor slob comes in for a loan. Bass goes through the application bullshit, waits a day or so, then makes up some excuse why the bank won't lend the money. Just when the guy's about to give up, enter a private lender. The chump gets his money, Bass gets a grand and the lender gets rich. Everybody's happy — except the bank."

"He got caught."

"When you get greedy, you stop being careful. Stupid. You can't be greedy and stupid both — oil and water, Mike. He tried his little game on the friend of a friend of a man in high places. The bank sent over a couple of stoolies. Bob's your uncle! Good-bye Newton Bass."

"How do you know all this, Kirk?"

"You kiddin'?" Jack Kirkpatrick smiled through his cigar for the first time. "I'm like this with the new manager." He crossed his fingers. "My worries are over. We're working another deal already."

"I have the strangest feeling that you may have had a part in the demise of Newton Bass."

"C'mon Mike, you know better. I gave him a few bucks to help me with Comet Cabs. But that deal went through the bank. Thanks for helping with that, by the way."

"Don't you ever get tired of living to make money?"

"The more the better. I've told you before, it's like padding — a cushion. It softens the bumps and grinds along the way."

"Some of them, maybe."

If the news of his friend's collapse depressed Mike, his partner was making his depression worse.

All the signs were there that the split between them was wider, deeper now. Kirk was chewing on more expensive cigars. After 10 years, he had carpeted his office. He had a custom Cadillac on order from the factory in Oshawa. No doubt, they were moving on — in opposite directions.

"Speaking of money," Kirkpatrick said, trying to sound disinterested. "A guy called from Gem-Star. He said to remind you that your mortgage payment is overdue."

"I'm making it today. Damn him." Mike shook his head. "You know, I'm afraid the lodge is going to suck me dry."

"I warned you! Don't look at me. I told you that from the beginning. I guess you weren't listening. You've got to have lots of bucks to make a place like that pay."

"I would do it again. You don't understand." Mike said. "Just make sure *you* don't suck me dry."

"Me! What is this? I don't want your money! I don't need it."

Still, trip sheets and deposit slips don't lie. Kramer was losing a hundred a day, no mistake — nothing overt, nothing concealed. There was no fraud, no theft. His deposits were simply down $100 per day. After the Comet takeover, he no longer had access to Kirkpatrick's financial affairs; Jack had separated everything. For all Mike knew, the difference in the bank deposits from their King Street operation might exceed that amount.

By late afternoon, Mike Kramer concluded his business at the lot. He had an appointment with his attorney at half past four. Curtis was going to be furious — once again, no hand-ball. To aggravate the trauma, Mike was going to be late. He waited for Tesky to come for his cab, then settled into the front seat as his most trusted driver picked a path through the rush-hour traffic on Avenue Road.

"Have you seen anything of Jimmy?" Kramer asked. "I haven't seen him around for quite a while. How's he doing?"

"A streetcar hit him."

"God! No!" *I didn't feel a thing. Where was I? Three weeks ago. What was I doing? I should have felt something.*

"Three weeks ago."

"Did he… "

"He lived. They took him to General. He may have died by now, though. I haven't heard."

What kind of conspiracy was this? What nefarious forces were at work this hot June day? They were hunting like a pack of wolves, running in the shadows, coming out only to strike — Newton, Kirk, now Jimmy. That's three; maybe its over… Serendipity was a country home compared to this. His trips to the city were like visits to a zoo.

When the taxi stopped on Bloor Street, Tesky looked bewildered when Kramer took out his cheque book.

"You can't wait here," Mike said as he wrote. "Drive around. Go have a coffee. Pick me up in a half an hour." He handed Tesky the cheque.

"Boss! This says five hundred. It should be five."

"No. It's right. And there's another one for the same amount in September."

"Why?"

"I'm being screwed at the lot — royally."

"I know."

"I can't do much about it. Not right now. I want you to keep your eyes and ears open. I'll check with you every week. Here's my number at the lodge. If anything serious happens, you can call me there. I have to know what's going on."

"Yes, sir. You can count on me."

Tesky held out his hand. Mike took a firm grip on it. Instantly, by contrast, he recalled shaking hands with Ronnie Greenberg. That handshake had bothered him, still did. Tesky's was honest.

"I'm not sure you should see him." The nurse at Toronto General Hospital was politely hesitant. "I don't think he's going to make it. Since you're the only visitor he's had, I guess it will be all right, as long as I go with you."

"Doesn't he have a family?" Mike asked as they walked to Jimmy's room.

"Apparently not. Aren't you a relative?"

"A friend. I've been out of town."

Jimmy was unconscious. It wasn't the same person who had smiled up at him with a cup in his outstretched hand. That man was gone, but not his image. Mike Kramer clearly saw him scooting over the sidewalk like someone with a mission.

Speed adds beauty to the deer.

"He's fading," the nurse whispered from the door.

"Yes." Going... going. Kramer stood at Jimmy's bed. He reached out, touched his hand, then placed a quarter on the corner of the night table beside him.

"By any chance, are you Mr. Crammer?" the nurse asked when they reached her desk.

"Kramer."

"Here, he left this for you." The nurse handed him a plain white envelope with MR. CRAMMER written on it by a shakey hand.

The envelope contained an address and a confusing, scribbled note that eventually indicated that there was something of importance hidden in a compartment under a flat rock. Tesky stoopped his taxi in front of an abandoned building which had probably been Jimmy's home. Kramer found the rock and, under it, there was a canvas bank bag, wrapped in plastic. The bag contained $156.25 in coin but they didn't bother counting it. There was also another note asking that the bag be delivered to Jimmy's daughter at a Rosedale address.

Tesky watched his boss walk up the driveway of a tudor-style home in Rosedale. Bag in hand, he avoided two children playing with a wagon. He had the posture of a man carrying weight on his shoulders. Tesky watched him ring the doorbell. A woman answered, listened intently for a moment, then slammed the door shut. As the taxi pulled away from the curb, the children smiled and waved goodbye.

"Wrong house?" Tesky asked on the way to Mike Kramer's hotel.

"Right house," he said. "Wrong neighbourhod."

"I know a family that's really down right now. Their house burned. No insurance." Mike handed him the bankbag.

At the hotel, Mike shook hands with Tesky again and reminded him of the agreement. He slipped twenty dollars into Tesky's pocket and held the door open for a fare to the airport. He picked up his key at the desk. Linda had called; so had the hospital.

"Mr. Kramer." It was the same nurse. "You asked me to call you if there was any change."

"Jimmy's gone, isn't he?"

"I'm sorry."

"I'll look after his burial." Mike's voice trembled and the nurse paused a moment.

"One other thing, Mr. Kramer. I saw you touch Jimmy's hand before you left his room. Did you put anything in it?"

"No."

"That's odd."

"Why?"

"He was clutching a quarter."

Linda McDermott was at her apartment by the time Mike reached her. She listened without interruption as he reviewed the event of the day. She always listened. He could count on that. If there was a singular reason why he loved her, that was it.

Kramer had a method of defining exactly how he felt about people. He insisted that the entirety of his experience with them, all his impressions be reduced to one word — not a sentence, not a prase — *one word.* It was difficult to do with some, but not Linda.

Linda McDermott, from the first — *sincerity.*

"I don't feel well," he apologised.

"I'm not surprised. You've had quite a day. Can you imagine — Jimmy's daughter behaving like that!"

"If you don't mind, I think I'll skip dinner tonight and get a good rest. We'll be together in a week anyway. I can't believe opening is only nine days away."

"It's just as well I don't see you tonight," Linda agreed. "I have some work to do for Maxwell."

Of all the things Mike didn't want to hear, his name was atop the list.

Maxwell Taylor — *power.*

"Mike... I love you."

"Thanks for listening. I'll pick you up next Thursday." The triangle turned and stung him.

Mike didn't have to look for Newton Bass's number; he knew it. Still, he hesitated dialing, trying to think of an excuse for calling him at home. One of his college instructors had defined an excuse as the skin of a reason, stuffed with a lie. He decided to let their conversation take its natural course.

"The number you have reached is not in service."

Newton Bass — *Foolish.*

Alone. Quiet. Mike Kramer rubbed his aching forehead. He could feel the lines in his brow — wider, deeper than they should have been. He massaged his tired eyes with his thumb and forefinger.

He hadn't wept. But they were moist.

Chance and change. Scallywags both.

A hundred years from now, he told himself, nobody will care what has gone on in the world in the past 24 hours. That didn't help. *His* world still shook from the events of the preceeding day — a travesty of life, the life he wanted: just a modicum of peace and contentment, like everyone else.

Chance and change.

Was there a human alive who would survive unscathed the chicanery of those two indiscrete bed fellows? Anyone he knew? Jake, maybe. Yes, probably Jake in his cocoon. But for the rest, the best they could do was structure their lives so that they moved in a general direction and hope for the mercy of chance and change.

Linda had called before he left the hotel. She was going to look after Jimmy. Remarkable, that woman. The things she could do, once she set her mind to it. Very resourceful. He decided to use the extra time to visit Newton Bass before he left the city. The house was for sale, including an almost finished swimming pool in the back yard. According to a neighbour, the Bass family had moved out suddenly at night. They were living with relatives in St. Catharines, she thought.

Kramer regretted stopping. There was a finality about the sign on the lawn. He grieved the loss of his friends — one to foolishness, one to death, one to greed. Kirkpatrick had been a partner and a friend. That was gone. Mike was through kidding himself. Maybe he still belonged on King Street. So be it. But not with Kirk. No way!

Ten years together, each preparing in his own way for what they hoped would be a smooth passage through life. Ten good years gone to where all good years go. The security and stability for which they had strived — like kettles to boiling water, banks to the turbulence of Thunder Falls — could frame, but not contain the steady pressure of those two rascals, chance and change

At Barrie, the city which seemed to be his point of no return (the boundry between his two worlds, the line that, in a sense, cut him in half), he stopped for a coffee. Already, the sun was uncomfortably hot and the beverage made him sweat. Yet he drove with the air conditioning off and the window down. He didn't mind the heat. Those same emetic rays that had turned Toronto into a solar furnace, had also worked a fascinating catharsis upon Muskoka. He hoped, if only by osmosis, it would do the same to him. In any event, when people came pouring out the furnace door, he and Serendipity would be waiting.

Barrie was behind him before he was able to clear his mind of the city and turn his attention to Serendipity and the very sharp horns of an uncomfortable dilemma — Linda McDermott and Toni Warden. He didn't completely understand his relationship with either one of them; but he understood enough to realize that the latter had to be told of Linda's arrival and its implications. He was prepared to compromise honesty if it helped restore Toni's pride, to give as much as he could if it was well received, to offer encouragement so long as there was a positive response. He knew he wasn't Mr. Clean, no knight in shining armour. He was a man on the make, hoping that something good would come of it. If the dilemma wasn't resolved in one week, before Linda came to Serendipity, it would certainly be settled after her arrival.

Yes, all he could do was structure his life so that it moved in a general direction. If he stubbed his toe, *when* he stubbed his toe, he must remember not to bow his head, not to be diverted.

Turning onto Sidney Road, he recalled Anna's words: *If you look behind, you will see that the speed of the deer is paled by the speed of thought. You should most be concerned with the leap.*

By the time he passed Jake's garage, Mike Kramer had abandoned hope of understanding the meaning of those words for his life.

XVII

Finally, still hard and wet from her, holding her because their naked bodies were exchanging energy to keep warm, he felt things specific about Toni Warden. They came to him in waves with the drum-rolls of Thunder Falls. Even while he held her, Mike Kramer knew that she was a mirage, there to quench a thirst that she could not relieve. He told himself — or something told him — that this had to be the end of it. Had to be!

"Toni," he said. "I told you that there was someone else." Not a word from her. Not a movement. "She's very special."

"I know."

He was surprised by her reaction. It took a moment to recover. "I would have told you this before, but I didn't think… I wasn't sure we would… Toni, she's coming to Serendipity. Next week. She's going to help me with the lodge this summer."

"I know."

"You know? How?"

"Ronnie Greenberg told me. While you were away, I went for a walk, to come here. Ronnie followed me. He caught me at the bottom of the path and tried to force me. I think he knows about us."

"How could he possibly know?"

"He's clever. He cornered me against the big tree and tried to force me."

"That creep! I'll beat the snot out of him."

"No! Please, Mike! Leave it be. I shouldn't have told you. I handled it. He wasn't much different than any other man I've known. More of a pussycat maybe. No wonder I..." She stopped.

"What happened to you? Did he hurt you?"

"A torn shirt. My shoulder was scratched." She left him and started to dress. "A slap in the face. A knee in the groin. He got the message. He took off yelling something about this being his lodge and he could have whoever he wanted." Toni paused. "He's all screwed up. I know how it is."

Mike realized the incident was finished.

"A torn shirt is the least of my worries," she continued. "I can handle any number of Ronnie Greenbergs. The question is, can I handle one Mike Kramer."

"What are you talking about?"

"Never mind."

He dressed. "Reubin, the maitre d', will be here tomorrow," he mentioned casually. "I've told him about you. You'll like Reubin. If anyone knows the business, he does. Take my car to Gravenhust tomorrow. I've made arrangements for you to pick up some clothes. They'll bill me."

Toni didn't answer.

"Good luck," he said.

She took his hand and kissed the back of it, as though she didn't understand, had never known, a man's kindness. They walked together to the edge of the falls. "I feel so happy here," she said.

"It's the water. I think the spray creates some type of ions in the air that makes us happy."

"No. It's me, not the water. I'm happy here with you. Inside. Deep."

"It's the water."

"Don't hurt Ronnie... Please."

"I won't."

For the life of him, he could see no obvious reason for her lack of self-esteem. He resolved to help restore her confidence any way he could. She was not like Linda: not in appearance, not in attitude, not in ambition. But they were both striving — Linda to expand, Toni to consolidate. The attraction was that he was striving too.

Before they separated at the bottom of the path, Mike asked: "If you knew about Linda, why did you come here today?"

"I told you last week. There's a chance. A fair chance, that's all I ask of you."

Make this the end of it.

"There's not much of a chance, Toni. I'm sorry."

"Let me be the judge of that."

"You should begin to concentrate on your new career. I could open many doors."

"I feel strong enough to handle both. I think I can!"

They parted.

"I tried," he muttered. "God knows, I tried."

Everybody knows at least one Pepi Riveras — a person with insatiable zest for life who survives quite nicely without a lick of common sense, the one who cuts a swath through life like a whirling dervish, the harbinger of commotion and chaos, predictable as silly-putty.

When Pepi Riveras arrived with his band — The Latin Lovers — Monday at noon, they proved to be the catalyst that began the transformation of the lodge from a quiet, peaceful haven to a madhouse. They had been the resident musicians two years ago — a smashing success according to Sam. They were "loose" like Sam had said. Pepi led the entourage; the "Lovers" followed like a hatch of ducklings. They strutted around the grounds, opening doors, looking in windows. They whistled in harmony when Toni Warden passed. She was walking with Rick Gerrard. Pepi snatched the football Rick was holding. The game was on! The Lovers huddled around their quarterback and Pepi threw a pass that bounced down the terraced lawn to the beach.

"Let me see that, nosy," he yelled as the piano player retrieved the ball and threw it back to him. He handed the ball to Rick. "You can't play basketball with this," he said. "It ain't round."

While they completed their orientation tour, the wives and girlfriends who had accompanied them, toted the luggage to their rooms and set their instruments up in the entertainment hall.

The Boychucks were bringing truckloads of groceries up for the Tuck Shop. Pepi and his Latin Lovers helped them unload until Mr. Boychuck became angry and asked them to leave.

The Tuck Shop was below the lounge and Pepi had stationed his troops along the steps. He took boxes from the truck and passed them clumsily down the line. Inevitably, the trombone player dropped a case of Fig Newtons.

"You'd better go," Mr. Boychuck warned. "Before you break something."

"Okay," said Pepi, shrugging his shoulder. "One day you'll need us and we won't be around. "C'mon men. We know when we're not wanted."

The dance team would not arrive until July 5, because of commitments in Toronto. But they sent a truck ahead with the sets they were going to use while working on stage. Pepi and the Lovers helped the truck driver back up to the stage door. Unfortunately, they backed him into a tree.

When the driver became belligerent, Pepi retreated.

"No violence," he warned. "These men are pacifists, but be careful of the last half of the word." The driver stood scratching his head as Pepi sauntered away. "C'mon men. We can take a hint." He didn't turn back. "Never try to help anymore," he said loudly to the group.

Ray Mildenhall also arrived Monday with his girlfriend Bubbles, who may have been so named because of the baths she took or the champagne she drank, but more likely because she seemed to bubble out of the tight clothes she wore. In his heyday, Mildenhall had toured with some of the best. Now, after too many liquid breakfasts, he arrived a spent champion. All of his possessions were in a rusted station wagon — a magnetic sign on the side of the door:

RAY MILDENHALL
PROFESSIONAL EMCEE
HAVE MOUTH — WILL TRAVEL

When Pepi and his group spotted him, they had a dandy reunion, right there in the parking lot. Eventually, Mildenhall fled to the office. While The Latin Lovers got to know Bubbles, Pepi removed the magnetic signs from the doors of the station wagon and replaced them upside down.

Each day, no one would see or hear from Ray Mildenhall until two in the afternoon... exactly. Then, he would phone for a scotch and a raw egg. And Bubbles' routine would be just as precise: every morning that it didn't rain, even if it was cloudy, she would appear at the beach at ten o'clock, spread her blanket and settle-in for the day. When it was wet, she would opt for the lounge to do her nails and listen to music on her portable radio until Mildenhall phoned for his breakfast.

In the evenings, before opening, Pepi set up his group in the entertainment hall and practised on the staff: Reubin, the maitre d', and his staff; Joshua, the chef, his cooks and kitchen help; Olga, the head-chambermaid and her girls; Rick Gerrard and the counsellors; Larry Parkinson, the Boychucks, Sam and Anna Greenberg. Funny thing about Pepi — though he sang with a noticeable Spanish inflexion, he spoke without trace of it. Accent or no, when he was through with them, they were a family. It was a relaxing time. Jake and Pal and Ronnie Greenberg were the only three who stayed away.

On several occasions during that final, hectic week, Mike caught himself thinking: "If I have enough money, what glorious fun this will be." Just as often, he wondered if he and Sam had created an entity which functioned without them. He knew better, of course, but when activity became frenzied, seemingly out of control, the organized work rose to the top like cream.

Things apparently connected themselves, as though, even without Mrs. Cohen, Serendipity had a triangle of its own for a conscience.

XVIII

Ordinarily, there was something secure about being in a car, snug and insulated — a safe feeling, like watching a storm from the inside of a house. He could sing if he wished, talk to himself, answer the radio, behave with impunity. That moving space was his and nothing reached him there unless he chose it.

Not so this trip; Mike Kramer had company. Linda sat close to the passenger door, reading, seldom looking up. Occasionally, he glanced at her admiringly — proudly. There was moisture on her lip. He wanted to stop the car and kiss her, but didn't.

The woman never ceased to amaze. She was a standout from the day of the transport strike when he first saw her walking, stopped for her and took her to work. Just when he thought he had her pegged, she surprised.

When he ventured to predict, she changed: never would she see him again if he refused to talk with Father Kelly; never would she leave Maxwell Taylor and come with him to Serendipity; never would she accept or even try to understand what he was doing.

Yet, there she sat, another of the many tiny miracles that had mysteriously worked together for his good.

When perplexed, she tilted her head to the side like an inquisitive puppy.

It was tilted now. That was all he could divine regarding the workings of her mind.

After Barrie, Linda stopped trying to read. He insisted on telling her about the lodge, heaping antidote upon antidote — a nervous, premature introduction to Serendipity. Detail after detail, trying to explain — rubber bullets bounding off her stern composure. Not once did her disposition mellow. What was going on between those delicate ears? So close as to be touched, yet hiding. Where did she go to be so alone? Where did anyone go?

As they turned onto Sidney Road, the turn that meant so much to him, Mike became silent. Words had not touched, probably nothing would.

Jake and Pal watched their arrival from the kitchen steps. They didn't move as Mike parked the Thunderbird. "Some reception committee," Mike thought. "Talk about first impressions."

Mike and Linda sat quietly for a moment. "That's Jake," he said, shaking his head apologetically.

Linda reached for his hand. "I understand now," she said. That was all.

When they emerged from the car, Jake and the dog hurried toward them. Jake shook hands with Linda while Pal wagged his tail — his whole behind — and circled her with frenzied delight. Finally! At last! After all these years, his master had found someone they both could like.

Jake followed Mike to the trunk of the car. "C'mere Pal! Stop that!" The dog was rubbing himself against Linda's legs.

"Leave him," she said.

"She's good," Jake said, looking at Mike "Where d'ya want them bags?"

"210."

Jake looked surprised. "Your room?"

"Mike!"

"201 then. It's a nice corner suite."

Jake smiled his widest, toothless smile. Mike wasn't certain, but he thought he saw Jake's own backside wiggle a bit.

That evening, when they went to meet the Greenbergs, there was no mistake. Sam's ass wiggled all over when Linda complimented them on the painting above their fireplace.

"Ahh..." Sam Greenberg pushed himself back from the table. "It's true we *are* what we eat."

"No Papa!" Anna meant business. "Not that speech again." She looked apologetically at Linda. "Papa gets carried away."

"I don't mind," Linda smiled.

"No," Anna insisted. "Not his 'we-are-what-we-eat' speech again. Not tonight."

"It's true. We *are* what we eat."

"I have some work to do downstairs," Ronnie interjected.

"But you haven't touched your pie," Anna argued. "You didn't finish your meal. You've hardly spoken a word all evening. Are you feeling well?"

"Excuse me," Ronnie said flatly and he left the table.

"That boy is going to come along fine," Sam commented after an uncomfortable moment. "I can feel it." Even as he spoke, they could hear hammering start up in the basement. "Like I said, he will be the cornerstone of our foundation."

"Ronnie has changed," Anna said. "I would feel better if we were the cornerstone of *his* foundation. We must not push too hard. We must be patient."

There was a sudden break in the conversation at the table. Mike was in awe of Linda's poise. She finished her pie and coffee as though oblivious to the undercurrent of unrest that pervaded the Greenberg house.

Anna rose to clear the table and Linda excused herself to help. The two men kindled the fireplace and settled back. The sound of laughter and the jingle of dishes came to them gently. When the fire quit crackling, they could hear Anna explaining the details of her responsibilities regarding Serendipity. Linda was responding with enthusiasm. There were many good sounds and feelings in the Greenberg home that night, all punctuated by the erratic wham-wham-whamming of Ronnie's hammer.

Sam winked. "He's making something important this time." Mike nodded and Sam motioned toward the kitchen. "The girls are getting along splendidly."

"I think so."

"My friend," Sam sighed, "can you believe how quickly time has passed since we met?" Mike simply smiled at the bromide. "Can you believe your first guests arrive tomorrow? How do you feel?"

"Like I am going to have a baby." Mike answered. "Like I should be doing something — like running around double checking everything, making sure nothing goes wrong." He paused. "Like there must be some way I can express my gratitude to you and Anna for all you've done. Without you, there would be no opening."

"Without you, my friend, there would be no lodge. Anna and I have said many times that we are in your debt. You've given us hope we thought was gone."

"Then let's say we're even."

"It's a deal."

"Let's have a drink together — one last quiet time before the sky falls."

"Good idea."

While Sam was gone, Mike heard a commotion on the beach and went to investigate. Pepi, the pied piper, had lured his fans out of the entertainment hall. They were building a bonfire. Mike watched them and listened to a round of *Row Row Row Your Boat* before Sam called from inside.

"You know," Sam said when they had settled, "this may be inappropriate, especially tonight, but I would like to talk to you about money."

"Not tonight, I have a headache," Mike joked.

"I hate to see you hurting financially."

"So do I."

"How bad is it, Michael?"

"Bad enough that I already know I'll never make my August payment. July is almost booked solid and still I'll be short. It seems I overestimated revenues and underestimated expenses."

"A common fault, my friend. I probably should have helped you more. What are you going to do?"

"Throw myself at the mercy of Gem-Star Mortgages. What else? Maybe they'll wave a payment. I don't think they want to operate a summer lodge. We'll work something out."

"I almost went under three times trying to get the lodge established. At one point, my brother-in-law bought into it to keep it solvent. It took me years to buy his share." Sam managed a smile. "I never said it would be easy."

"Don't worry about it."

"Michael, I... I hope you understand why I can't help you. Old age talks to me these days. It tells me that I'm through with taking chances. I owe it to Anna and Ronnie to see that they are looked after. I know we have covered this ground before, but I want to be certain you understand. You are a very special friend and I would hate to see you hurting, but I can't help you financially."

Mike raised his glass. "To our friendship," he toasted, "may it continue to grow."

"Good luck tomorrow," Sam replied.

Weary Sam Greenberg poked his head through the doorway that led to the basement. He hoped not to have to negotiate the steep narrow stairway. He was tired... very tired.

"Ronnie" he called.

Wham! Wham!

It wasn't the climb down. It was the struggle to get back up that took so much out of him. He had never questioned his weight. He had always been himself. Lately though, since he had been struggling with simple functions like walking briskly and climbing stairs, he wondered if he shouldn't cut out desserts for a while.

"What are you building, son?"

"Nothing much."

"It sounds like something much. What is it?"

"A new desk for the reception office. The old one should have been thrown out before I left for school."

"Did you check with Mr. Kramer? Maybe he doesn't want a new desk. It's his place now. We can't go on acting as though its ours."

"You do, Sam."

"I try not to."

"He won't mind. I want it to be a surprise."

"Mr. Kramer and Miss McDermott have gone. Your mother and I would like you to come up now."

Wham! Wham! Sam waited until the hammering to stopped.

"Do you think you would like to go back to school in the autumn?" he asked, trying unsuccessfully to sound casual.

"We'll see, Sam."

"Well, son, if you want to talk about it, come to me anytime."

Sam stopped at the bottom of the stairs. "Mr. Kramer asked if you would report for work at eight tomorrow evening."

"Next, I'm going to make new seats for the benches on the lawn," Ronnie announced proudly.

"Check with Mr. Kramer first." Sam admired the work his son was doing. It was good and he thought he should say so. "I insist!" He waited for an acknowledgement that didn't come. "Tomorrow evening at eight."

"I'll be there."

As the old man struggled up the stairs, Ronnie drove a final nail so hard it split the wood.

A brave frog croaked from the ravine and two more answered from the long grass near the boathouse. The first wave of crickets were tuning on the lawn; it was war to them and their din would increase until Pepi Rivera's guitar was silent. After, their victory chant would force some to sleep with windows closed.

When they left the Greenbergs, Mike stopped on the footbridge and drew Linda to him. They kissed, but Linda backed away.

"What's the matter?" he asked.

"With Serendipity... nothing. Nothing at all. With us... everything. This is a fantastic place. A dream. I love the Greenbergs already, just as you do. I love Serendipity already, just as you do. But us? We have a lot of ground to cover before we can truly love each other."

"At least you're here. That's a start."

"That's why I came," Linda agreed. "By the time this summer is over, we'll know... I'll know, anyway. One way or the other."

"Let's talk in my apartment."

"No!"

"Yours?"

"No!" She turned away. "That won't help, Mike. It will only confuse us. We have certain things to resolve that require concentration, concerted effort from both of us." She sounded apologetic. "Not yet."

He acquiesced. "When?"

"When we've covered enough ground — not before." Linda replied sternly. "It's been a long day. A good one for me, but I'm very tired and I'll have to work long hours tomorrow."

"You're right," Mike agreed. "I should have thought about that. I'm relieved to see you get along so well with Anna."

"She is a marvelous person. She's going to help me all day tomorrow."

"Do you realize how much I owe those two?" Mike took her hand and they left the bridge.

"They think it's the other way around."

When they passed in front of the dining room, Pepi Riveras spotted them. "Hey boss!" He called from the beach, "Come on down here. We've got something for you. Both of you, come on down!"

They looked at each other and shrugged. "It's all right," Linda assured him. "I'm not that tired." She held his arm as they walked down the lawn.

"Listen to this!" Pepi was excited. His cohorts sang a song in Spanish. "Ya got a hotel full of canaries here, I'll tell you that," he bragged when they had finished.

"That's nice Pepi. Excellent! Thank you, everyone. Thanks for all your work. Tomorrow is *the* day. Thanks for everything."

Mike Kramer pretended not to notice that Toni Warden had left the group in the middle of their song; he tried not to follow her movement as she ran up the cement steps, tried not to stare at the lighted window of her room above the dining room.

Bertha had followed her immidiately and Rick Gerrard shortly after.

The others seemed not to care.

If he lay very still, drifting in tranquility to the quickening tempo of the first raindrops, things of tomorrow would come to him in peace; if he fell asleep with them, they would be there, gentle in the morning.

He didn't hear the master key turn in his apartment door; but he heard Toni Warden enter his room and felt her move beside him.

They loved. "I love you, Mike." And loved. "You're gorgeous." And loved. "You musn't leave me." And more love.

She lay with him a while and stroked his temples.

"Tell me I'm more than just a pretty face."

He told her.

Then, she was gone.

Part 2

Serendipity

I

Can Pal come in too?"

"He's wet."

"Dried him off before we came up."

Early Saturday morning Jake stood at Kramer's door in a puce shirt and green trousers. It was the same outfit he had worn for Serendipity's opening the day before — the same shirt at least, because the brown stain on the pocket had been there yesterday. Friday morning had been the first time Mike had seen Jake shaved. The stubble had returned, the odour too. It could have been Pal. He wasn't sure.

"Very well," Mike relented.

Pal didn't wait for orders. He led Jake into the room, inspecting each piece of furniture.

"To pee or not to pee. That's the question."

"It had better be 'not to pee,'" Mike snapped. "Or you'll be minus one dog."

"C'mere Pal. You'd better wait in the hall." Jake let the dog out and gave him something from his pocket.

"Atta boy."

"I'm in a bad mood," Mike apologised. The odour was Jake's.

"Me too."

"It's the rain. Some opening. Rain all day."

Mike looked out the window. The rain was forming puddles before it reached the ground. "Will it ever stop?" Actually, the first day had gone remarkably well in spite of the rain. Linda and Anna had proven to be a formidable combination.

"Yep. It'll quit by noon."

"Good." Mike took it as fact. "Jake, I asked you up here because we have a number of very important matters to discuss. I thought we could clear them up more quickly without interruptions."

Mike poured coffee and Jake took a cup. They heard sniffing at the space beneath the hall door. They could see a portion of Pal's wet snout and two or three of his whiskers.

"Take him a saucer of coffee," Mike offered.

"Likes it with milk and sugar."

"I know."

"He'll be quiet now," Jake said. "Doc Rogers op'rated on it. Saved his life."

"Business Jake!"

"Doc says ya should watch out fer Ronnie Greenbug. Says he's trouble. Doc knows 'im from way back."

"So do you, Jake. You sold Sam this land, plus a hundred acres around it."

"Yep. Helped Greenbug build the lodge too. Pal an' me, we seen it all."

"Why do you work here, Jake?"

"Got my reasons."

Mike wondered why he allowed his conversations with Jake to drift, if indeed he had any control over them at all. He was intrigued by this simple man who seemed so impervious to the changing world around him.

"Why work at all? You could retire. Why don't you. Do you have some goal in mind? Is there something here that you believe in?"

"Don't b'lieve in nothin'."

"Nothing? Come now, Jake."

Nothin' — 'cept Pal an' Doc. Everybody's crooks."

"Except you."

"Me too!"

Mike shook his head. He decided to abandon that approach. Why not try to get right down to business?

"The health inspector will be here first thing Tuesday morning. Do you know what to expect?"

Jake appeared to be thinking. Mike assumed that was the reason he waited so long before answering. "You'd like Doc Rogers," he finally remarked. He talks 'bout things the same way you do."

"Bring him over sometime. I'd like to meet him."

"Soon."

"Jake! The health inspector!"

"Kitchen an' laundry, that's all he cares 'bout. Leave the rest."

"I received a complaint from the kitchen foreman. The porcupines were at the garbage again yesterday morning."

"Ain't hurtin' nothin'."

"I thought you got rid of them."

"Pal tangled with a porkypine once. Only once."

"Are you going to eliminate the porcupine problem or not?"

"Leave it to me."

"Good. Now, I've received another complaint. One of out guests stopped at your garage for gas last night. He got the old five-gallons-twenty-bucks routine."

"Gotta make a livin'."

"Not at four dollars a gallon, you don't. Cut it out, with my guests at least."

Jake didn't answer. He visibly didn't like the way the conversation had turned.

"Next." Mike took several pieces of paper from his pocket and sorted through them.

"Mrs. Cohen," Jake said sourly. "Ain't seen her yet. She comin' this year?"

"She phoned yesterday. She'll be here in a few days."

"That ol' man o' hers sure thinks he's hot stuff."

Mike was tempted to ask Jake more about Peter Cohen, but the conversation was drifting again. He shuffled the papers until the one he wanted came to the top.

"The flowers you put in the lounge and office, Miss McDermott just about had a fit."

"What's wrong?"

"They're plastic."

"Got 'em from Boychuck's store. They owed me. Might as well use 'em."

"So you brought them here and submitted a bill for one hundred dollars for flowers."

"Boychuck's owed me a hunnert."

"Miss McDermott will pick up some plants in Gravenhurst." Kramer tore up the bill. "Take them away," he ordered, noticing that Jake didn't seem at all disturbed. "And this next bill is for a hammer."

"Ours busted."

"So you brought one from your garage and billed me for it."

"Yep." Jake farted. "Oops. 'Scuse me."

"Here's a bill for nails… and seeds… and …" He went through the papers one by one. "I'll pay these," he conceded. "They don't amount to much. But no more! No more bills without getting my approval. I won't pay them."

There was no doubt in Jake's mind that he had scored a major triumph. His employer didn't realize it, but if even just one of those bills had been approved, Jake would have regarded it a victory.

"That's all for now then, Jake. Here's your list of work for today. You'll notice porcupines are at the top."

Jake took the list and read it. "There ain't no money beside Porkypines."

"That's right! You've been paid once already."

The phone rang and Jake made his exit, his escape, while Mike discussed a reservation problem with Linda. When the conversation was finished, he could hear Jake scuffling with Pal in the hallway. He called Jake back into the room. The bowlegged, unkept man stood at the open door and waited.

"Jake... I'm going to say something and I want to know what you think about it... honestly.

"Okay."

"What does the phrase 'Speed adds beauty to the deer' mean to you?"

Jake grinned and scratched Pal behind the ears. "Only when it's runnin'," he said.

"Thanks Jake... Goodbye."

It was still early. There would be time for him to stand at his window if the rain would ever stop.

At least the cabbies in the city would be going crazy.

The phone rang. Linda again: would he come down to the office right away? Ronnie Greenberg was taking out the reception desk.

True to Jake's forecast, the rain stopped by noon. Bubbles was the first to hit the beach, to bare her body to the sun that steam-dried the sand around her blanket — a Cadillac frame with plenty of miles on it. She owned her section of beach and the guests soon learned to leave it open for her.

Ray Mildenhall called for his breakfast at precisely two o'clock. By two-thirty, the shuffleboard courts were dry for play and a few guests were on them, while Rick Gerrard set up the volleyball net on the beach, keeping it well away from Bubbles.

A few brave souls were swimming, though it would take a day or two for Limberlost to warm again.

Larry Parkinson opened the boathouse. Within an hour, he had phoned the office to report that all the canoes were rented.

What fun!

On Saturday, a second wave of guests began to arrive — those who had chosen not to participate in the Friday night's July 1 holiday traffic jams. They arrived *en masse,* converging on the reception office like a locust swarm. Linda and Anna handled everyone in an efficient, professional manner —

even those unglued parents who had been trapped in their cars with squabbling children for hours. Counsellors whisked the children away immediately and held them, by force if necessary, until the haggard parents felt like claiming them. The bellhops showed guests to their rooms, ducking behind the first tree on the way back to count their tips.

By six o'clock, there were still families not reunited — Bannermans, Jacksons. Linda phoned the Bannermans and Mrs. Bannerman appeared a short time later to gather up her three little jewels. The Jackson's phone was off the hook, so Linda walked over to 111 Chestnut House. The DO NOT DISTURB sign was posted. On their way to dinner, at seven-thirty, the Jacksons retrieved their children and after they had eaten, Mrs. Jackson stopped by the office to find out when the counsellors would be around in the morning to pick up Jason and Jennifer.

Each day and night was strung together like shining beads by an endless kaleidoscope of people and their problems — sectioned by crises large and small, real and imagined.

Great fun! If only…

ABRACADABRA — the bottom line turns from black to red. HOCUS-POCUS — the cash-flow that had been there on paper initially, wasn't there now. There wouldn't be enough money.

No time to sulk. Linda was at his office door. "We have a problem with Mrs. Baschmann. She insists that when she wrote for reservations, she asked for a view of the ocean."

"The ocean?"

"The ocean," Linda said. "Her room overlooks the parking lot."

A placebo was in order. "No problem." Mike glanced at the reservations board. He knew that board well. "204 Maple House cancelled. Put her there. And tell the bellhop to open the curtains and comment on how blue Limberlost Ocean is today."

Within ten minutes, Linda was back. She sat across the desk from him and leafed through her notes. I'll have to make a list each morning and leave it on your desk," she remarked. "There are too many problems to handle this way."

Mike nodded.

"The health inspector finished," she began. "He left this." She handed him a list of things to be rectified. "He promised he'd come back in two weeks and close the place down if there isn't some improvement. I showed the list to Jake. He says we should throw it in the garbage; he says the inspectors always starts out tough and become soft later on. He says if the inspector closes these places, he's out of a job. Makes sense, I suppose."

"We'll do as the inspector wishes," Mike said flatly.

"Ronnie Greenberg keeps asking when he can install the new reception counter."

"The next rainy day. After check-out time. He'll make more noise, more mess, more dust than is necessary. Be prepared."

"I wish he wouldn't hang around the office in the mornings. He tries to help, but he's a nuisance."

"Let it go for now. The less we have to do with him, the better."

Linda was obviously dissatisfied with his answer, but she checked the item on her pad and went to the next. "Rick Gerrard needs help at the driving range. He can handle the golf lessons because they are by appointment; but he can't operate the range and look after the athletic programs at the same time. It's too much."

"I can't hire anyone. There's no money." Mike looked for a reaction, but there was none, not a blink. Linda sat rigid, ready to make a notation on the margin of her pad. "Some of the others will have to fill in."

"What others? Everyone's busy."

"I'll work it out," he assured her. "Even if I have to spend time there myself. I'm cutting back on the stage shows too. I've cancelled the comedian. Ray Mildenhall has agreed to fill in." Not a flinch. Nothing.

"Times are tough," he said. "What's next?"

"Well... I've had at least a dozen calls asking if we're going to have a bingo night."

Mike slapped his hand on his forehead. "Bingo! I completely forgot! I'll be burned at the stake if we don't have bingo! Let's make it every Thursday night in the games room — starting Thursday."

"You'll be in Toronto Thursday," she reminded him.

"Sam offered to look after it."

"I will if he can't," she said.

"What a good friend he is, Linda."

"I know. Anna and I are going to be very good friends too," she added.

"I can see that. You always amaze me. I thought Anna would be the last person you'd chose as a friend. In fact, I was concerned that you might not get along."

"Why?"

"Knowing you as well as I do."

"You don't know me! Not how I feel! Not what I think! Anna has learned more about me in a few days than you have during our entire relationship. I've learned more about myself, as far as that goes."

"Forget I mentioned it."

Linda returned to her note pad. She wrote something before she spoke; "Toni Warden slapped 117 Chestnut House in the face — in the dining room. Reuben says the guy pinched her when she was showing his family to the table. You had better check with Reuben first. Apparently there was quite a scene."

"I'll look after it."

"I don't quite understand this next one," she said. "The owner of the fishing camps phoned. He said that Jake has been trapping porcupines and letting them out of cages onto his property. He's been seen doing it twice. If he catches him again, he's going to... I wrote it down." She showed him the pad.

"He wouldn't dare," Mike laughed. "How uncomfortable for Jake. I'll drive over there after a while. I want to meet him, anyway."

Mike Kramer walked with Linda to the door. He put his hand on her rump and she stuck him with her pencil.

"You seem to be settling right in," he said.

"I wish everyone here thought that." She handed him a plain envelope. "Sorry to have to give you this."

"Your letter of resignation?" he asked, opening it. "So soon. I won't touch you anymore, *during working hours* . I promise."

"Someone slipped that under my door. It was there when I got up this morning."

He unfolded the paper, which contained a sinister message. The letters were cut from a newspaper and pasted neatly together: GET OUT AND STAY OUT

Toni Warden! Toni for sure! Damn her!

"I'll keep this," he said, folding the paper and replacing it in the envelope. "You don't seem to be bothered by it." He found it difficult to disguise his alarm.

"I love it here," she said. "I'm not going anywhere. But I thought you should see the note."

"Try not to worry. We'll find out who's doing it."

"I'm fine." She was.

"It doesn't sound too serious." Mike kissed her before they opened the office door. "Any other problems, before I let you go?"

"Not that I can't handle," Linda said, waving her note pad at him as she returned to work.

Peter Cohen was a rich man's nabob. Unlike Maxwell Taylor, who had parlayed a store into an empire, Cohen had started with an empire and parlayed it into a network of real estate and development holdings that spanned the globe. He was not what Mike Kramer expected — younger, balding, slight of stature with a high, soft whispery voice. Mr. Cohen seemed a bit of a milquetoast, really. Probably was, except at board meetings. He had a ring fetish; there were rings on the fingers of both hands; there were two rings hanging from a gold chain around his neck, which made a tinkling sound when he moved. When it came to deference to his wife, there was a ring through his nose as well. No amount of coaching from Sam could have prepared Mike Kramer for the Cohens.

Mrs. Cohen — Ruth to her friends — was not what Mike had expected either. She was very short and very plain, plump but not dumpy. She had an attractive face out of which came an endless stream of crisp, precise words and sentences. She spoke forcefully but was not belligerent. In the time that he knew her, Mike would never hear her raise her voice.

"There you are, Mrs. Cohen." Mike handed her a key. "Spruce Cabin is yours for the summer."

"Spruce Cabin? Where is that?"

"We replaced the numbers with names this year."

"Leave the numbers. Replace the cabins. I hope it's better than last year."

"So do I."

"Remember the cabins last year?" she asked her husband.

"Yes."

"Terrible — cold, damp. Where is old Sam?"

"He's around. His son, Ronnie, is working here as a night clerk."

"Remember Ronnie Greenberg, Peter?"

"Yes."

She looked back at Mike. "One day, Mr. Kramer, I will tell you about Ronnie Greenberg."

She wouldn't, because Mike learned very quickly to dodge her, unless he wished to waste an hour chatting. He would become so adept at sensing her whereabouts, he developed the power to see around corners, to see in the dark.

Mrs. Cohen didn't like the sun, nor the water, so when his keen senses failed him and he found himself trapped, he would run for the beach.

Strange that either of the Cohens would come to Serendipity. There had to be a motive, but they were both misfits here.

"Mr. Cohen," Mike said, "You'll be staying upstairs — 202 or 204."

"Take 204 Peter," Mrs. Cohen interjected. It's a much better room."

"204 then."

"And you wanted a wake-up call tomorrow morning."

"Sev —"

"Six, Peter. So you can eat a proper breakfast."

"Six, please."

Mrs. Cohen followed her bellhop out the door. Mr. Cohen followed them up the stairs.

About 30 minutes later, the phone rang in Mike's office. It was Mrs. Cohen.

"Much better, young man," she said. "Much better." And hung up.

II

No need to knock. The screen door always slaps three times against its casing. Sam will hear it and come to the porch.

Mike waited. Eventually, Anna answered instead. She was drying her hands on a rose-patterned apron.

"I have to talk to Sam about a few things," he explained.

There it was, as he knew it would be — that sudden excitement he always felt in her presence, the cloud of uncertainty he always felt... as though each of their meetings was a perilous adventure. Mike loved her for it, but was afraid at the same time.

Papa and Ronnie had gone to the movies in Huntsville. They had made arrangements for the day-clerk to work two hours extra. Ronnie would be in two hours early tomorrow.

That was fine. He'd catch Sam in the morning.

"A cup of coffee, maybe?"

"Uh... no... I'd better go. There's so much to do."

"It's already made, and I'll throw in a plate of freshly-baked peanut butter cookies as well."

Always the sucker for peanut butter anything, he gave in and followed her into the house, realizing that, by invitation, he was about to enter Anna's world. He was only minutes away from that inexplicable, asexual process whereby they made love. She asked him to light a fire before disappearing into the kitchen and he complied.

"Now that I have you," she said upon returning, "sitting before the fire with coffee and cookies, it is time we had another talk."

"There are loose ends," he agreed.

Ronnie was one of them; it was him she wanted to talk about.

"How is he doing? At the lodge, I mean."

"I don't know, really," he hedged. "I don't see that much of him. Linda would know better than I."

"Ronnie has always been a withdrawn, basically shy fellow, but he's different now than before he ran off. His moodiness frightens me. Like the rumblings of a volcano, I know there is an eruption smouldering beneath the surface. Please tell me if he causes trouble."

"Certainly," Mike lied. He had no intention of running to her every time their full-grown son stepped out of line. If so, he would have mentioned homecoming and the abuse of Toni Warden. He was inclined to suggest they treat Ronnie like an adult, instead of a little boy, but thought better of it.

"Tell *me*," she cautioned. "Not Papa."

He wondered if she sensed his insincerity. Who knew? Anything was possible with that pest, Ariel, around.

"There is little chance that we can influence him. After the teens, the forces that shape our lives keep our path reasonably steady; it is doubtful that, at his age, he will change. At your age, almost impossible. For Papa and me, it would take a miracle."

He waited while Anna sipped her coffee and nibbled a cookie.

"Something very important is going to happen. It involves Ronnie. I don't know exactly what it is, but Ariel has asked me to speak to you about it. We must not be distracted."

"Tell me about Ariel," he coaxed. "He? She? What?"

"*It* has been with me since childhood — as a being of light at first. Gradually, like the lamp I told you about, the light faded until all that is left is a voice... and that has been fading too. Perhaps that is why I feel this sense of urgency about Ronnie. There may not always be Ariel to guide me. My dear mother loved her garden. For the first time since her death, Ariel didn't bring her to dig in the flower beds with me this spring."

Mike held out his cup for more coffee, then set it down to scratch a mosquito bite that had already begun to swell. Mosquitoes were thick this year, so thick as to make it uncomfortable for his guests to venture out after dark. He had come to ask Sam if he had ever sprayed to get rid of them. But this was to be Anna's night.

"So you can see my predicament. When I feel something as strongly as I do this, I cannot remain silent. There are remarkably few important events in our lives on earth; this may be one of them. We will soon find out, if we are not distracted."

"We?"

"You and Papa, Linda and me. You know by now that Linda and I have become fast friends. Already, we are very close. She is much like me when I was her age — especially in matters of religion. I know that her devotion to Catholicism has been an obstacle in your relationship; it is a hint of what is inside, like the trimming on a gift."

"Amazing! The two of you seem so different. I was worried you'd have nothing in common."

"Friendship does not require similarity... or disparity, for that matter. It is simply a mirror, that reflects value. Unlike the window. Love, there is no looking through friendship. That is why we must strive, collectively, to be the mirror Ronnie needs. Our friendship might help him see the goodness in himself, might encourage him to stay and face his problems here. He will try to divide us, no doubt, but we must be strong. You, Michael, are the key."

"Do you think I would do anything to harm our friendship?"

"Not intentionally. But you are the catalyst to the four of us, the quickening ingredient to our unique chemistry. You created Serendipity because of certain needs in your life and your creation has revitalized us all. Don't lose sight of the goals that brought you here. Hold tight to the speed of your deer. Keep believing that all things will work together for good; they simply will not happen according to your terms. I have told you what is at stake. Do not become distracted!"

Here she comes! Damn! Anna, the mirror.

"Toni Warden," he whispered abashedly, looking away as though standing naked before her. Thunder Falls... notes under Linda's door... the dining hall incident, which still hadn't been resolved. "Toni has a right to live her life here too! Serendipity is not just for an elite few. She is a friend, like the rest of you," he maintained defiantly, hoping to God that the phone would ring.

Anna had taken the phone off the hook while serving coffee and cookies. "Miss Warden also is a gift which, through your physical relationship, you are unwrapping. I am suggesting that inside you will find apiece of glass that could cut very deeply into the relationships you have already established. I make no apology for talking like this, for wanting to bring the battle to an end. Nor am I surprised by the presence of a disruptive force such as Miss Warden. Ariel —"

"To hell with Ariel! Where was precious Ariel when Fran died? When Ronnie took off? Why not Gem-Star? Kirkpatrick? Father Kelly, for God's sake! Why single out Toni? Lonely, confused, harmless Toni." He was of a mind to tell the truth about her beloved Ronnie, what he had done to her at Thunder Falls, but the triangle turned in his temples and he could not.

"... trailing clouds of glory do we come, from God, who is our home."

The master had spoken. Anna's lips moved, but it was his voice. Mike would have been a fool to doubt that Wordsworth was near.

Anna wasted little time defending her spirit guide. We are often too much in awe of the spirits was here warning. Think electric, her advice. The physical world is a hodgepodge of conductors, slowing the spirits down, channelling the power of good and evil here on earth. No master blueprint, no intricate building code.

"It is a Tinker Toy world," she insisted. "Without me — or someone like me — Ariel ceases to exist. Ariel could do no more to save Fran then I — except warn me, as she warns me now that these conversations of ours are numbered."

"Anna, I can promise you that, whatever else happens, I will make time to sit and talk with you." *Make love to you,* Anna!

"I have learned to trust Ariel. Remember, you are a fetus now, without a mother-concept, a spiritual unborn — kicking at the walls — without a concept of God. Do not think unkindly of me for saying so. You are the one responsible for the 10-year delay. I am asking you to help with Ronnie and to stay after the speed of your deer." She glared at him. "The four-legged kind."

Easy for her to say, he thought, after leaving her to the screen door's three claps on the Greenberg porch. As much chance of leaping clear of this cesspool as a fish had leaping clear of Limberlost. Anna had made herself comfortable among the gremlins. They gave him the creeps.

Gem-Star threatening to destroy him, Kirkpatrick behind — new broom in hand — to sweep the broken pieces into the trash, Maxwell Taylor waiting patiently for Linda to give up on him, and Anna expects him to be the cornerstone of a friendship that will save her worthless son, to go romping around her ridiculous playground after the speed of a bloody deer.

What was the point of it all? Pimples on a bump on a bug's backside! Coming from nowhere... going nowhere! Stewing in our own juice! A scene in a plastic bulb. Something wrong, like bathing with your socks on. Something missing, like kissing your sister. Like the Zoo!

LEAP, she says — from one dung heap to another!

Still, there must be more... *has to be!* It would not escape him tonight. He would go to his apartment, hide under the comforter on his bed and stay there until he decided what it was.

Anna must have hung up the phone after he left. From the footbridge he heard it ring twice, then she came to the porch and called to him.

It was Linda. Would he go to the office right away? There was a serious mix-up with one of the reservations.

III

Probably his imagination. He hadn't slept well; Anna's words and coffee had kept him awake most of the night. Well rested, there would have been no recognizable difference, no overnight change in her.

"Why do I have to come here like this?" Toni Warden complained. She glared at him through squinting eyes. Her lips were pressed tightly together. The set of her delicate visage belied the fact that her teeth were clenched. "Can't we talk in your apartment?"

"No. We can't."

"Why not?"

"This is business."

"So what?"

Kramer didn't respond. It would have been easy to lose his temper, feeling as he did — rotten. "How is Bertha?" he asked.

"How should I know?"

"You're her friend, aren't you?"

"Why don't you ask her how she's doing?"

"I will." Who was this stranger? "Toni, we had a problem with one of the rooms last night — one of Bertha's rooms. The Bronsons checked into 218 Maple House and the room wasn't ready. It hadn't been cleaned. That room has been vacant for two days. It should have been ready."

"Why tell me?"

"Since you and Bertha are close friends, I thought you might know if something was wrong."

"Nothing's wrong. Bert's fine. I know I'm not here to talk about her."

"No."

"Then can we get on with it? I have to get ready for lunch."

"Very well." he sighed. "The man you slapped has checked out."

"Good!"

"He was booked into Chestnut House — two rooms for three weeks. I can't afford losses like that. You broke his glasses. I'll have to replace them as well."

Toni stood up quickly. She raised her skirt above her waist, tucked it under one arm and pulled one side of her panties down to expose the bruise the size of a silver dollar. "That's what I got for my trouble," she snapped.

Mike watched as she straightened her clothes. He involuntarily glanced at the window to reception to make sure no one had seen her. "I can't afford those kind of losses, I tell you. In future, you'll have to control your temper. After all, you knew this sort of thing was bound to happen."

"Yes, sir!" she mocked. "Yes, sir! I knew."

"Linda has asked me to —"

"I hate Linda! She's a creep! What do you see in her?"

He ignored her outburst, pretended to ignore it. "Someone — a member of the staff — has been slipping messages under her door. She would like to have them delivered to her personally at the office."

Toni's expression didn't change. "Linda's a bitch," she said.

"The menus are ready for tonight," he said. "You can pick them up on the way out."

Toni stood up to go. She deliberately moistened her lips before she spoke. "Will I be joining you tonight?" Her voice had softened suddenly and her countenance with it.

Mike looked at her, trying to remember Anna's counsel. Bad enough that she should hoist her skirt and drop her pants in his office... in broad daylight... for God and man to see. Now she was after him again to crawl in the sack. Anna was right! The brazen bitch!

"Of course," he replied. "Please ask Linda to come in when you're leaving."

"Well, well," Linda said as she entered his office. "Quite the girl. Interesting, don't you think?"

Mike shrugged. Who thought anymore? Who gave a damn?

"Did you get the dining room incident settled?"

"Who knows?"

Linda crossed the item off her list. "You look terrible," she said.

"I couldn't sleep last night. I think I'll go back to bed for an hour."

"Not today, my dear." She dropped the list in front of him. "These things have to be taken care of immediately… if not sooner."

Glancing over the list, he could see she was right. Even if there was no list, something would happen before he could sneak off to his apartment. "You haven't got Bertha on here. I'll have to speak to her about the Bronsons' room."

"I already did that," Linda said. "Bertha insists she cleaned that room two days ago."

"Obviously she's mistaken."

"She doesn't seem to be the kind of person to make a mistake like that."

"We'll just forget about it then. Don't even mention it to Olga. As long as the Bronsons aren't upset."

"They're not."

"I was looking at the reservations board this morning," Mike remarked casually. "I noticed you pencilled in one of the special guest rooms for the first weekend in August."

"You don't miss much do you?" Linda smiled. "You watch that board like a hawk."

"I hope the initials M. T. don't mean what I think they mean."

"They do."

"Maxwell Taylor is *not* coming here! He is *not* staying at Serendipity. That's final!"

"It is *not* final! And he *is* staying at Serendipity for three days in August. We already have his deposit for five hundred dollars."

"Return the money and cancel his reservation."

"I will not!"

"Cancel it!"

"No!"

"Why would he want to come here?"

"I don't know. I don't care."

"I don't want him around."

"For three days?"

"For three minutes!"

"Too bad. He's coming and the other rooms I've reserved are for people he's bringing with him. That's why the deposit is so much. Do you need the five hundred dollars or not?"

"Shit!" There were days when Mike Kramer enjoyed a good fight, times when he knew he could hold his own. This morning wasn't one of those times. "Why would you invite Taylor here, when you know how I feel about him?" He had retreated. Ever so slightly.

"I didn't invite him, believe it or not. He phoned to see how I was doing. I still work for him, remember. He asked me to make reservations. I could see no reason not to."

"Because I don't like him! That should be reason enough."

"He is also a friend. I often wonder if you really understand friendship. He's going to run for mayor of Toronto, I think. He said he'd like to spend a quiet weekend here... to decide."

"You're right about one thing," he admitted. "I need the money. I'll arrange to be away that weekend."

"Don't be silly!"

"If you were in my position, you would think differently. There are things you don't understand."

"There certainly are. Like why you would invite Jack Kirkpatrick to bring his wife and three kids here for a week."

"Kirk's a friend," he quipped, pleased with himself. "He's only staying the weekend. Marcia and the kids will be staying on."

"Free of charge! I guess they *will* stay on. No wonder you can't pay the mortgage."

"Kirk will give me something, don't worry about it."

"Yes. He'll give you something. A kick in the ass! This guy is robbing you blind, Mike. And you permit him to stay here for nothing. What's wrong with you?"

"Please, Linda," Mike pleaded. "No fights. To hell with Maxwell Taylor. To hell with Jack Kirkpatrick. I don't feel well. I feel awful. Let's talk about something else... like what's going on outside. What *is* that incessant noise, anyhow?"

"Why don't you go out and have a look!" Linda slammed the door as she left.

After waiting an appropriate length of time, Mike walked out of the office as nonchalantly as possible. Linda refused to look up from her typewriter as he passed.

He strolled out to the front lawn. Pepi Riveras, guitar in hand, had gathered a line of 50 men, women and children; he was bunny-hopping them around the grounds. Immediately, Kramer spotted at least a half dozen of his employees who should have been working. But there was no such animal as work for Pepi; he was no beast of burden. If it wasn't play, if you couldn't make a game of it, you just didn't bother doing it.

The line proceeded nicely except for Mrs. Cohen. She couldn't keep up and finally dropped to the lawn, exhausted. She sat in the sun and rested, clearly uncomfortable, fanning herself with her wide-brimmed sun bonnet.

Pepi manoeuvred the line so that it passed in front of Mike. "Jump in here, boss," he puffed. The woman behind Pepi grabbed Mike's arm and pulled him in. They bunny-hopped through the front door of the office, around Linda at the reception desk and out again, past the lounge to the entertainment building, across the driving range, between Maple and Chestnut House, down the lawn to the beach. Bubbles wouldn't join the line, refusing to leave her blanket, turning on her stomach and pretending to fall asleep.

When Pepi, without warning, led his charges into Limberlost with his guitar high above his head, the line broke. Most of the children followed, but many adults declined. "Don't pee in the lake!" he yelled. "Don't pee in the lake!" He nudged Mike: "Too late," pointing to a child standing motionless in water up to her waist. "She peed."

On the beach and dripping wet from the knees down, Mike looked up. The ubiquitous Mrs. Cohen had stopped fanning herself. Jake was standing beside her, shaking his head, no doubt disgusted with the performance and telling her so.

And he caught a glimpse of Linda, just before she disappeared from the top of the steps to return to work.

When Toni Warden came to him late that night, it wasn't business as usual; she wanted to talk. She told him that there were frightening things going on inside... things that had her scared and confused. She needed him more than ever, these days. Maybe it was only the intricate aberration of an over-tired mind, but before she left him, he thought he heard her whisper "I love you."

Well after Toni's ephemeral visit, just before he fell asleep, Mike remembered that he hadn't mentioned another threatening note under Linda's door, that either they would have to stop, or she would have to leave.

⁂

Fire! FIRE!

Why would someone be yelling fire? We know there's a fire. We lit the damn thing.

FIRE!

Such a grand reunion it was! Pepi yelling at everyone; Jimmy scooting over the sand; Gus spilling drinks, trying to balance a tray on his bald head; Newton Bass gathering wood for the bonfire; Father Kelly skinny-dipping.

FIRE! FIRE!

The dream ended subtly, gradually merging with the reality of a commotion on the lawn. When he went to the window to investigate, it took a moment for him to admit that there was no bonfire on the beach, that the reunion of his old acquaintances was actually a cluster of lodge guests milling on the lawn in their pyjamas and nightgowns. Some of them were running with pails of water from Limberlost.

FIRE!

It didn't take Mike long to get there. Smoke was pouring from the window of the back corner room in Maple House. Mrs. Cohen, suddenly beside him, reported: "Ronnie and Jake are inside, trying to put it out. Pepi's in there too, waking all the guests and getting them out of the building."

As Mike instinctively started for the front door, he heard the sound of broken glass and turned to see Ronnie and Jake throw a smouldering mattress from the second story room to the sidewalk below.

"Everything's out," Pepi announced, emerging from the building. "Prob'ly a cigarette." Mike tried to remember who was staying in that room, but couldn't. "Just the one room. There's no damage to the rest."

"Thanks Pepi. I'll have a look at the damage in the morning. I'm not up to it. It's three o'clock! Let's get everybody back to bed."

Jake and Ronnie offered to stay and help do that, while Mike returned to the office, Pepi following behind.

"Hey, boss. Think this'll make the papers."

"Why would a room-fire reach Gravenhurst? Who would care if it did? I doubt it."

'A little publicity is a good thing. Want me to call them?"

"Forget it Pepi. It's over."

"Well, if someone from the newspaper should happen to call here, be sure to mention me... and the Lovers too. Say 'Pepi Riveras and the Latin Lovers.' Okay? That way, people'll know there's a band here. Mention our album, too."

Mike wanted to know how Pepi thought he should go about mentioning an album while reporting a mattress fire.

"Dunno," Pepi admitted. "Say a case of 'em got burned in the fire."

"Good night, Pepi. Thanks for your help."

"This ain't night, boss. I'm just waking up."

"Where's Jake?"

Mike accosted Ronnie Greenberg the minute he returned to the office. While waiting, while looking over the guest list to see who had been in 200 Maple, he had answered the flood of calls and the personal inquiries as well. "While I'm up, could I get a book from the tuck-shop?" "Do you have an extra blanket?"

There wasn't time to think about what had happened, only time to confirm what was already suspected — the room with the smouldering mattress had been vacant since 10 a.m. the previous morning.

"Where's Jake?"

"How should I know?" Ronnie shrugged. "Gone home I guess."

"I want to thank you for what you did tonight, Ronnie. The damage could have been far more extensive if you hadn't acted as quickly as you did."

"I didn't do it for *you.*"

"Then why bother?"

"I have my reasons."

"Listen!" Mike slammed his hand on the reception desk — too hard, because it stung for a long time after. "Something serious has happened here tonight and I'm going to get to the bottom of it. I'm going to ask you some questions and I want straight answers or I'll boost you out of here so fast your head will spin!"

Ronnie didn't answer. Mike looked at his watch — 3:45 a.m.

"Are you aware that 200 Maple has been vacant since ten o'clock yesterday morning?"

Ronnie hesitated. "Sure."

"It doesn't take that long for a cigarette to burn a mattress. Even if it did, Bertha would have seen something when she made the bed."

"Strange, isn't it?"

"Very! You weren't the first to spot the smoke, were you?"

"Jake was. He phoned from the room."

"What exactly did he say?"

"He said get over to 200 Maple quick. There was a fire."

"Isn't that odd?"

"What?"

"That Jake would be here at two o'clock in the morning."

"No."

"No? Why not?"

"Because he hangs around here a lot at night. I have to chase that stupid dog of his away from the garbage cans. If you ask me, he's sleeping at the lodge." *218 Maple House. It wasn't clean when the Bronsons' checked in.* "He lets himself in with his key, uses the room, and no one's the wiser. This time, he fell asleep with a cigarette. I'd fire his ass out of here. He's a trouble-maker."

"I'll take care of Jake."

When he passed Linda's door on the way back to his apartment, he realized that she had slept through all the commotion. Her reputation as a sound sleeper was still intact.

For a moment, only a brief time, he stopped in the hallway and considered slipping quietly into her room, gently laying down beside her. Just to see what would happen.

He decided against it.

Which of Anna's gremlins was in charge of lining up the events of his day? Probably the same one who arranged for the bread to always fall buttered side down. Mike knew he should have returned to bed after the fire; he chose instead to wait up and have breakfast with Linda, to watch the sun rise above the hill that rimmed Limberlost. The way he used to watch.

Rise! You sucker! Rise. Fifty billion years to go.

Be diligent, Anna had said. *Be diligent.*

What did she know?

The out-of-shapers began to assemble on the middle terrace of the lawn in front of the dining halls, so they would be close to breakfast after Rick Gerrard coaxed them through their exercises. There weren't as many as usual. Mike and Linda watched them struggle from their table at the front window, listened to them grunt and groan.

Mike spent considerable time briefing Linda on the peculiar events that had happened while she slept. "I'm going now to take a look at the fire damage," he said dryly. "I'll get Jake started on the repairs right away."

"Jake?" she questioned. "Shouldn't you confront him before this goes any further? After all—"

"No!" He thought a moment. "No," he repeated less emphatically. "I shouldn't."

"Surely you have to put a stop to this while you have the chance."

"I'll have to think on it," he said with finality.

"Very well, you do that. You think about it," she responded sarcastically. "In the meantime, your lists keep growing longer."

"You type my lists. I'll worry about them."

"Lets hope this sort of thing doesn't happen again."

"I'm going back to bed for an hour," he announced. "I've been up since two o'clock."

Linda shook her head. "Uh, Uh, not today. You have enough to keep two men busy."

"C'mon, sleeping beauty. Have a heart!"

"Start with this." She took a piece of paper from her purse and handed it to him.

"Another one?"

"It was in an envelope, under my door when I got up this morning."

Same format. Slightly different message:

GET OUT OR ELSE

The sender had underlined OR ELSE in pencil.

"It's going to be tough to figure out who is doing this," he said, folding the paper and putting it in his pocket.

"Not too difficult," she answered tersely. "I think we both know who's probably responsible. But you think about it."

"OR ELSE," he said.

"It will take more than an OR ELSE to get me away from Serendipity."

"Or away from me?"
"*Or* away from you."

❧

When Mike Kramer reached Maple 200, a fire inspector was already there — measuring, making notes, trying to look important, He might have been successful too, had he remembered to zipper his fly. The only explanation he offered for his presence was that someone from the lodge had called him. News travelled fast, mysteriously fast: The inspector admitted that he had received a phone call, but he insisted that he was not at liberty to reveal the identity of the caller. The results of the inspector's visit were very disheartening; he handed Mike an official-looking slip of paper which ordered that smoke alarms be installed in every room, as well as other strategic locations around the lodge. The installations were to commence within three week's time; if they didn't have the thousansds of dollars required for such a project, the inspector replied that it was not his job to be concerned with a few dollars when precious lives hung in the balance.

Before Mike left, the inspector mentioned that he would be spending the balance of the day drawing a detailed sketch of every building. He would leave copies of the sketches and the red dots would indicate exactly where each detector was to be installed.

As Mike was walking away, the inspector casually asked if it might be arranged that he have a bite to eat around noon.

From there, the day deteriorated.

❧

Pepi's wife was a text-book introvert. She was shy and soft spoken — so soft that few could say they had actually been present to hear her put a complete sentence together. She was so unlike her husband, it was not unreasonable for one to suppose that Pepi loved her because, by stark contrast, she actually complimented his effervescence. It was an art, the way she had learned to survive with facial expressions and physical gestures.

If Bubbles could have her blanket on the beach, Mrs. Riveras could have her tiny table in the front corner of the entertainment hall — *no man's land.* She never joined the Lovers' wives and girlfriends who sat together at a more prominent table. She sat alone each night, waiting for Pepi to join her between breaks in the stage show and during the 20-minute rests between dance sets later on. He never did, of course. He would shed his guitar, tuck two or three albums under his arm, head for a table with new faces and, more often than not, make a sale — pure profit, since the albums were donated by the studio for promotion.

Mrs. Riveras was a good looking woman and could have been even more attractive with a bit of attention to her appearance. It was not uncommon for a guest to make a play for her. She would smile, nod, shrug until the intruder left. And, if he persisted, she would offer him an album from the stack that Pepi had left at their table. That always did the trick!

Though they seldom appeared in the entertainment hall — only when there was a change in format — Mike and Linda enjoyed watching Mrs. Riveras operate. For them, her routine was an attraction. Because of their rigorous schedule and long working hours, they didn't stay for dancing unless trapped as they were now, by an aggressive, arrogant contractor from Montreal. He had completely revamped the dining room, demolished the office and was in the process of rebuilding it when Toni Warden approached their table.

She didn't speak, just held out her hand. Inexplicably, he took it. He left Linda, who seemed not to care, with the contractor and followed Toni to the dance floor. The manner in which she held onto him was embarrassing. Mike was certain the murmuring behind him was gossip. And to make matters worse, each time they passed close to the stage, Pepi Riveras would rattle the maracas and wink at him.

So pretty. Such potential.

She was still the best looking woman he knew. He wished his desire to have her would disappear.

But it wouldn't. It was there — *always.*

"Tonight," she whispered finally, relaxing some. "I need you tonight."

"Not tonight."

He felt a toughness returning to her, like holding a soft, then calloused, hand.

"Why?"

"I'm not in the mood."

"You're in the mood for Linda. Bitch!"

"I'm in the mood to be left alone. I'm tired and I have a busy day tomorrow."

⁂

"Linda said you wanted to see me."

"Yes Bertha, come in and sit down."

"What happened now?"

"I want to change things around. I'm going to put you in Chestnut House instead of Maple. I've discussed it with Mrs. Oleifson already. She agrees."

"I've always worked in Maple House. Always."

"There is no difference."

"There is so! It's because of the trouble, isn't it?"

"Bertha, are you absolutely sure you made up the Bronsons' room? Is it possible that you could have overlooked it?"

"I didn't overlook it. I cleaned it."

" I'm asking because there have been a number of other incidents — all in the Maple House."

"Like what?"

"The fire."

"What's that got to do with me?"

"Probably nothing. But the fire was caused by a smouldering cigarette. You cleaned the room the morning before."

"That's right. And there wasn't no smouldering cigarette."

"And you cleaned the Koffman's room before they checked in?"

"Yes."

"You're sure?"

"Yes."

"They complained that cigarette butts were left in the ashtrays."

"Not by me."

"Another room had paper in the trash cans and the bathroom hadn't been cleaned. Linda has the details."

"Maybe I should find another job."

"No! It's unfortunate that these things are happening in your rooms, but I'm not holding you responsible. Still I think you should switch to Chestnut House until I can get to the bottom of it."

"Okay."

"One last thing. When you cleaned 105 yesterday did you happen to see a ring laying on the night table?"

"No."

"Mrs. Morris claims her diamond ring is missing."

"I never saw it."

"Don't worry, it'll probably show up. They're staying for two weeks."

Bertha was different now too — a similar toughness that he hadn't seen before.

What the hell was going on?

Linda came to the office door after Bertha had gone. "Mr. Jordan is waiting to see you."

"Oak Cottage? Can't you handle it?"

"I think you had better talk to him."

Mike waited for Mr. Jordan to settle into his chair. "How are you enjoying Serendipity?" he asked.

"Fine... just fine. The wife and I have travelled a lot since my retirement. This is one of the best."

"Thank you. That's good to hear."

"Except for one problem. Someone is prowling around the cabins late at night. Early morning really — two or three o'clock. Whoever it is makes enough noise to waken us. We lay in bed and listen to him moving around outside. When I go out to have a look he's gone. The trees are pretty thick. He must hide in the ravine. The wife is terrified."

"How do you know it's a man? It could be an animal."

"No, it's not. It's a man. I know the difference."

"I'll have it stopped. Immediately."

"I hope so Mr. Kramer. The wife and I were wanting to stay on an extra two weeks."

Mike saw Mr. Jordan to the door. When he left the office, Linda remarked that there had been a second complaint about late-night noise around the cabins.

"This place is a zoo," he complained. "I had better not go to Toronto this week."

"You'll be sorry."

"No... Kirk will be here next weekend, anyway," he rationalized.

V

The only imaginable thing that Ruth Cohen and Jack Kirkpatrick could have in common was an aversion to the sun. Kirk, unlike Mrs. Cohen, would brave the beach rather than face his wife's disgust, and on occasion, had been known to enter the water to play with the kids. But a minute too long under the ultraviolet and, because of his ruddy complexion, his body looked like it had been gone over with a blowtorch.

"Sun an' fun, eh Kirk?" Mike laughed as he approached his partner, who was stretched out on a beach chair with one wet towel draped over his head and shoulders, another covering his legs. "You're the only person I know who packs a tent to the beach."

"I feel like a fuckin' hot dog. I'll look like one, too, if I sit here much longer. My cigar is starting to smoke."

They shook hands, but Kirkpatrick couldn't get up, because of the towels.

"I'll have Rick Gerrard bring you down a beach umbrella."

Jack's wife and three children were playing in the water. Mike waved to them. Rachel Kirkpatrick was a big woman, broad of keel, with ample breasts. Good with the kids. Not apt to stray.

"Don't bother," Jack said. "I'm going inside in a minute. I just want to make sure the family gets settled in."

"Sorry I missed you last night," Mike apologized. "How come you were so late?"

"Damn accident. Traffic was backed up for miles. Took us two and a half hours to get off 400. What a trip! Try sitting in a car with a wife and three kids for a few hours. I nearly went crazy! Nice spot you've found here though, Mike. Very nice. And *very* expensive! No wonder you're feelin' the pinch."

"I'm hurting, I admit it, Kirk. Really hurting." It was difficult to discuss business with someone covered with towels. "We'll talk after dinner, if you don't mind a bit of business mixed in with your weekend."

"What weekend? I'm heading back as soon as it's safe. Rachael and the kids have *almost* forgotten I exist. I figure about another hour should do it." Kirk shifted his cigar and looked over at Bubbles. "I'd like to come back on my own, though."

"Why leave so soon?"

"I've been pushin' DAY AND NIGHT to sell their cabs. I heard one partner wants out, so I put a healthy bid in last week. The shit will hit the fan any time now and I want to be around when it does. They've been squabbling and fighting for months. I may pick up a bargain before I'm through with those two. That's one thing about us, Mike. We may have had our differences, but we've never let it last long enough to hurt either of us."

There was the crack in the armour! The one Mike had wanted. "You know Kirk, you remind me of a story about the miser who fell in the water holding a sack of gold. He refused to let go of it and it took him to the bottom."

Kirkpatrick's response was delayed because his youngest daughter threw a pail of water on him. It was even more difficult to be serious when the towels were wet. "Maybe you're right," he agreed, "but I'd rather go to the bottom than get to the shore empty handed and end up begging."

With a tin cup? Like Jimmy?

"Like me?"

"That's the way you'll end up, before you're through. If you'd stuck it out with me, we'd of had the cab business right there." Kirk held out the palm of him hand.

"Then what?"

"Big money."

"Well, it's too late now, isn't it? But because I chose a different way, that should be no reason for you to steal from me."

"Steal?"

"Yes, steal Kirk — at least a hundred a day, maybe more."

"You call it stealing. I call it looking after my interests. We've already discussed it."

"No. It's stealing. And you know it. If one of your drivers shorts his sheet ten dollars he calls it 'looking after his interests' and you call it stealing. If you short me a hundred bucks a day, I call it stealing."

Jack took the towel off his head and removed the cigar from his mouth. "I'm sorry, Mike. I'm sorry that you feel that way. After all we've had going for us, I'd never deliberately hurt you. I've always figured that turnabout's fair play. If the situation was reversed, I would expect you to treat me the same way."

"I think you've gotten greedy, Kirk. And I also think you realize how much I'm hurting. I think you know how much I'm going to need that hundred-a-day before this is all over. I couldn't make the June first mortgage payment. The representative from Gem-Star is coming here in early July to pick up two payments. What do you suppose he'll do when he finds out I can't make the July payment either?"

"That bad, eh?"

"That bad."

"I can't understand why a company like Gem-Star would take a chance on a place like this," Kirk said. "*I* wouldn't."

"If I had the hundred dollars a day you're siphoning off the top of my business, I might make it."

"Why should I do that?"

"Because you want my business."

"Don't be stupid. Why would I want your cabs?"

"For the same reason I've seen you bend down to pick up a penny."

"Too bad you feel that way, Mike, after 10 years of trusting each other. Maybe I *have* been too concerned about my affairs at your expense. You have my word that when I get back to Toronto I'll turn things around, even them up."

Kirkpatrick held out his hand. Mike took a firm grip on it. "What are you going to do in the meantime?" Jack asked, giving an extra firm squeeze to their handshake.

"I'm going to wait for the for the guy from Gem-Star to make a move. I may come up with some cash. Who knows?"

"I wish I could help you, Mike. If I had it, I'd give it to you now. No questions. But —"

"No! I may have to sell some cars." Mike hung his head. He would rather pull out his own wisdom teeth. "All I ask is that you treat me fairly, Kirk — honestly. And if I have to sell, I'll sell to you at a fair price."

"No problem! No problem at all. I'll be ready! I'll take the whole lot if you want."

"I haven't decided yet. I don't know what to do."

"Well," Jack Kirkpatrick said abruptly. "I'm leaving now. Keep in touch."

"Before you leave, Kirk would you like to meet a couple of really fine people? They live in the house across the ravine. They built this lodge."

"No, I gotta go. I want to get back in time to do a few things."

"I'll be down to the city before the end of the month."

"Good luck, Mike... could you bring Rachel and the kids with you when you come?"

As far as Mike Kramer could determine, Kirkpatrick departed without saying goodbye to his family.

He simply left.

"Wanna buy some plastic plants?"

Linda McDermott glanced up from her typewriter. She could hear Jake's voice, but it was coming from outside the office door, which had been propped open because of the heat. It was only mid morning and already the fans were going.

"Come in, Jake," she said, returning to her work.

Jake's unshaven face appeared in the open doorway. There was a freshly rolled cigarette stuck between his lips. He hadn't lit it and didn't appear to be in a hurry to do so. He entered the office and leaned over the counter. Pal pushed his way through the swinging door and settled behind the counter near Linda's desk.

"C'mere Pal!"

"Leave him. He's fine. He likes the breeze from the fan."

Jake watched Linda work. "I'm startin' to melt," he said dryly, pointing to the sweat marks on his shirt. The cigarette had stuck to his bottom lip and it wagged when he spoke. "Where's my list?" he asked.

"There isn't one today. Mike isn't back from the city yet. He said just keep working on that room. But here are a couple of bills that Mike wouldn't approve." Actually, she hadn't bothered showing them to Mike. He wasn't likely to approve bills for Jake's work clothes.

Jake took the bills, crumpled them up and deposited them in an ashtray. "Other clothes got messed up in the fire," he grumbled.

"I'll bet," she said. "What were you doing around there at two o'clock in the morning anyway?"

Jake didn't answer. He continued to lean on the counter and watch her work. Pal had settled in too; he lay with his chin on the floor between his outstretched paws and followed the flow of conversation with mopey eyes. "Boychuck ain't takin' those plants back," he complained. "Looks like I'm out a hunnert bucks, eh?"

"Looks like," Linda agreed. "Why don't you try to sell them at your garage?"

"Hey! Yeah! Prob'ly get a hunnert an' fifty for 'em that way!" It was one of the few times Linda had seen him enthused. "C'mon Pal. Let's get our work done."

"Why don't you leave him here with me?" Pal hadn't intended to leave anyway. "He likes the fan."

"Won't stay. Maybe if I tell 'im."

"He'll stay. Just go and don't say anything."

"Maybe if ya gave him your coffee. Got cream in it?"

"Yes."

"Good. Love's cream in his coffee."

Jake didn't leave. He played with the pen at the registration counter. "You know Doc Rogers?" he asked.

"I've heard about him."

"Like to meet him?"

"Sure."

"He's sick."

"Bring him around when he's better."

"Good."

Mike Kramer passed Jake on the sidewalk outside the office. Jake appeared to be in a hurry.

"Them clothes got ruined in the fire," he grumbled without looking up and went on his way.

Mike wiped his forehead with his shirt sleeve. "My bag is in the trunk." he said to the bellhop, handing him the car keys. Then he turned his attention to Linda, who greeted him with the same enthusiasm she had Jake. "Lord it's hot! That's the last time I'll *ever* have the Kirkpatrick kids in *my* car. They started up as soon as we left: 'We don't wanna go! Do we havta mommy? When can we come back? Can we come back tomorrow mommy.' Their bickering drove me nuts — all the way from Sidney to Don Mills! They didn't bother Rachel though; it was like background music to her. She never shut up once the whole trip — talk, talk, talk. When we got to Kirk's house, she had the nerve to ask me in for a cup of coffee... Not likely! In fact, I think it may be a while before I go to Toronto again. What a trip!"

"What about your business?"

"I had a good talk with Kirk when he was here. It seems to have done some good. The bank deposits are up already. Even Tesky has noticed a change in attitude around there."

Mike pointed at Pal who had slept through his complaining. "What's he got that I haven't?"

"Fleas." Linda smiled but didn't look up. "I wouldn't stay away from Toronto too long," she warned.

Mike appeared annoyed. "Kirk and I are friends, above all. In the end, that friendship will keep things in order."

Anna and her mirrors. Nonsense.

"I put a list on your desk. Things that need your immediate attention, Mike. And a young lady has been anxious to see you about a very important matter. If you'll attend to the list, I'll call her and tell her you're back."

"Lucky dog," Mike said to Pal as he disappeared into his office. He could see the list. Linda had itemized the problems she couldn't handle and left spaces after each for his written reply. Since he had been away for a day, the paper was filled. He could hear the bellhop returning his keys to Linda as he began to study the items:

Friday - July 20, 1973

Please attend to the following:

i) cabins — Mr. Morris is checking out because of the noises at night
No comment.

ii) Tuck shop — broken into while you were in Toronto
— nothing stolen except a few magazines
I know. Shirley met me in the parking lot.

iii) Boat House — lock broken last night, nothing missing
Shit.

iv) Fire inspector — please call, wants a progress report
Shit.

v) Rooms — new guests in Chestnut House
— another room not made up
Shit.

vi) Toni Warden — Reuben says she wants a raise
No.

vii) Mrs. Morris — wants action re: her diamond ring
I'll call her.

viii) Another note — one word this time — BEWARE
There is more — tomorrow

What the hell is going on?

Where had it gone? The vision? The dream? The speed of the deer? Mike put the list on one side and shook his head — like a stung boxer — as if to clear it. He had already made up his mind to at least hang on through the summer, to pay wages and operate Serendipity, even if it meant selling a portion of his business to Jack Kirkpatrick. What happened beyond that depended upon his meeting with the representative from Gem-Star, who undoubtedly would arrive shortly after the August mortgage payment became overdue.

His phone rang. It stopped self-pity from slithering into depression.

Linda: "There's a young lady here to see you."

"Send her in." Mike smoothed his hair with the palms of his hands.

Linda opened his office door. "This is Mary Anne Croft. She has something very important to discuss with you." She waited for the small girl to enter and winked at him.

"Come in Mary Anne." Mike waited for Linda to close the door. Mary Anne climbed into a chair. "What can I do for you?"

"It's my birfday tomorrow."

"Good for you! How old will you be?"

"Umm... fife."

"You're a big girl now, you know."

"Mr. Pepi an' Nosey."

"Who is nosy?"

"A man who works for Mr. Pepi. Mr. Pepi calls him that 'cause he always picks his nose."

"I see. What about Mr. Pepi and Nosey?"

"They want to... mommy says they can come to my birfday party if Mr. Pepi gets out of bed... Mommy will pay him to come 'cause he plays nice music... an' he knows magic... Mr. Pepi can make things disappear."

"I know."

"Mommy says to ask you if Mr. Pepi can come... an' can we go inside 'case it rains."

"Sure. Tell your mommy I'll phone her."

"Can I have my party here next year too?"

"Of course you can."

"After little Mary Anne struggled out of her chair and hurried from the room, Linda looked at him through the open window in the wall between them.

"Someday, buster," she said, beaming.

"When?"

"Whenever you're ready!"

XI

It was surprising to see that, from the waist up, Peter Cohen's diminutive body displayed a generous assortment of colourful tattoos, even more surprising that his entire body was covered with thick, curly hair; there was even a ring at his neck where he shaved it off which caused his head to appear detachable. More amazing than that, however, was the amount of time he spent with Maxwell Taylor.

"They're not strangers," Sam had remarked. "I know Cohen well. When he spends that much time with someone, you can bet they aren't discussing the price of balloons in Bombay."

They both arrived Friday evening, Cohen alone and Taylor with his band of assistants. They took an early breakfast together Saturday with Mrs. Cohen and Linda joining them. Then the two men set up their headquarters at a table on the beach and spent the day passing papers to each other, reading and signing them, sunning themselves and swimming. They dined together in the evening, again with the ladies, and the foursome took in the stage show afterward. They requested that Mike join them; he politely declined.

Peter Cohen left Serendipity early Sunday but by mid morning, Maxwell Taylor was back at his table on the beach. Linda joined him. From his apartment window, Mike watched them for an hour. He felt uneasy and afraid and he blamed Linda for it. After all, she was the one spending time with Maxwell Taylor when she knew exactly how he felt about him; she was permitting the monster to reach across the table and touch her hand. It was Linda who...

There was a knock at the door. "Mr. Taylor and Miss McDermott would like you to join them on the beach," the bellhop said in a monotone voice.

"Tell them to —" Mike stopped. "Don't tell them anything."

"But Mr. Kramer, they're expecting an answer. I'll lose my tip."

"Very well... tell them I'll be right down."

"Ah Mr. Kramer!" Maxwell Taylor didn't offer to shake hands but he did pull out a beach chair. "Sit down. Glad you joined us! We've been a long time getting together."

"Not long enough."

"Mike! Behave yourself," Linda said.

Taylor seemed very jovial — too jovial. "Too much sun yesterday," he explained, to account for the fact that he was fully dressed. "I'm burned all over." He hesitated and then a veil of seriousness passed over his face, like a cloud passing over the sun. "I've been trying to persuade our Linda here to come back to Toronto with me. I have several very important projects in the works. I need her help. She's a fine assistant. I've had nothing but difficulty since she left."

Mike glanced at Linda for some response.

"Why tell me?" he asked?

"She hasn't agreed… not yet."

"Not yet?" Mike looked to Linda again for some reaction. There was none.

"That's where you come in, Mr. Kramer. That's why I asked you to join us. I don't particularly like you any more than you like me. But Linda will be going back to Toronto with me and you are the one who is going to convince her."

"You love to win, don't you? Anything for power, right?"

"Let's put it this way, Kramer. I only pass this way once. I might as well travel on top of the heap."

Top turd of the dung pile.

There was still no response from Linda. Not even a change in her expression. She either expected this or wasn't listening.

"Beautiful," Mike said. "Excuse me."

"No! No! Sit down, Kramer. I'm not through with you yet. Not by a long shot."

Mike sat, curious.

"Let me begin by saying that this is a fine lodge you have here. Very nice. You've done quite a good job with it."

"Skip the *nice* stuff. What's this got to do with Linda?"

"Well, I was wondering how you are making out financially. Does this lovely woman here know how you are making out financially?"

"I'll manage. What does that have to do with Linda?"

Maxwell Taylor stared straight out at the islands with an intensity that Mike had never seen in a human before. His entire body tightened. "I'm not so sure she'll want to go down with a sinking ship. You see, I know more about your affairs than you might think. They don't call me "Trigger" for nothing. I doubt that she'll want to stick around when she finds out how you've botched and bungled your way into real serious trouble."

Still, Mike could not tell if Linda was listening. She seemed to be far away.

"I'll look after my affairs," he answered indignantly. "Don't *you* worry about them."

"But I *am* ! I *am* worried."

"About what?"

"Well, your mortgage payments, for instance. Does Linda know that you missed the last one? Does she know that another was due last Tuesday? Tomorrow is the sixth, and, last word I heard, it still hasn't been paid."

"That's between me and Gem-Star. Leave it alone," Mike warned. "Stay out of it."

"My dear man! Stay out of it?" Maxwell Taylor reached into the pocket of his shirt. "I am Gem-Star, sir! I own it!" He handed Mike a business card. The gold letters identified Taylor as the president of Malor Investments. "You're looking at Gem-Star! Shutting you down is going to be a messy business. I'm here to take Linda away, to spare her that."

No wonder Linda had nothing to say. She knew. All along. She was part of the conspiracy to destroy him. He felt that if she came to him now, and kissed his cheek, he would vomit. The shock was too sudden, too severe for an immediate response. He felt withered by betrayal, yet strengthened by abandonment and he waited for the two to sort themselves.

Anna. He felt her presence. *Oh Anna.*

Maxwell Taylor's feet were barely touching the sand. He was almost suspended in mid-air, nearly flew to the water. Mike had him by the shirt collar and the seat of his pants so quickly that he was into Limberlost before he could protest. He came up sputtering and floundering. "My glasses! My pipe! You bastard!" The children stopped their playing and came to dive for his pipe and glasses.

The adults on the beach gasped in unison and murmured to each other. The shuffleboard courts fell silent and people were standing on the dining room steps pointing. Only Bubbles ignored the incident; it was not yet time for her to turn over on her back.

Kramer enjoyed the time it took Maxwell Taylor to walk back across the beach. He went to Linda and stood before her, dripping. "Get your things," he said. "We're getting out of here." He motioned in Mike's direction, but didn't look at him. "This loser is going down! Done!"

"Go away, Maxwell," Linda said, showing no emotion. "You are a disgrace."

Maxwell Taylor turned. "You'll be hearing from me," he warned Mike as he passed.

"I'll have the kids bring your pipe and glasses, *if* they find them."

"Mr. Kramer, I'm sorry to bother you at a time like this." The bellhop tried to mask a smile. "There's a long distance call for you in the office."

Mike smiled back to make him more at ease. "Not now. Get a name and number and I'll call them back."

"The man said it was very important."

"Very well," Mike agreed. Anything would be better than facing Linda at this particular moment in his life. He followed the bellhop up the stairs.

"I'll take it in my office," he informed the desk clerk.

He waited for his phone to ring.

"Hello."

"Boss? It's Tesky."

"Oh-oh."

"Yeah. Thought I'd better give you a call. I can't believe what's happenin' here. They tried to send me over to Queen Street yesterday. You know, the old Comet lot. They said my car was broken down. It was fine when I parked it the night before and no-one had it out during the day. There were other cars I could have used, but it was either go to Queen Street or not work. I went. I thought it would be best not to make waves."

"Who sent you? Kirkpatrick?"

"Jackson."

"Same thing."

"Right. Kirkpatrick was at Queen Street when I got there. Word's out that he's looking for a dozen more licenses. I've heard that Diamond and Yellow are both after him to change colours."

"He can't do that, not at King Street anyway. We have a contract."

"That's why he's usin' all the good bookers over at Queen Street. Somethin's up. I'm just tellin' you what I hear."

"Thanks, Tesky."

"What if it happens again? What should I do?"

"The same thing you did yesterday; don't let on you suspect that anything is wrong. I'll get down there as soon as I can."

"I don't like working for that pecker-head."

"Hang in there."

Speed adds beauty to the deer.

Within the hour, Maxwell Taylor had assembled his entourage and left Serendipity — without checking out... without asking for a refund... without Linda. The kids found his glasses, so he could see where he was going. But he didn't wait for his pipe.

XII

What kept ya, Sam?"

"You only phoned 15 minutes ago. I came as fast as I could." Sam Greenberg put his hand on his chest. "My ticker, you know. Got to be careful. What's wrong?"

There was a half-bottle of Canadian Club on the table. Mike grabbed it and waved it high above his head. "The last hurrah!" Sam wasn't impressed.

"Let's have a drink and a serious talk."

"I don't know about the talk my friend. But it would appear that you are three or four drinks ahead of me."

Mike drank from the bottle, then held it out to Sam.

"That's it? No glass? No ice?"

"Drink! It'll be my birfday in a few minutes."

Sam feigned drinking and returned the bottle. "I understand that you've had a difficult day," he said, sinking into the sofa. "Trigger can make things difficult at times, can't he?"

"Difficult! *Difficult,* he says! I've been screwed by everyone around me, and he says difficult.

"I call it *betrayed!*" He took a healthy drink and passed Sam the bottle. "By you! By Linda! By Kirk! By everybody! I wished I never saw this place!"

"How did I betray you?"

"Ya sol' me a bill o' goods. Jus' like ol' Jake. No differ'nt. Ya dumped this place on me. Ya knew I'd end up like this."

"And your partner. How did he betray you?"

"Kirkpatrick's a stealin', cheatin' bastard, who wants me to go under so he can pick up my cabs for 10 cents on the dollar."

"And what about Linda? How has poor Linda betrayed you?"

"Poor Linda! Always poor Linda! Poor Linda had to be in on it from day one. How else could Maxwell Taylor get his hooks into me. They planned this together from the start."

"Then why didn't she leave with Trigger?"

"Dunno." He snatched the bottle from Sam and drank. "Prob'ly staying' to take care of Trigger's lodge."

"Why would she be with Anna now then, trying to get over the same shock you have had? Do you think for one minute that Anna would have anything to do with her, if what you say is true? *You* have betrayed her!"

"Bullshit!"

"You begged her to chase your dream, then quit running. You have been unfaithful and deceitful. Yet, she stays. I'm not proud to admit that I have done the same thing to Anna in my time. We are plodders, you and I — lucky men to have strong women to haul us out of the muck from time to time. They are most unfortunate to be stuck with a pair of mockers."

Mike let the drained bottle fall onto the carpet and staggered. From the sofa, Sam caught his hand and steadied him, then struggled to his feet and faced him squarely.

"I ain't quittin', Sam," Mike said with a slur. "He's got me down and it's only a matter of time until he finishes me off. But I ain't goin' out without a fight. I'm seein' this thing through the summer, then Taylor can do what he wants."

"Good boy," Sam praised enthusiastically. "I ain't quittin' either."

Mike grabbed Sam by the shoulders and pulled the squat man to him, so that his face was buried in Mike's chest. "Yer a good fren," he said. Suddenly, Mike released him. "Lishen!"

"What?"

"Loon!" Mike answered, falling back. "Shtupit Loons!"

It was midnight when Sam finally got him to bed and returned him to the house to report Mike's condition to Anna and Linda. If someone had told him Kramer would be sitting on the front lawn of Serendipity — nursing a fresh bottle — an hour later, singing "Happy Birfday To Me" and cursing the loons, Sam would have laughed.

Why not a bluebird? How about a mighty eagle?

"Shtupit Loons."

The guests on the sidewalk at the crest of the lawn clicked their tongues, shook their heads disgustedly and moved on.

"Fuckin' crickets." What the hell was going on? Couldn't a man rest in peace? Should have named the place Muskoka Zoo. "Shaddup!"

Mike was vaguely aware of the chilly midnight air and the moisture that had settled on his bare arms and on the grass around him. He heard a clutch of busybodies giggling at him from the shuffleboard courts. He didn't give a shit and told them so, though they giggled all the more. It was all he could do, sinking his fingers into the thick grass, to hold onto the carousel without falling off.

Some one, he didn't know who... a woman, covered him with a sweater that felt soft and was still warm from the heat of her body. She took the bottle from his hand, drank from it, then snuggled in beside him and put her head on his chest.

"I love you Mike," she said. "I need you."

"Nah."

"I want you."

"Nah."

"Take me to your bed. Make love to me."

"I'm thirsty."

She tried to get him up, but he was dead-weight.

"Come on," she said, tugging at his arm. "I'll put you to bed."

"Leave him alone."

The voice startled Toni Warden. It took her a moment to adjust to the unexpected intrusion. She kept pulling at Mike. "He's coming with me."

"Get lost, I said... I'll look after him."

"I love him. I need him. He needs me."

"If you aren't gone within 10 seconds, you'll end up in the lake. Now go! And stay gone."

Toni Warden looked out toward Limberlost as her antagonist counted... two, three four... She waited. Six... seven... . eight. At the count of nine she turned and walked a few steps. Then, she began to run, putting her hands to her face as though to hold back tears.

"I love you Linda."

"I love you too," she said. "I never knew, Mike. I never knew what Maxwell was doing."

"Listen!"

"What?"

"Stupid loons."

Mike leaned on her and she helped him cross the lawn. "Ain't love grand!" Pepi Riveras shouted from the sidewalk in front of Chestnut House. "Hey! You dropped your sweater!"

Linda didn't answer.

"Shtupit loons."

The bombs inside his skull exploded in sync with the pounding on his door. With each beat of his heart, there was such pain that he feebly tried to will that pump to stop. He heard Linda's voice and a muffled response from the hallway. When the glue that held his eyelids shut finally broke, he saw Linda standing bedside him with a breakfast tray. Blurry image, but it was her all right — in *his* bathrobe! Fuzzy voice, but he *had* heard her tell the bellhop to advise the desk clerk that Mr. Kramer was not to be disturbed for the balance of the day.

He got up on his elbows, but didn't stay there long. They hurt, everything hurts — even the hairs in his nose hurt. Never again, he promised himself.

Never, ever, again!

"Happy Birthday." She sat on the bed and balanced the tray on her lap. "Take this," she ordered, offering two aspirins and tomato juice.

"Just the coffee," he pleaded.

"Not until you take this."

"Just coffee."

"Take it."

Mike succumbed. He was too weak to fight. "Stupid loons," he said.

"What do the loons have to do with it?"

"I was in bed. I got up to listen to the loons. I would have been fine if it wasn't for them."

"Now the toast."

"No."

"Do you want coffee or not?"

He struggled with the toast. Linda allowed him to leave the crusts. "Pal will eat them," she said. Mike cupped the hot mug in his hands and sipped. "Anna's minding the store."

"I don't remember much about last night," he remarked, timidly. It hurt to talk. "But I do recall a couple of things."

"I doubt it."

"I know I can't wait too long before I apologize to Sam."

"What else do you remember?"

"I remember something cuddly in bed beside me."

Linda let the robe fall from her shoulders and slipped under the covers. "That was me." She punched him in the ribs and he cried out.

"Did we… ?"

"No! We didn't!"

"Why not?"

"Because it wasn't time. You wouldn't have remembered anyway."

Mike couldn't argue that.

"You snored all night," she complained.

"I don't snore."

She moved close to him. She punched his ribs again. He *had* snored. And *he* complained about the loons.

"When is it going to be time?" he asked, trying to sound unconcerned.

Tell you what. You have a shower — hot, hot — brush your teeth and I'll wait here. We'll see what happens when you get back.

"Do I have to?"

"Don't press your luck."

That was one thing he didn't intend to do! She was naked in bed beside him — a fortuitous turn of events that he wouldn't dream of questioning. She reminded him that the odds against her being there were extremely high. Reluctantly, he left the warmth of her, the softness, the shape of her, for the shower.

Linda kept warm beneath the blankets, listening to him grumble in the bathroom that his teeth hurt and groan when he stepped into the shower.

"Hotter! Hotter!" she called out.

"I'm not a damn lobster," he replied.

After a reasonable period of adjustment, he began to sing and she suffered through several choruses of Down By The Old Mill Stream.

Not the river, but the stream.

She loved whoever it was in the shower, wouldn't trade him for a dozen Maxwell Taylors; that had been decided on the beach. She imagined him as her husband, as the father of her children, and was comfortable with the image — even with all his nonsense. She had Anna to thank for that, would have given up and walked away from it all if not for her. Last night, Anna had talked with her for hours, insisting that something vital was imminent, something important was going to happen which involved her. Anna had been adamant that she must not leave Serendipity and that she must preserve her relationship with Mike. Mysteriously, Linda had yielded, clearly seeing herself as part of Anna's peculiar tryst and accepting her love for Mike as an integral piece of the puzzle.

It was what she had wanted anyway. Exactly what she had wanted, except on Anna's term's. Father Kelly or no Father Kelly, Serendipity or no Serendipity, her time with Mike Kramer had come.

Now he came to her, steaming from the shower, working the front of his body into the unmistakably female grooves of her back and buttocks. "Logically, we shouldn't be here," he remarked.

Who gave a damn about logic?

"You *do* know that I had no idea what Maxwell Taylor was up to," she probed. "He was interested in what you were doing and I suppose I told him things I shouldn't have, but I had no idea —"

He reached out with his fingertips and hushed her, then told her he was sorry. His fingers glided over her chin and neck, down to her breasts; her nipples swelled and so did he. "The important thing is that you are here."

Linda moved into him as his hand glided over her flat stomach, down the inside of one thigh and up the other to rest in the heat between her legs. "Does this mean you'll move in here with me?"

Another shot to the ribs, with her elbow. "No! We still have a long way to go."

"Let's get started then."

"It appears," she said, turning to him and touching his hard penis, "that you have a running start already."

When he finally entered her, he did so eagerly, but as gently as he could after waiting so long, after wanting her so much. A fleeting thought of Toni Warden came to him, but he disposed of it. "I love you," he whispered to Linda, then the roar of Thunder Falls, the panic of orgasm, swept everything from him, even the triangle turning.

After, nestled on his shoulder, Linda told Mike that she never did have any quarrel with his lovemaking.

It was late afternoon by the time Mike learned of Toni Warden's disappearance. She had not reported for work, hadn't been seen by anyone all day and she was not in her room.

He knew exactly where to look for her. Still hung over, scrambled eggs for brains, blood like syrup, the climb to Thunder Falls almost did him in. Toni was sitting motionless on a rock near the edge of the falls, resting her head on her knees, lost to the commotion. She must have been there all day; there was something scary about that.

"I've hurt you," he said, sitting close but not touching. "I'm sorry." Nothing... no answer, not even when he asked if she was all right. "This won't help." Painful silence, in the midst of noise. "Can't you try to understand?" No, without an answer he knew she couldn't. "What we had was good for both of us. I needed you. You needed me. But it's over. Just over. I told you there was someone else." He waited... still nothing. "Don't stop here, Toni. Not now. This can be a new beginning, if you want it. You can start a better life, a good career. I'll personally see to it that... "

Useless.

"I have to go," he said, getting to his feet and extending a hand.

She didn't move. "You 're just like all the rest," she said. "You... Ronnie... there's no difference."

He let his outstretched hand fall to his side and left her there.

XIII

Never again.

His pace was a little slower than usual. He wasn't looking forward to facing Sam Greenberg.

And he still felt like a rag doll.

Never again.

Mike met Ronnie Greenberg at the footbridge, on his way to work. The two stopped at either end and stared... glared... at each other.

"Good evening, Mr. Kramer," Ronnie said when they finally passed. That same, sardonic tone. Always there. "Got a little pissed last night. Quite a show."

Mike didn't respond.

"Do something about that dog," Ronnie whined. "Or *I* will."

"Jake's dog."

" It's in the garbage almost every night."

Mike continued toward the house. What would Pal be doing at Serendipity at night? What would Jake be doing?

"Way to go, Mr. Kramer," Ronnie called out derisively after he had crossed the bridge. "You've turned this place into a loony bin."

Sam Greenberg came to the door when he heard the snap-crackle-ping of the screen-door spring. That sound always reminded Mike of ricocheting bullets in T.V. westerns.

"Could I speak to you alone?" Mike asked. "Maybe here on the porch?"

"Of course." Sam joined him and they sat together as they had so often four years — no, four months ago. Only four months?

"I don't know where to start," Mike began. "I'm embarrassed. I don't recall everything that I said last night, but considering my mood, it couldn't have been very nice."

"I don't remember much myself, my friend. I ended up as drunk as you were. I'm not used to drinking whiskey straight out of the bottle."

Thank God! Mike unconsciously accepted the lie as a matter of convenience. He relaxed. "I wouldn't deliberately hurt you, Sam. You know that."

"Yes. I know."

"Yes, you should." Sam appeared dejected.

"But never let it be said that Mike Kramer did the logical thing. I've decided to keep the lodge open until Labour Day. Everything I've put into Serendipity is lost anyway. I won't lose any more here by keeping it open. Gem-Star will have to make a move before the end of the month for sure. I'll let Curtis handle it. He can delay foreclosure until after the holiday. Then, I don't give a damn about what happens."

"What about Mr. Kirkpatrick?"

"Well..." Mike sighed in desperation. "If I'm going to continue with Serendipity until the end of the summer, I should stay here. But nothing more can happen — nothing worse, I should say. So I'm going to spend two days a week in the city to keep a harness on good old Kirk until September. I was wondering if you would help me out while I'm away."

"You know I will."

"Linda runs things, generally. That's not a problem. But a number of small, unrelated incidents have been happening repeatedly. They have me worried, especially when I'm away."

"What kind of incidents?"

"Fires, thefts, break-ins, prowlers, notes, rooms used without permission — on and on, over and over. When I start to look into one area it stops there and breaks out somewhere else."

"Sounds like Mrs. Cohen could help."

"I've already thought of that. Believe it or not, she knows nothing, not even about the prowler hanging around the cabins."

"I must admit, she hasn't been quite as active this season. I'll never understand why she comes here in the first place. *Never!* "

"Did Ronnie mention that Jake's dog has been hanging around the kitchen in the middle of the night?"

"No."

"I thought you might have some idea why Jake might be around here at that hour."

"None."

"Well, as I said, these incidents, if isolated, wouldn't be all that serious. Put them all together… it's a bad time to be leaving Serendipity. You can see I have no choice. I'll feel better about it if I know you are keeping an eye on things?"

"Of course I will."

"Good. I'll tell Linda she can work with you when I'm away. I *am* sorry about the lodge, Sam. I've really screwed things up."

"You know, Michael, I told you about some if the difficulties I had with Greenberg Lodge over the years. It's the kind of investment where everything has to run smoothly to pay off. That takes time and patience."

"I've run out of time, therefore patience is irrelevant."

"I wonder then, why you are holding on. Why are you willing to risk your taxi business in order to stay on here for another three weeks?"

"There will be a lot of people out of work if I close now."

"Is that the only reason?"

"No. Linda wants to keep it open. Anna has asked me to stick at it. And you… "

"You are worried about my son, aren't you? If you close, you're afraid I may lose him again."

"It had crossed my mind. I won't deny it."

"So you have just said that you are willing to chance serious personal losses for the benefit of us at Serendipity, so that each of us can get what we want out of it. I'm saddened to think that you feel there is nothing left for you."

"My savings, the money I borrowed, all the work — gone. Maxwell Taylor will take care of that."

"What about your dream? Do you remember your dream, my friend? You can salvage that."

"Nightmare, you mean!"

"I mean the deer's speed. Anna said to ask you about the speed of the deer."

"I'm farther away from it now than I was before I came to Serendipity. That's the saddest part of all."

"You are closer, if your path is a circle."

"Let it go, Sam. The only thing I've salvaged from this mess is Linda. That's enough to make a fresh start after Labour Day."

"You have gained my friendship... Anna's too."

"Sam!" Mike showed his annoyance.

"Very well," Sam conceded. "I'll say no more about it."

He remembered how Anna had told him that friendship was a mirror and relented. Here was good old Sam, once again making him take a good look at himself, talking to him about dreams and friendship, not caring that he had been an unconscionable jerk last night.

"Sam... there is one thing I remember saying to you last night that I really meant, drunk or not."

"What is that?"

"You are a special friend. Very special."

With modesty, Sam chuckled and said that he had the flat nose to prove it.

XIV

Why would anyone pound on his door in the middle of the night? *Go away... It can't be time to leave for Toronto already.* The pounding stopped. Within seconds, Mike began wondering if he had imagined it. He turned on the lamp beside his bed to look at the clock. He lay back and rubbed his eyes. *Why at 2:00 a.m.?* The pounding had stopped.

Eventually, out of curiosity, Mike went to the door. The Messenger had struck again. He picked up a folded note, no envelope, pencilled in block letters:

TAKE A LOOK IN CHESTNUT 215

This is a nightmare. Has to be. I'm going to wake up and be back in my Toronto apartment.

Mike dressed and went to the reception desk. The place was empty except for Ronnie Greenberg.

"Has anyone come through here in the last few minutes? Mike asked.

"No."

"You're sure?"

"No one."

"Someone banged on my door. They must have come through here."

"They could have used the back stairs."

"If they had a key."

"Lots of them around. Bellhops, cleaning girls."

"Hand me the key to 215, please."

Ronnie passed him a key. "Not Maple house," Mike said. "Chestnut." They exchanged keys. "Who's in there?"

Ronnie leaned back in his chair to check the board.

"Nobody," he answered, sounding bored. "It's been vacant for two days." He handed Mike the key. "While you're out there, take a look around the kitchen. I think Jake's dog is visiting again tonight."

Time passed slowly at the door of Chestnut 215.

Mike listened. There was movement inside the room and muffled voices making low, unintelligible sounds.

A vacant room?

Kramer decided not to knock. He quietly slipped the key into the lock and pushed the door open, so that it slammed against the wall.

Bertha instinctively reached for a sheet to pull over them and hid under it. But Toni Warden sat straight up.

"Oh my god!" she whimpered. "Oh no!"

Mike didn't bother closing the door. Without a word, or a visible reaction, he left the building. Understandably, he would have forgotten about Pal if he hadn't spotted Jake moving along the back of Maple House, toward the kitchen.

"What's up?" Mike asked, obviously surprising him. Jake didn't answer. He farted as he walked. "What's going on here?"

Jake stopped. "Gettin' Pal."

"You'll find him going through the garbage."

"Nah... Pal don't eat garbage."

"What are you doing here at this time of night?"

"Movin' the sprinkler."

"At two-thirty!"

"Gotta be moved regular."

"Jake, Jake, Jake."

"Sprinkler's gotta be moved."

"Ronnie can do it."

"Ain't trustin' no Greenbug! Had ta come over anyhow. Left my saw. Doc Rogers needs it first thing this mornin'."

"That's enough, Jake! If either you or Pal are seen here after dark again you're fired. Both of you!"

Jake walked away, moving like a penguin on his bowed legs. "Don't forget your saw," Mike called, grinning. He felt strangely relieved and at ease. There was surely some good to come from the disturbing events of the last hour. Maybe Linda's lists would be shorter now.

Mike checked the lawn sprinkler. It was sitting, unused, circled by a coil of plastic hose at the base of a tree by the boathouse. He didn't go back to bed; he sat on the beach for an hour and left for the city just as the lights in the bakery were going on.

XV

Dispatcher Jackson was at the King Street lot when Mike arrived. Customer calls were handled by central dispatch downtown. But he was responsible for assignments and collections when Kirkpatrick wasn't around.

"Mr. Kirkpatrick went straight to Queen Street this morning," he explained. "But there's an urgent message here for you. A Miss McDermott wants you to call her right away."

Mike made the call from his office and he could tell by the clerk's voice that all was not well at Serendipity. It was a while before Linda came to the phone.

"Mike!"

"What's happened? What's wrong?"

"Toni Warden! She's dead."

Death is good.

"I'm sorry," she said.

"How?"

"We don't know exactly. A fisherman found her early this morning at the bottom of Thunder Falls. Pushed? Jumped? Fell? We don't know. Pepi is over at the fishing camps now."

"Pepi? Why Pepi?"

"I don't know. I had to have someone. I wanted Pepi."

"I'll be back right away, unless there is something I can do at this end."

"No. Bertha has quit. She's on her way back to Toronto right now. She's going to take care of everything there. The poor girl was devastated. They must have been very close."

"They were."

"Rick Gerrard quit too. I don't know why. He's packing now."

"Ask Rick to stay until I get back. I'm leaving now."

He didn't bother speaking to Jackson on the way out, just went to the car and drove away.

"This is Sergeant Walker," Linda said. She was dishevelled, and obviously shaken. "Ontario Provincial Police."

"Let's talk in my apartment," Mike suggested. The sergeant nodded. "Is Rick still here?" he asked Linda.

"He agreed to wait," Linda said. "But I don't know where he is."

"See if you can find him and ask him to wait down here."

The officer followed Mike up the stairs. "What has happened here?" Sgt. Walker asked when they were sitting comfortably.

"You tell me."

"We don't know, sir. She could have fallen, jumped or been pushed, At this point we have no way of knowing. I had hoped you might know something that would help us."

"I know nothing," Mike said, obviously thinking as he spoke, "no more than you do."

"At this point, it appears to have been suicide."

Mike's head bowed.

"I realize you may not be in the mood for this, Mr. Kramer. But it would have helped us a great deal if you had kept an employment application for Mrs. Amanna."

"Mrs. Amanna?"

"Warden was her maiden name. It is an offence not to have completed applications for all your employees. It is the law! If I were you, I would look after that right away. Make sure all employees complete applications."

"I will." The sergeant was right. Mike insisted upon his cab company employees completing applications. Why should Serendipity be different. It *was* a business.

"No harm done. It seems that this Bertha girl knew the deceased in Toronto. We were able to get quite a bit of information from her. The Toronto police have located her husband. I have a report of their interview with him. It seems to support our suicide theory."

Mike said nothing.

"Mr. Amanna wants nothing to do with his wife. He said he has washed his hands of her since she walked away from him and their two young daughters three or four months ago. He said that their marriage had been a series of clinics and hospitals. There were two previous suicide attempts. There is even a history of lesbian activity here. I suspect that the Bertha girl fits in there somewhere. The short of it is that Mr. Amanna had already explained their mothers' disappearance to the children. He flatly refuses to have any further involvement. We are sending the body to Toronto and this Bertha girl is looking after it from there. I'll keep you advised if there are further developments."

"Thank you."

"You be sure to get those applications up to date. You can see that it's very important."

Rick Gerrard was waiting when Mike shook hands with Sgt. Walker and entered his office.

"Thanks for waiting, Rick. I had hoped to get a chance to talk with you."

"Don't flatter yourself!" Rick Gerrard was livid. "I only waited to tell you what I think of you. Now that I can, I can't." He paused and some of the redness drained from his face. "She was just a poor lost girl, in search of a bit of kindness, a little understanding and a glimmer of hope. She needed a friend. Someone who could help her understand what was going on inside."

"Simple as that?"

"Yes, simple as that. The last thing she needed was someone like you."

"Who? Mrs. Amanna?"

Rick shook his head. "No, damn it! Toni Warden!" He grasped the lamp on Mike's desk and threw it against the wall. Mike expected Linda to investigate, but she didn't. Rick sat down again. He clasped his hands and let them hang between his knees. He leaned forward and stared straight down at the floor in front of him. When Mike saw tears drop from the young man's eyes, he went to the outer office. Linda was at her desk. God! Of all the places she could have been — should have been — that day! She was there. At her desk.

"Shirley Boychuck knows a local girl who is looking for work," Linda said. "She can replace Bertha. Anna is helping Reuben. Sam is at the driving range."

No deer can run through a tangle of barbs and brambles.

"Rick will be out in a minute," he said to her. "He's leaving. Please see that he has money for his trip home and tell him we'll forward his cheque." Mike bowed and kissed Linda. "Pay him to the end of the month," he said. "I'm going to the fishing camps. With any luck, I'll fall asleep at the wheel."

"Too late. The body's been moved to Gravenhurst. It may even be on the way to Toronto. Pepi's back already."

"Where is he? I'll talk to him."

"He and Nosey are on the beach with the kids. They're building two lemonade stands."

"Two?"

"One for the kids to sell lemonade."

"The other?"

"Are you ready?"

"Probably not."

"Well... Pepi has it figured this way: the kids sell lemonade from their stand; Pepi sells albums from his stand next door. The kids sell their lemonade for a penny a glass and Pepi subsidizes them ten cents for every glass they sell. Still with me?"

"Carry on."

"So Pepi figures that when customers come to buy a lemonade, they won't believe the bargain price. Before they recover, they'll associate the bargain lemonade with Pepi's album. For $5.01 they'll whet their whistle and whistle to Pepi Riveras and his Latin Lovers. How about that!"

"He should have asked me first."

"He asked *me.* I told him to go ahead. This country was built on ideas like that."

Soon. The whole dream will go " poof."

Alone, picking over a breakfast he couldn't eat, occasionally looking out the dining room window, his mood lightening momentarily when he thought of his quarrel with the loons. It seemed the entire lodge was still in shock from the untimely death of Toni Warden… Mrs. Amanna. Mike could see it in the movements of the people on the lawn and beach — not the children though; they either didn't understand the death or understood it completely, he didn't know which. Nonetheless, he had slept well, an exhausted sleep that was in part still with him.

There were certain benefits to be salvaged from the rubble that surrounded her death: His fortuitous early-morning encounter with Jake would stop the mysterious incidents of which he was obviously a part; with Bertha gone, there would be no more problems with unmade rooms; Toni would put no notes under *anyone's* door. Yes, Linda's lists would be shorter now.

The triangle turned a bit — because of his complicity for Toni's demise. But it was difficult to mask the traces of satisfaction that showed on his face as Anna approached.

"May I join you?" she asked. She carried a cup of coffee.

"Please."

"You are looking smug this morning."

"It's only temporary."

"I thought it would be nice to sit for a moment, while there is a break in the action." She smiled at him. "You know, Michael, when Papa and I started, I used to be hostess and secretary both. I would work in here, then rush to the office to do my typing, then back here. We knew that every second of our day was filled. What fun those times were."

"The fun has gone, I'm afraid."

"Really?"

"It's no fun knowing that you and Sam are back working regular shifts because of my mistake."

"It *is* for Papa and I."

"You should be home relaxing, enjoying your retirement."

"Knitting."

Mike looked at the frail woman. He remembered their serious conversations and realized that he had neglected the afterthought they required. One day, when this was over, he would assemble the bits and pieces.

"Well… I appreciate your help. Linda has a line on someone. I'll be talking to her today. If she's suitable, she can relieve you right away. I can't begin to thank you for helping out. You won't take money. There must be some way I can pay you."

"You have already."

"Pardon?"

"Papa tells me you have decided to keep Serendipity open until Labour Day, even though you should be looking after your business in the city." Anna stopped abruptly. "Excuse me," she said, "there are guests waiting to be seated." Anna left her coffee on the table and didn't return to finish it.

While Anna was in the kitchen, Mike left the building. The morning walk between the dining room and his office was routine. Too routine. No need to lift his head.

Just walk.

"Hang in there, girl," he said to Linda as he passed her desk. "Three more weeks, and it's all over."

She seemed harried this morning, more stern than usual. "I'm hanging," she snapped back.

"You okay?"

Linda nodded. "Larry Parkinson's brother called. He can look after the driving range... starting tomorrow, if you wish."

"Tell him to be here at ten o'clock."

As always, Linda had arranged the mail neatly on his desk. Her list was on the top. He looked forward to reading it:

Saturday, August 11, 1973

Please attend to the following:

1) Porcupines — they returned last night

If they like it here that much, they can stay.

2) Fire inspector — very upset at lack of progress re smoke detectors and alarms

Project suspended indefinitely. Stall him.

3) Cabins — two complaints already this morning about noises in the night.

No! I refuse to accept it. Impossible.

4) Rooms - i) Mr. Waters took his family to the movie last night. While they were gone, someone with a key stole a very expensive watch.

ii) Mr. & Mrs. Johanson checked into an unmade room last night. They are not upset. They thought we should know.

Now we know.

5) Boathouse — lock broken again. Nothing missing.

I'm running out of ink.

6) Jake — Ronnie left me a note this morning. He said Pal was here last night. I spoke to Jake this morning. He said he was at the garage all night and the dog was with him.

I wonder.

7) Another note — see envelope attached.

TO BE CONTINUED...

Mike opened the envelope. Again, when he unfolded the note, the message was formed from newspaper cuttings:

YOU ARE NEXT

He called Linda and she appeared with pencil and pad. "Somebody had a busy night," he said.

"Apparently."

"I thought we were through with all this cloak-and-dagger business. I guess not. I don't know exactly where to start. Perhaps we should close, before this gets out of hand."

"No, please. Don't do that." Her response was a plea; there was a disposition of begging there.

"Maybe the police, then. This last note is more serious than the others... "

"I'm all right, Mike. Honest I am. I'm shocked, as you are, but the things that are happening but I want to see it through. I want *us* to see it through. To tell the truth, I was hoping you might find a way to keep Serendipity — I mean even after Labour Day."

"There is no way, Linda. The lodge is gone. I've lost it. I could sell some of my cabs to Kirk — a finger in the dike as long as Maxwell Taylor's calling the shots. He'd get me sooner or later."

"You're right. And I'm sorry."

"Don't be! This is of my own making. But we have three weeks and nothing to lose. So let's make the most of it. I promise you, before we leave, I'll find the person, or persons behind the thefts, the break-ins, the notes, everything! And I start now. If I have to stay awake day and night, I'm going to find out who is behind all this."

"Where will you begin?"

"I know exactly where to begin. I'm going to have a talk with Ruth Cohen. She must know *something*."

The telephone rang and Linda returned to her desk.

"It's Tesky, boss. Thought you was comin' down."

"I've been down, but something serious happened here. I had to turn around and come right back. Didn't Jackson tell you?"

"Nothin'... but you should get back here right away. There's a big deal in the works. I've heard rumours and I can feel it, Kirkpatrick is up to somethin'. They have me workin' out of Queen Street steady now. That's where the action is, so I get to hear. Nobody's wise. I keep my mouth shut."

"I can't leave the lodge on the weekend. I'll be there Tuesday or Wednesday."

"I hope that'll be soon enough, boss."

"So do I."

XVII

The next three nights — Saturday, Sunday and Monday — Mike slept in the early evening and spent the hours between midnight and dawn walking the grounds, waiting in the shadows for a break — something, anything.

He had spoken to Ruth Cohen and the results of their discussion had left him more discouraged than ever, for he felt she knew more than she was telling.

"Your husband didn't come to Serendipity this weekend," he had remarked, to open the conversation. Usually, with her, that was all you had to do and the rest came naturally.

"Who cares?" she said.

"I thought it might have something to do with the argument I had with Maxwell Taylor."

"I doubt it. Make no mistake, young man, my husband has Mr. Taylor in his pocket. Peter is the one who is setting up this major business. Maxwell Taylor is only the pawn. In any event, young man, good for you! Mr. Taylor needed that dousing. I could have kissed you. My husband needs one too, but he's a little smarter. One day, perhaps. But don't worry about Peter. I can handle him."

"I was really hoping you could help me."

"How?"

"There have been complaints of noises near the cabins late at night. Have you heard anything?"

"Uhhh... I'm a very sound sleeper."

"You're sure?"

"Positive."

"Your cabin is closest to the boathouse. The door lock has been broken twice. I thought you may have."

"Uhhh... no... nothing."

"Well... I'm not trying to scare you, Mrs. Cohen but I have to trust someone. If you do hear or see anything — anything at all — please let me know."

"I certainly will, young man."

On Monday night, Mike made himself as comfortable as he could inside the boathouse and waited. Through the west window he could see the first few cabins, those closest to the beach. With the window open, he would certainly be able to detect any curious movement in that area. There was none. There had been no trouble for three full days and nights.

By noon, Tuesday, he left for Toronto.

XVIII

"Come off it, Kirk! Cut the crap! What happened to our conversation at Serendipity? Huh? What happened to the 10 years of trusting each other? The turning things around? The evening-up you were going to do? My deposits are shorter than ever!"

"Things change. Even in a couple of weeks, they change."

Kirkpatrick rolled his cigar proudly. "Good ol' Smilin' Jack is onto something big."

"So you take my best men and use them for your cars at Queen Street!"

"I had no choice, Mike! No choice at all. A major chain is expanding. It's my chance to get in. Do you know how long I've waited? Of course you do. The catch is, they've set a quota based on gross income. They'll negotiate with the first operator who reaches the quota two months running. That's the deal. No favourites. I may reach it this month. But I'll never do it in September without three more cars."

"Great! Then buy more cars, but don't steal from me to make your quota."

"You've got to be joking. There are two other companies besides me who are after the same thing. Word is out that we all need more cars to make the quota. The city has declared a three-year moratorium on new licences. The supply has dried up. And I told you before, I'm not stealing anything."

"I'd like to know what else to call it! Taking money out of my pocket and putting it in yours!"

"Call it borrowing."

Mike laughed, but Kirkpatrick was serious. He could see that.

"Yes, call it borrowing," he repeated. "Borrowing against the outrageous price I'm going to have to pay you for three of your cars."

Mike didn't react. He stayed silent, contemplating the inevitability of time. The circumstance that he had hoped to avoid was upon him. The decision he had postponed a dozen times — hoping for miracle, not overtly, but still hoping — was now to be made. Mike Kramer could see that his partner, unlike himself, had relished this moment, had planned for it with eager anticipation.

"Twenty thousand, Mike. Take it or leave it."

"Forget it. I'm not interested. That's less than seven thousand apiece."

"Twenty thousand each, Kramer! Twenty thousand each! We're talking sixty grand, partner."

The figure staggered Mike.

"Enough to save Serendipity," Kirkpatrick suggested. He was moving in for the kill. "And plenty to spare."

Serendipity! Linda! Sam! Anna! My dreams.

Ah, my friend. You dream your dreams and then put a price on them.

"You'll still have a fair-sized fleet," Kirkpatrick added. "Twelve cars these days is nothing to sneeze at."

The moment had come. There would be no more excuses, no more procrastination. "No deal, Kirk. Sorry."

"Twenty-five!"

"No."

"Eighty grand for the three. My final offer."

"Sorry."

Kirkpatrick slammed his fist on the desk with such force that everything on it hopped like Mexican jumping beans. His cigar was wet and his face was the colour of his hair. "What's the matter with you, man? You crazy?"

"Probably."

Kirkpatrick sighed deeply. It was a stuttering sigh, like a child after crying.

"I want all my drivers back from Queen Street, too. Immediately, if not sooner."

"Just a minute here! We've got the tail wagging the dog. If you want your men back here, stick around for a while and see to it yourself."

"No. I'm going back to Muskoka tonight. But let me ask you one question, Kirk. If one of your drivers was openly stealing from you, openly, and daring you to do something about it, what — "

"I'd fire him!"

"Now, how do you think Diamond or Yellow would react if I could show them that you've been openly stealing — sorry, borrowing — from me. You could double your quota and they wouldn't touch you with rubber gloves."

"You wouldn't!"

"Try me. I have facts and figures and witnesses."

"Some partnership!"

"There never really was one, I guess. I've always liked you, Kirk. Still do. It hurts to have to resort to threats and innuendo. I owe you for this summer, I know that. It's been a disaster, but that's not your fault. If you make the quota on your own in August, maybe there's some way I can help you in September, when I get back. Like I said, I owe you. But between now and Labour Day, I want my drivers back and my cars out."

"Bastard!"

"Don't worry, partner," Mike said, smiling knowingly, "you'll find a way to make the quota. I only hope that you don't decide to eliminate an independent to get his licences. See you next week."

"Thanks, partner!"

XIX

There would be no point in telling Linda that he had refused an opportunity to save Serendipity. She would be disappointed; she would prob ably expect an explanation and Mike would have liked one himself.

He didn't know the reason for acting as he had, but he supposed that continuing to do business with Gem-Star and Maxwell Taylor was out of the question.

It had been like taking a spoonful of poison: you could take something after to sweeten the taste, but death was inevitable — if not next year, then the year after that. On a hunch, Mike Kramer phoned Linda from his hotel the following morning.

"How are things there?" she asked, thinking that his unexpected call meant trouble.

"Good..." he said, without thinking. "Well, change that to fair. I was wondering how you made out last night. I thought there might be some activity with me gone."

"You were right."

"What?"

"More of the same. The usual list."

"Another note?"

"I was hoping you wouldn't ask."

"What did it say this time?"

"There was no note, Mike," her voice sounded more uncertain than usual. "Perhaps we should wait until you get back to discuss it."

"No... now. That's why I phoned."

"Well wait then. I'll put you on hold... Linda picked up the phone in Mike's office. "I'm back."

"Is it that serious?"

"Someone went into my room last night. Sam wasn't feeling well, so I had to call bingo. It must have happened then. Certain things are missing."

"What kind of things?"

"Personal things."

"How personal?"

"Very!" She hesitated. "Mike... I'm scared. For the first time, I'm scared."

"Maybe you should leave."

"No. I'm staying here. But that doesn't mean I can't be scared."

"I called because something told me this might happen. These incidents are all connected and I have the feeling that if we solve one, we solve them all. Will you be okay alone?"

"Yes."

"I'm going to stay here at the hotel for a while. I'll leave so that I arrive at Serendipity after dark. I'm going to park up by the fishing camps and walk back. I'll be in the boathouse tonight. I want you to act as though I'm still away. Let as many people know as possible without being obvious."

"Maybe we should just call the police."

"No. Not yet. Let me do this my way."

"I love you, Mike."

"Me too you."

Never, never, never, even in his most bizarre fantasies could he have imagined himself sitting in a boathouse — curled under a coat in a corner by the west window — on a lake, in the middle of Muskoka. Never, if someone had warned him five months ago that he would be there at midnight, waiting for God knows what, he would have laughed.

Yet Mike Kramer was there — cold, tired, hungry — certainly not laughing. Waiting, for phantoms, shivering, hoping for a clue to some of the mysteries that had plagued Serendipity. Was that it? Waiting for a clue? No. He was waiting for the sun to rise. Praying for the sun to rise quickly.

It had been cloudy during the day and now there was a light mist, the kind preceding rain, to dampen his weary bones. Regardless, there were people on the beach — teenagers. He couldn't see them, but he heard them talking and giggling about school, mocking the instructors and mimicking their idiosyncrasies. Mike guessed that there were six or eight of them, all far away from him, all living in another world.

The front of the lodge was visible, from the dining hall to the path that led to the cabins. Three times, at intervals of approximately forty minutes, Pepi Riveras and the Latin Lovers appeared out of the shadows in front of Maple House, stopped and sat on the benches near the shuffleboard courts, then disappeared again. By two o'clock, Pepi and his gang were gone for good, the kids had left the beach and it was still. The loons were at it again and Mike watched the lights in Maple House go on and off like a large switchboard. He could see a man, at one of the windows, removing his shirt, motioning erratically with his arms as though arguing with someone.

Then all the rooms were dark and there was silence — even the loons. Somewhere between 2:30 and 3:00 a.m. the lights went on in 200 Maple House, the room that had been gutted by fire. He was pleased that Linda had not waited for his return to book the room. There must have been a rush, or she would have waited.

A man — a young lad in his late teens, Mike guessed — came to the window. He wore a red shirt, and his hair was blond, almost white. After a few minutes, the light went out and shortly thereafter, the young fellow appeared at the entrance to Maple House, accompanied by a girl approximately his age. They were in the glow of the lawn lights and Mike could see them clearly. They kissed and parted; he visually followed the boy in the red shirt into the darkness beyond the dining hall. Within a few minutes, Mike once again detected movement near the dining hall. He watched Pal come out of the shadows and move listlessly along the sidewalk. The dog stopped near the path that led to the cabins. In time, he could discern a figure emerging from the trees. There was no mistaking that walk. It was Jake.

There was no question in Mike's mind regarding what his reaction should be — fire Jake and Pal before they reached Sidney Road. But he sat and thought, procrastinated really, knowing he was doing it but not knowing why, until Jake and Pal were well clear of the lodge.

There was something nagging at him, he didn't know exactly what — like the feeling of having forgotten something — a name, a place. And the harder he tried to remember, the more muddled it became.

The lad in the red shirt reappeared on the sidewalk; he passed in front of Maple House and took the cabin path.

Mike left the boathouse then, careful to fasten the padlock securely so Larry Parkinson would not be alarmed in the morning.

He made his way to the edge of the trees around the cabins, crouching low to the ground. After sitting behind a tree he waited silently, listening, moving only when his limbs became numb. There were no sounds other than those he invented.

Half an hour later Mike was walking, slump-shouldered, back to his apartmtent. He used the rear door, to avoid Ronnie; he wasn't in the mood for Ronnie Greenburg.

Depression, undesirable though it is, can deepen a sleep. And in his sleep, Mike Kramer had no way of knowing that he had been given the clue that would take him to the vortex of his nightmare.

XX

Upon hearing of his head-on confrontation with Jack Kirkpatrick, Linda was visibly piqued. It had taken a clever interrogation to worm the truth out of him — that he had turned down eighty thousand dollars and a chance to save Serendipity. She was somewhat assuaged by his explanation: Maxwell Taylor would find a way to get him sooner or later; there was no point in throwing good money after bad.

Nonetheless, it hurt to realize that the dream that had become as much hers as Mike's was lost, that the summer was almost gone and they would be back in Toronto for good in a couple of weeks. Serendipity, like a bad tooth pulled, would leave an empty, throbbing socket to heal.

Mike looked at her and thought how much like Anna she had become in less than two months. He wished for her that he could keep Serendipity, but there was no way.

"No notes last night?" he was asking.

There were none.

"No uninvited visitors?"

"No... but I thought you might have stopped in on your way to bed."

"Tonight, I'll stay with you. Since the last note threatened your life, and since you have a visitor stealing your underwear, don't you think it would be a good idea to move in with me?" he tried.

No, she didn't. Not yet. But she thought there must be a better way to catch the culprit than sitting up in that ridiculous boathouse half the night.

"It's Jake. I'm convinced of it," he confided. "Both he and Pal were around Serendipity at three o'clock in the morning again. It must be Jake — most of it, at least."

"Most of it?"

"The fire in the room. Something has bothered me about that since it happened; something I was leaving out or forgetting. It hit me on the way over to the office when I saw one of Jake's cigarette butts on the ground. A cigarette in the mattress caused the fire and most of us, including me, thought it was Jake."

"I still do," Linda confessed.

"Not likely," Mike said. "Jake's cigarettes are hand-rolled. There is nothing in the tobacco to keep them burning like the packaged ones. Even if he had slipped into the room to sleep and if he had dozed off with a lighted cigarette, it would have gone out right away. There's no doubt in my mind that Jake is responsible for the disturbances down by the cabins. He's probably behind the break-ins, even your notes. But Jake is not responsible for the fire in that room."

"Why, Mike? Why would he — "

"I don't know for sure. He used to own this land. You know how he thinks everyone is out to skin him. Maybe he feels Sam cheated him. Or I cheated him. Who knows."

"Not Jake. I don't believe it. Not the notes."

"We'll soon know, because I'm going to fire him today. If the nonsense stops, we'll know it was him. Where is he, anyway?"

"He hasn't come in yet," Linda said. "There isn't that much work for him, now that the room is finished." She was sad. "That room — 200 Maple House — is ready to use, by the way. It's finished and you can put guests in there now."

"What!"

"200 Maple is finished. You can start renting it out. What's the matter?"

Mike reached for the room board. He spotted immediately that the room had been vacant since the fire, had been *marked* vacant since the fire.

"Nothing's the matter," he said calmly. "Tell me, do we have a young fellow — in his late teens, I think — with very blond, almost white hair?"

"Several, I guess. I'd have to think."

"Please try. It's important. His hair is almost white. He might be staying in one of the cabins."

Linda thought a moment. "Mrs. Cavanaugh in Cottonwood Cabin has a son with fair hair, Robert. They've been here — just the two of them — for about a week I think."

"Can you arrange for me to talk to him?"

"Of course. What's going on?"

Mike told her it was simply a routine matter.

Robert Cavanaugh *was* the boy in the red shirt. No mistake. He was eighteen and on his way to college in September.

"I'm getting a sports car for graduating," he announced proudly. "Mom promised."

"Is your father here at the lodge with you?" Mike asked deliberately.

"He died."

"I'm sorry. So you and your mother are alone now."

"My sister took off to the States with some creep," Robert offered openly. "Mom's pretty shook up. We're just getting away from it all for a while."

"What were you doing in room number 200 at Maple House last night?"

"Nothing." He was startled and obviously nervous. "I wasn't there."

"You were. I saw you. I want to know how you got into the room."

"What is this? I wasn't in any room!"

"I don't need to know what you were doing. I know that already. How did you get into that room?"

"I don't know what you're talking about."

"You've got trouble, Robert, big trouble. If you think I'm going to play games with you, you're mistaken. I've asked you a question. You have one last chance to answer before I call your mother."

The Cavanaugh boy glared at Mike, but made no effort to answer.

"Very well," Mike said, picking up the phone. He spoke to the clerk. "Cottonwood Cabin, please… "

"No!" Robert stopped him. He hung his head. "She'll scrap the car. For sure."

"Never mind," Mike told the clerk and then turned his attention to Robert Cavanaugh. "I told you, I only want to know how you got a key to that room. That's all. Then you can go."

"I paid the desk clerk for it."

"Which one?"

"Ronnie."

"How much?"

"Twenty dollars. Lots of the guys do it. If they meet a girl here and need a room. You know."

"Not any more they don't."

Ronnie Greenberg didn't work his shift that night; one of the bellhops filled in for him. When Mike confronted him with the information he had extorted from Robert Cavanaugh, Ronnie answered him defiantly: it was his lodge, not Kramer's, and he could see no good reason why he shouldn't rent out rooms; Sam was going to be very upset.

"I suppose so," Mike responded. "He'll have to be upset. You've worked your last shift."

"You prick!" Ronnie shouted. "We'll see!"

Mike expected to hear from Sam that night. But the call never came. He found out later that Ronnie had told his father he wasn't feeling well enough to go to work.

Next morning was the first time in a long while that Mike had awakened in a euphoric frame of mind. He was up at six, like in the beginning and had disposed of a considerable quantity of paperwork before breakfast.

Now, as he sat at his table in the dining hall savouring one last cup of coffee, it was mid-morning. There were many people on the beach, though it wasn't hot and the sky was spotted with large fast-moving cotton clouds.

Bubbles had set up shop and Ronnie Greenberg, who had not used the beach before that day, was off by himself near the boathouse. Unemployed now, Mike supposed he had nothing better to do.

A clammer that sprang from the steps near the office diverted Mike's attention. Jake was descending the stairs with his metal detector, and Pepi Riveras was following him with a spade. There weren't many things that could entice Pepi to an early rising, but treasure hunting was one of them. And Pal's excitement was growing too. This was a time when he understood the reason for his existence; it pleased him. He ran to the bottom of the stairs and up again five times before they reached the beach, then ran full-out across the sand to the boathouse and back in time to help the men set up.

Mike took his coffee to a bench on the lawn and sat to watch the show — a ringside seat, free. No harm would be done by letting them finish, although it bothered him to think that, when they were done, Jake had to go.

Jake started at the stairs and worked the metal detector in zig-zag fashion across the beach while Pepi followed with his shovel and an empty coffee can to hold the booty. When Jake found something, he marked the spot with his heel; Pal began barking and digging; Pepi sifted through the flying sand, found the object of their search, dropped it into the coffee can, then filled in the hole. The three would stand — twinkle-eyed and so excited as to almost wet themselves — to admire their treasure before moving on. No one knew what arrangements had been made for division of the spoils, but Mike guessed that Jake would get the largest share because it was his machine... for sure, Pal was the odd dog out; it was enough reward for him just to be in on the hunt.

There was an unwritten law that during the treasure hunt, Jake and Pepi and Pal owned the beach and everything under it. Those who knew it, passed it on to those who didn't. When the trio approached they were to move. The law was by no means carved in stone, because Bubble ignored it and refused to move. In timem they had learned to take a large detour around her blanket. A person would have to have their porch light out to tangle with Bubbles when she was sunning herself.

The early hunt had not gone well and Jake decidedto take a chance. He swung the detector close to her blanket. Sucess! Jake marked the spot. Pal barked as he dug and Pepi sifted through the flying sand to come up with a metal toy truck.

He held it up to show Bubbles. "Close, but no banana," he said to her.

"Move on, Pepi," she growled. "You're in my sun."

The procession worked its way toward the boathouse. They had retrieved a half-dozen items, an average hunt. As they approached Ronnie Greenberg, it became obvious he had no intention of moving. They chose to ignore him, and he them; they approached the blanket as though he wasn't on it. Jake marked the spot with his heel three feet from the blanket and Pal, sensing that the hunt was almost over, dug with renewed fervour. The sand flew and struck Ronnie Greenberg.

Disgusted, Ronnie brushed the sand off his legs and shook as much as he could from the blanket. It only took a few seconds for him to snatch the shovel from Pepi, raise it high above his head and bring it crashing dowm full-force on Pal's skull. He threw the shovel far into Limberlost and screamed maniacally at Pepi and Jake: "Take the fucking dog and get off my property. I don't want either of you around here again!" Before they could react, he was across the foot-bridge and into the Greenberg house.

At the crest of the lawn, Mike blinked, not believing that the joyful play he had been watching could so quickly turn to tragedy. By the time he started down to the beach, he met Jake coming up — walking slowly, staring straight ahead like a zombie — with pal in his arms.

"Doc Rogers can fix 'im."

Mike looked at the dog, laying limply in his master's arms. He told Jake, who walked past him as though he didn't hear, that Pal was dead.

Before him, Mike could see that Pepi already had things under control on the beach. He noticed that Bubbles had not moved from her blanket during the excitement and that the commotion had brought Linda to the top of the stairs.

In the background, beyond all the noise and confusion, Mike heard the twang of the Greenberg screen door and the three receeding slaps as it closed. Across the ravine, he saw Ronnie standing on the front porch steps, striking a Napoleanic pose -- no doubt surveying the condition of his kingdom, gloating over the havoc he had wrought.

Part 3

ARIEL

I

Though there are times when we wish our bodies could move with the speed of thought, it is doubtful that we would have an advantage; we would probably make more mistakes in a shorter period of time. Immediately after the beach disaster, Mike had a multiple-choice decision — go to the Greenberg house, go down to the beach, go to Linda, go after Jake. Why couldn't he be like Pepi Riveras? Decide what needed to be done and do it?

He opted to go after Jake, but there was no trace of him; he drove Sidney Road a dozen times, parked at the garage and waited in vain. No Jake.

Linda was at her desk when he returned to Serendipity. Though she didn't speak, he detected a demeanour that seemed not to belong to her, as though, with a chameleon sense of self-preservation, steady Linda had finally realized the sinister forces that pervaded the lodge. She could deal with Toni Warden; Pal, she couldn't.

It was late afternoon before he heard from Sam. Without warning, clouds had rolled in over the hills of Limberlost, dumping steady rain on Serendipity. Mike was sequestered in his apartment, watching guests and workers scurry about to keep from getting wet, when the phone rang. Sam's stern, officious voice told him to come to the house with Linda.

A strong wind had risen by the time they reached the footbridge; it whipped the treetops to a frenzy and pelted rain at their faces, causing Linda to seek shelter from it by cuddling close on Mike's leeward side. "We're in for it," he remarked. "Sam sounded pretty angry on the phone." When she didn't respond, Mike wanted to know why her disposition had changed so suddenly. It was nothing, she said; she thought her period might be early.

God, there were a thousand places they would rather have been than on the Greenberg porch, waiting to catch hell from Anna and Sam because their pampered, precious Ronnie had been upset. Anna came to the door, showed them in, cleared the furniture of books and magazines so they could sit down, then took to her rocker. Sam didn't greet them; he sat in his corner chair and scowled. Ronnie was there too, with his saddest beagle eyes and head low. Linda took a chair close to the fireplace, to warm her hands and feet.

"Excuse me," Sam said, leaving the room. A difficult silence followed until he returned with a small suitcase. "We have all had a long day," he said, laying the suitcase on the coffee table. "I am sure it has been just as long for Jake. But we are going to resolve this matter here and now. Today! Not tomorrow or the next day." He looked menacingly at Ronnie. "Now!" Sam opened the suitcase, then turned toward Linda and Mike. "I understand that my son has been renting rooms at Serendipity without your knowledge."

Mike nodded.

"Then this belongs to you." He extracted a roll of bills and laid it on the table. "Obviously there is more than that owing. We will get to that later."

Mike wanted to look at Ronnie, but he couldn't.

Anna rocked.

"And would you please return these items to the tuck shop?" Sam removed some magazines and sundries from the case. "It seems that Ronnie has been helping himself." His voice quivered. "And there is this item. I think we know where it came from." He held up a diamond ring. "And this," he said disgustedly, producing the missing watch. Sam held up a clear plastic bag containing a pair of scissors and some clippings. "I presume you will know the significance of this. I don't."

Linda let out a cry of astonishment, then quickly put her hand to her mouth to cover the rest of her emotion. She was sitting in the same room with a person who had threatened to kill her.

"That's enough for now," Sam said to no one in particular.

"No!" Anna interrupted. "It is not enough! All of it!"

"Well... there are certain feminine items here, of a very personal nature. Perhaps you know where they came from. You may as well take the case with you and sort it all out," he said, replacing the items.

"There is more," Anna said and both Mike and Linda wished she would shut up. Neither of them could take any more.

"What do you mean?" asked Sam.

"Perhaps Michael has a few more questions for Ronnie."

"Go ahead then," he said to Mike. Then he ordered his son to stand.

Ronnie didn't move.

"Stand up!" Sam screamed at him and Ronnie slowly got to his feet.

"Papa!" Anna was annoyed. "Calm yourself! Your heart!"

"Maybe we should just forget it," Mike offered.

"Ask!" Sam ordered.

Mike gathered his thoughts. "The fire. It wasn't Jake, was it?" Ronnie shook his head. "You put a lit cigarette in the mattress and it was you who called the fire inspector the next morning." Yes, it was him. "The messy rooms?" Yes. "The late-night disturbances around the cabins?" Yes. "The boathouse?" Yes.

"Just one last question, then. Someone slipped a note under my door one night telling me to go to 215 Chestnut. Was that you?"

Ronnie sat motionless and remained silent, but they could see that it was.

"Answer!" Sam insisted.

"Calm down," repeated Anna quietly.

"Never mind my heart!" he glared at Ronnie. "Answer!"

"Yes," Ronnie murmured.

"Why?" Sam asked, shouting and shaking with rage. "Why have you done all this?"

"Please don't," Linda offered, seeing that Sam had worked himself into a lather, not really wanting to hear the answer, thinking that it was a family matter now, better discussed privately. "It's done as far as Mike and I are concerned. Let's try to forget it."

"I won't forget it!" There were tears on Sam's cheeks. The fire made them gleam. "Not this time." He walked over to Ronnie. "Why?"

"I want what's mine. You had no right to sell out to him," Ronnie answered, pointing to Mike.

"So you would lie and steal and cheat and even *kill* to get what you want!" Sam wept openly. He raised his hand and struck his son flush on the face with all the force his weary body could muster. Ronnie reeled from the blow, but maintained his balance and stared back at his father defiantly. "My son! Where have you been these past few years?"

"Running... hiding."

"To what part of God could you run, where in him could you hide that I couldn't reach you? Running from what? Hiding from what?"

"From Fran."

"Fran is dead!"

"No! She'll never be dead." Ronnie pointed to her landscape. "Never!"

The painting moved on the wall — just an inch or two because that width of clean paint was showing at the left side of the frame. At that point in time, an inch was as convincing as a mile.

"Ariel is here," Anna told them, not alarmed. "Ariel is in this room."

Sam Greenberg fixed upon his son's eyes for a moment. Riveted, Ronnie could not look away. Then, without warning, Sam turned and went quickly to the fireplace. He snatched Fran's painting from the wall, leaned it against the fireplace bricks, put his foot through the canvas and with diminishing strength, twisted the frame to a more manageable size and stuffed the entire tangled mess into the fire.

Mike made a half-hearted motion to stop him, but Anna raised her hand; he was also aware of Linda's hand on his arm, lightly restraining him.

"Fran is dead!" Sam spoke those words with such emotion that he startled himself, as though he, for the first time, was finally convinced of it. Sinking into a chair, he took a handkerchief from his pocket and sobbed into it. "She's dead," he admitted.

For the moment, the room had grown uncomfortably warm; the oils were burning hard and bright with a rainbow of colours — Fran's final gift to the physical world.

There was a lingering odour in the air, like the smell of an over-heated furnace. Ronnie went to his father and bent over the broken man.

"Papa... I'm sorry. I'm really sorry. Something inside me... I... it's gone now..."

He kissed Sam's forehead, then apologized directly to Mike and Linda. Turning back to his parents, he told them he would see Jake first thing in the morning. "I love you both."

Then he ran from the room.

Though devastated and weak from the ordeal, it didn't take Sam long to regain his composure. If any one of them was visibly distraught, it was Anna. She had stopped rocking and sat rigid, as though strapped into an electric chair, awaiting execution.

"Jake must be suffering, poor man," Sam said sadly.

Mike went to the window. The late afternoon, what was left of it, was dull and miserable and more depressing than before. Through the blowing rain, he could see Ronnie's distorted figure on the beach, throwing pebbles at the wind-puffed waves of Limberlost. Sam's droning voice was barely discernable. "Ronnie will work for you without wages to make restitution," he was saying. Mike had to decline, explaining that even if Ronnie had changed, he couldn't have him back at Serendipity after all that had happened.

"I understand, my friend. Then he will have to find a job elsewhere and work to repay you."

Mike returned to Linda and she took his hand. "That isn't necessary," she said. "The lodge will be closed soon and we'll be gone. It is best forgotten."

"I insist!"

"Very well," Mike conceded. "It's between you and Ronnie. I think he's going to be all right."

"He'll be fine now," Sam agreed.

"We have lost Ronnie," Anna said, trembling from head to toe, as though someone had thrown the switch to her electric chair. "He has gone."

"No," Sam argued. "He's just—"

From outside came a loud, sharp crack — like a tree splitting or the sound of heavy ice breaking on Limberlost in winter. Simultaneously, Sam's mouth opened wide and he gasped for breath when the pain gripped his chest. Anna was at his side immediately, but he straightened himself, pushed her back, insisting that he was all right and was out of the house and down the porch steps before the others had time to react.

"What was that noise?" Linda asked.

"I don't know. It sounded like it came from the beach."

"It was a gunshot," Anna told them.

Linda looked at Mike in horror. "Oh my God!"

They covered Anna's shoulders with a shawl and took their time helping her down the slippery lawn. At the middle terrace, they could see Sam sitting on the beach, holding Ronnie in his arms, rocking back and forth with him, like he would cradle a doll — a drenched, sand-covered, bleeding, dead doll.

By the time they reached the beach, Pepi Riveras had joined them. "Take Linda to the office," Mike asked him. "Get the police and an ambulance. Tell them there's been a murder."

"Murder?" Linda questioned.

"It isn't suicide. There's no gun."

"We didn't have a chance to talk," Sam moaned. "Not like I wanted." There were no tears. He just rocked, as if mesmerized, then took the body in his arms and tried to stand. Anna and Mike helped him to his feet and he carried Ronnie through the driving rain to the top of the lawn.

Sam was exhausted when he reached the top. He dropped to his knees, holding his lifeless son close to him. When Mike finally took the weight from him and laid it on the spongy grass, it was like removing a magnet. "My God, forgive me for doubting," he said.

There… genuflect. His glasses gone, the rain gleaming in the dusk on his bald head, at the altar of his dead son, Sam Greenberg ran and leapt as far as his creator would allow — far enough to be free of Anna's gremlins once and for all.

Maybe it was his imagination, but Mike thought he saw Ronnie move; he thought he saw a flash of light above the trees, heading in the direction of Thunder Falls.

"Come," Anna said to him. "It is done."

Mike thought they should stay until help arrived.

"Papa doesn't need our help. Come... leave them alone until the ambulance comes. They walked away together, Anna holding onto his hand. They stopped at the footbridge to look back. Sam was still on his knees. A cluster of guests had assembled under umbrellas in front of Maple House. They held their distance, content to murmur and mill about and begin the diverse rumours that would inevitably sweep Serendipity.

"Ariel has gone," Anna said. "My lifelong companion has left me for good."

Together, they went to the house to wait for the ambulance, Anna still holding tightly to his hand. If she grieved the loss of her son as much as the loss of Ariel, she didn't let on.

II

Without public gesture of remembrance, the Greenbergs had Ronnie cremated in Toronto, then put him away quietly. That was what they had done when Fran died and, it was stipulated in their will that they wished the same fate for themselves. Sam had stayed in Toronto to attend to business matters; Anna had returned home alone and closeted herself in the Greenberg house. Though Linda visited her regularly, it was almost a week after her homecoming that Mike found the time to knock on her door.

Anna greeted him with a gentle smile, a pot of coffee and a plate of peanut butter cookies. As they settled in the living room, Mike noticed that Fran's missing landscape had left a clean rectangle on the wall above the fireplace, outlined by the dingier paint around it. It was uncharacteristic of Anna to have left it.

"Ariel is gone. Fran is gone. Ronnie is gone," she mused from her rocker. "This house was not built to be empty. Papa called today. His business in Toronto will keep him there at least another week."

"Are you okay?"

"I'm fine." Her voice was stronger, reassuring. "Linda has been a great comfort to me."

"Would it help if you stayed at the lodge with us until Sam gets back?"

"No, thank you." She changed the subject abruptly. "Have you heard anything about Jake?"

"I'm afraid not. He's still missing. The police are convinced he fired the shot. They were here every day, asking the same questions, while you were away."

"This has harmed your business."

"A little. What does it matter? Serendipity will be closed in a few days. Gem-Star will foreclose. I'm surprised I haven't heard from them. They must be waiting until after Labour Day — a humanitarian gesture."

Anna offered more cookies, but he declined, explaining that he couldn't stay long. He just *had* to talk to her.

"About the speed of the deer?"

Yes, about that... and everything else that had happened. "There are so many questions."

"For instance?"

"Anna... you knew about Ronnie, didn't you? The things he was doing."

"In a general sense. Not everything."

"Why didn't you say something to me?"

"To what end?"

"I could have put a stop to it! This terrible tragedy would have been avoided."

"We would have lost Papa. He comes first."

Mike understood that, though he had to think about it. She must have known that there was no saving Ronnie. "You know, in the beginning, when I got up early to sit by the lake, when I stood at the shuffleboard courts to grasp an overall concept of Serendipity, I used to speculate about who of us would survive this first season unscathed. I concluded that Jake was about the only one who might make it. I was sure wrong there. *You* seem to be the only one who has survived unchanged."

Hardly a compliment, she thought, though she kept it to herself — to have purposely avoided change, to have been given knowledge and not act upon it. One pays a price for that!

"I was wondering," he said sheepishly, "if you know what Jake was doing at the lodge in the middle of the night. That's one question that hasn't been answered." If Anna didn't know, it probably would stay a mystery.

He forgot, Ariel had left her. No longer could she divine affairs of men. Without her guide, she was as mundane as he.

"Exactly what happened that day?" Mike asked, trying to appear nonchalant about it, in case Anna didn't wish to answer.

She knew exactly what had happened and was anxious to discuss it.

"You will recall when we talked of this before, how I told you that it helps to think of existence in terms of electricity. Just like the image of a lightbulb stays with us after it has been turned out, so the spirits of organisms linger after death — some good, some bad, some ephemeral, some strong enough, like Ariel, to stay with a human for a lifetime. The kind of spirits that we attract and hold are determined by our thoughts and attitudes, so that if we would be a particular kind of person, we must entice those particular kinds of spirits.

"They are easy to seduce, for they are self-serving; they need us to give them identity here on earth — like electricity needs a conductor. I was Ariel's conductor and conduit to the earth. When I wore out, Ariel left."

"Where?"

"I don't know. Where does electricity go when it has no conductor?"

"What happened in this room, the day Ronnie was shot?"

"Fran's landscape was the key, of course. When it was destroyed, her spirit was freed to make its way back to earth elsewhere. No doubt, what is left of Fran is already attached to a struggling artist somewhere on this planet. Ronnie's death freed Ariel; my lifelong companion wanted no truck with an aging recluse. Papa believes, when Ronnie was shot, that he actually felt the bullet entering his chest. That is why he doubled over when we heard the gunshot. I think he simply suffered a mild heart attack, but I would never tell him so. But then that's us, isn't it? He's forever questioning God's recipe, while I'm milling about in the stew. Whatever happened, he has changed. He is out of the stew. You can judge for yourself when you see him."

"Are you saying that he is no longer bothered by spirits?"

"Precisely! He is beyond their influence."

"So the only threads biding him to your world were the spiritual influences of his children. Once they were broken, he was free to leap clear."

Anna smiled at that... and smiled again when Mike said there must be a lesson for him in it all. There was, she assured him: to remember that all of the nonsense that goes on in our world is but a tempest in a teapot, that it is us stewing in our own juice. If we do not spring free of it, we are doomed to a narcissistic search for physical identity, doomed to an interminable attachment to one ridiculous human after another.

III

Any skepticism about the change in Sam Greenberg was dispelled immediately when Mike opened his apartment door. In the 10 days he had been in Toronto, Sam's triple chin had shrunk to a double; there was a healthy glow to his skin; his eyes gleamed and his smile was radiant.

"Fifteen pounds and falling," he said proudly, showing Mike the space between his belly and his belt. "Anna's taking in my clothes already!"

"Fantastic!"

"My friend, I suppose you have been busy making preparations to close Serendipity this weekend."

Mike shrugged. "I still haven't heard a peep out of Gem-Star. Maxwell Taylor must be up to something."

"Probably."

"It has been hard on Linda, knowing we've lost Serendipity, waiting at the jaws of the guillotine. She loves this place more than I do."

Sam wondered where she was.

"Calling bingo. The entertainment didn't show. We're having a bingo night instead."

Would he phone the bingo hall and ask her to join them? "I would like to see the two of you together before you leave."

Mike complied. "We feel guilty," he confessed, "complaining about our lot, when we realize what you and Anna have been through."

"Don't worry about us. We're fine."

"I've missed you, Sam."

"You've been at the bottle again," Sam joked, remembering Mike's whiskey-inspired sentimentality, the night of his birthday. "Anna tells me Jake's still missing."

"Not a trace."

"Thank you for dealing with the police. I'll get in touch with them tomorrow. I'm pleased they left Anna alone while I was away."

Mike mentioned his evening with her, over coffee and peanut butter cookies. How she had answered some of his questions that evening and left as many in his brain. With all the problems he would have to face in the coming days, "the speed of the deer" was the most important. Since Anna was convinced her husband had experienced it, was living proof of proper thought...

maybe, while they were waiting for Linda, he would elaborate.

Feigning helplessness, Sam held up his hands. "So many things have happened so quickly that I may disappoint you. I mean, I don't understand a lot of it myself. We may be a bit too close for either of us to recognize the significance of what has taken place. I can only tell you that the moment Ronnie was shot, I felt his pain; I felt the bullet entering his chest. Here!" Sam put his had over his heart. "Anna probably thinks it was a heart attack, though she would never tell me so. But it wasn't. I went to my doctor in Toronto — just to be sure. I knew it wasn't my heart; it was real and it was physical, the way it should be — if my reasoning about the nature of God is correct — when our understanding is stripped of diversions."

"Of emotion, you mean... and intuition?"

"On the contrary! They are a real and integral part of our functioning; but stripped of diversions, emoting or intuiting or reasoning is like eating fruit fresh from the tree, like drinking clear water from the stream above Thunder Falls."

When the triangle turned, it didn't hurt as much this time.

"We must recognize that we are part of the body of God; what part doesn't matter. If we are a toe, we should be at peace with that, for a toe we will always be. And I can only guess that the very last thing God wants to be concerned about is a toe."

Linda came, cutting off the conversation. Mike had intended to have Sam apply his philosophy to the speed of a deer, since Anna insisted that he was living proof of it. It would have to wait. Maybe he could figure it out on his own. The Masters — Berkeley, Whitehead, Wordsworth — had been around again lately; maybe they would help.

The two greeted each other with an affectionate hug, exchanging compliments about their appearance. "You look wonderful," Linda said.

"You ain't seen nothin' yet!" Sam bragged.

Sam didn't sit after that. He paced slowly at the window, with his hands behind his back. He had definitely lost weight; his stomach didn't protrude as far as usual when he struck that familiar pose. "I hope you will humour me," he began. "There are several things that I must tell you. First, I have convinced Anna that we should take a long vacation. It isn't good for us to stay in that big, empty house. We intend to leave next week to see the world and we won't be back until next spring."

"Good for you!" Linda said.

"Anna has found someone to live in the house until we get back. My main concern is Serendipity. I would like to know that the lodge is properly taken care of while we're away."

They exchanged puzzled glances at that. What did Sam Greenberg care about Serendipity? A year ago, he was prepared to let it rot. "I'm just going to walk away," Mike said, recovering. "I've lost my investment... including my personal savings. I can't see the sense in paying a caretaker to leave it in good shape for Maxwell Taylor. I'm sorry Sam. I know how much the lodge meant to you, but... "

"You would walk away from your dream?"

"We have no choice," Linda interjected. "Both of us have gained so much by being here, but now we have to get on with the rest of our lives. It's like being tied to a train track, listening to the train approach. You may wish that it won't come, but it does anyway. Gem-Star cometh!"

"Maybe on another track."

"No... it's only a matter of time," Mike said.

Greenberg took a document from his jacket pocket and laid it on the coffee table in front of them.

"Read this." Mike and Linda leaned forward. "Never mind." He returned to the window, staring out to Limberlost, with his back to them as he spoke. "I'll tell you what they say: they say that I, Samuel Greenberg, have purchased the existing mortgage on Serendipity Lodge from Gem-Star Mortgages; they say that Michael Kramer is released totally from his obligations to Gem-Star and that he will henceforth deal solely with me regarding such matters; they say that the mortgage payments are to begin next July and that the mortgagee and the mortgagor covenant for quiet enjoyment, which means the lodge is to be kept in good repair." He sneaked a look at the couple, holding hands, leaning over the papers, incredulously pretending to read. "You've hardly heard a word, have you? No matter. I'll leave the documents and you can return them signed in the morning."

Linda went to Sam and hugged him and told him that he was a wonderful man, a compliment he accepted without comment. Mike remained seated. "Why? How did you manage to... "

"Not many outsmart me when it comes to money. Jake perhaps. Maxwell Taylor, Peter Cohen and I are not exactly strangers. I knew that Trigger was thinking about politics and that he needed Cohen behind him if he was to get very far. I am not without acquaintances in political circles either, my friend. Taylor's enemies would think they had died and gone to heaven if word reached them that he and Cohen had conspired to destroy a struggling romantic like yourself. Imagine! It didn't take long to convince Mr. Taylor he was better off explaining to Cohen how he bungled this deal than how he had ruined his political campaign before it started."

"What deal?"

"You don't realize exactly what you're sitting on, do you? Property values are going crazy. The value of Serendipity has increased considerably, even since you bought it. Did you know that Peter Cohen had plans for a huge development there? No, I guess not. He has been after me to sell for years. He would love to take a dozer to this place and push it all into the lake. I would say you're sitting on a gold mine, my friend. Sometime in the future, Cohen is going to have to deal with you. I would be very disappointed if you were anything but difficult."

"You knew this before you sold the lodge to me. Yet you sold below market value."

"Don't be concerned about *my* welfare. Remember, I own a hundred acres here, including most of the shoreline between Serendipity and Sidney. The fact is, I have *you* surrounded. Sooner or later, Cohen is going to have to deal with me, too."

"What about my speech?"

"Speech?"

"To the staff. This weekend. I have it all written. My Serendipity-is-closing-for-good speech."

"Change it," Linda interjected, "to see-you-next-year." She was ecstatic.

On the way back from walking Sam home, Mike and Linda held hands to steady themselves against the late summer wind. They stopped walking at the shuffleboard courts; something about that spot was good for thinking. They looked out to Limberlost, couldn't see, but listened to the stupid loons. A peace settled on them, gently as the dew showed their footprints in the evening grass.

"I've missed the summer," Mike lamented. "I can tell you anything you want about the spring here, but I've missed the summer."

There would be other summers, she promised.

"There were so many problems that I lost the summer."

Since he was talking to himself, she didn't reply. And when he asked her to marry him, she simply squeezed his hand and told him that she would. "Where do we go from here?" Linda wondered, ever the realist.

"Back to Toronto," he answered half-heartedly.

"What are you going to do about Jack Kirkpatrick? You know I've always been afraid of him."

"Don't worry about Kirk. I have him exactly where I want him. I'm taking my cars off the King Street lot. I'm going to operate on my own."

"You can't! You have a signed agreement. He'll ruin you if you give him the chance."

"Kirk needs three more cars to swing a deal. I'm going to sell them in exchange for his release. I'd sooner operate on my own with 12 than keep 15 for spite and fight with him. We'll use some of the money to buy a house and the rest can go into Serendipity."

"You'll need help."

"Tesky's a good man. I'm going to give him a chance."

"I can help too… until the children come."

He was hoping that she would.

IV

To Bubbles' delight, the weather turned dry and hot throughout the hectic weekend; to Mike's delight, since Serendipity was filled with guests and overflowing. Linda packed her things and moved into his apartment to accommodate a stranded couple, and stayed there until they returned to Toronto.

The last of the guests hung on until Tuesday noon. Certain of the staff had pre-arranged to leave early, while some — like Olga Olefson and the kitchen foreman — agreed to stay a few days and help close the lodge.

As usual, Ray Mildenhall rang for his breakfast Tuesday afternoon at two. When he discovered there was no room service, he took Bubbles from the beach and left.

Pepi Riveras and The Latin Lovers weren't far behind. They were scheduled to work a Detroit lounge Thursday night. Still, Pepi found a quiet moment to chat with Mike before he left.

"Well boss, we made it!"

"Thanks to you, Pepi. You're a great guy."

"See you next year."

"For sure."

"I was wondering, boss. I still got Jake's metal detector. What should I do with it?"

"Keep it."

"Think so? What do you figger Jake's doin' now? Right now."

"He's on a beach in Hawaii. He's bought himself another metal detector and he's making a fortune."

"Hope so. I was wondering, boss. Think I could have the metal detector rights to your beach next year?"

"No problem. As long as you fill in the holes. I don't want the beach looking like gopher heaven."

Pepi had seemed relieved after that.

The Greenbergs left Wednesday. There hadn't been time to talk with either of them. So much to do. They went like honeymooners — joy in their going, madness in their wake. It would be six months before Mike and Linda saw them again, though they promised to phone and write when they could. Six months! An eternity to be deprived of their special friendship. Six months to sort through the orts of Serendipity.

Shortly after their departure, Sgt. Walker arrived unannounced, apologizing that he had tried to phone.

"The phones were disconnected yesterday," Mike explained, giving him a Toronto number. "Or, you can reach me through the Greenberg house."

The sergeant looked splendid in full uniform, his movements punctuated by the jingle of buttons, bars and chains, by the creaking of new leather as he followed Mike into the inner office. "I hope my people haven't been too much bother. We try to stay out of the way as much as possible."

"Not at all. They've been very considerate."

"I want to bring you up to date on our investigation before you leave. First, I should tell you that the file has been closed on Mrs. Amanna. Suicide... plain and simple."

He should have felt at least a twinge of pain.

Sgt. Walker continued: "As for Jake, we're convinced he shot Ronnie Greenberg. We found an area behind his garage where he used to shoot at tin cans. The bullets retrieved there match the one taken from the body. The rifle itself still hasn't been found. It's probably at the bottom of the lake. We're working on the assumption that Jake hasn't gone far. He has lived here most of his life and he owns considerable property, so it is unlikely, given his possessive nature, that he has gone very far. But he knows every inch of the forest around Sidney. Unless we get lucky, he could hide out indefinitely."

Mike wondered what would happen to Jake's garage, to his property.

"We're boarding it up until he is found or until the case is closed, whichever comes first."

Shit! There went the last decent place to eat in Sidney!

"We managed to find a relative... an older brother in Owen Sound. He wasn't too enthused about it, but he's going to look after things for Jake if he can't be found soon. I gather the two had differences."

"Jake has a friend — Doc Rogers — who lives on his property. Maybe he's hiding out there."

"Well sir, we've resolved that, too. I put some men in the bush to look for the rifle. They found an old cabin instead and we thought Jake would be in there for sure. I decided to take him by surprise. As one of the first through the door, I can tell you honestly that I was the one taken by surprise." The sergeant grew more uncomfortable as his story unfolded. He tugged at the knot in his tie and lost some of his colour. "There was a table in the centre of the room, with a skeleton sitting on it. Jake's mongrel was at the skeleton's feet. There was no sign of Jake. We kept an eye on the place for a few days, but he's too smart for that. He's in the bush somewhere, I'll bet a month's wages."

"Doc Rogers?"

"The skeleton was that of Walter Rogers, a long-time friend of Jake's. There was no foul play. It appeared that Mr. Rogers died of natural causes and Jake refused to admit it. He might try to get back there eventually. It seems that Rogers and the dog were the only two meaningful things in Jake's life."

"Are you going to continue searching?"

"I've called in my men. I need them for other work." He hesitated, wondering whether or not to continue. "Funny thing, though... I spoke with the Greenbergs before they left and neither of them seemed overly concerned about finding Jake. They apparently feel that his loss has been as tragic as theirs. They didn't come right out and tell me, but unless some new information surfaces, I'm not going to look too hard."

Mike was glad of that — not openly, but silently within himself, he was glad of that.

It was Thursday morning — after the last sheet, blanket and pillow case was laundered, packed and stored — before Mike and Linda could get over to the Greenberg house. They were anxious to meet the person who was staying there until the Greenbergs returned.

When they reached the porch, Mrs. Cohen opened the door. "Come in, come in," she said. "You look like you've seen a ghost."

"We thought you were gone," Linda said, trying to recover.

"It was a short trip from my cabin to this house. I'm the person who will be staying here until Sam and Anna get back."

"I… we've made arrangements with Shirley Boychuk and her husband to caretake the lodge this winter. We wondered if you would mind keeping an eye on things. If there is any trouble, just contact them." Mike noticed that the outline from Fran's picture was still there.

He wrote names and numbers on a piece of paper and handed it to Ruth Cohen.

"Are you joking?" she laughed. "With my nose! Nothing will happen that I won't know about! And the whole village too!"

They chatted briefly about certain details that Mrs. Cohen would have to know. Mike gave her keys that she might need. Their conversation laboured, like there was an extra weight that slowed, held it down.

"You want to know why I'm staying here, don't you?" Ruth Cohen asked finally.

"Only if you care to tell us," Linda said.

"I have to tell you, whether I care to or not. I think you can be trusted. Sam and Anna said you could." Mrs. Cohen's mood became sombre, distressed. "It concerns Jake," she said. "He told me that you were suspicious of him being at the lodge late at night. He worried that you were blaming him for some of the things that were happening."

Mike and Linda waited, without speaking.

"Jake was at Serendipity late at night because he was coming to see me. He was with me in my cabin."

"While Pal waited at the garbage cans."

Mrs. Cohen nodded. "I'm staying at this house because, sooner or later, I know that Jake will need me." She took a tissue and dabbed at her eyes with it. "He has to have a place to come — someone, somewhere. Someone who cares. I can't bear to think of him out there all alone."

Mrs. Cohen broke down. Linda brought her a glass of water. After she was calm, Mike asked: "What will you do if Jake does come here?"

"Keep him here with me until the spring. The authorities will never look for him here."

"And in the spring?"

"Run. Go away. Disappear. I've considered all my options, made all my decisions. Jake may be bow-legged and unkempt, he may have no teeth and murder the Queen's English, but I wouldn't trade him for a truckload of Peter Cohens. When he comes to me, he is the most beautiful man..." Her cheeks flushed when she realized her candor and she didn't finish, withdrawing into the protective shell she had grown during the years with her husband.

When it came right down to it, Mike admired her integrity, though he had some difficulty picturing her in bed with Jake. "Sam and Anna are aware of everything you've told us?" he said rhetorically.

"They are," she answered, implying that her plans for Jake had their blessing.

A kosher couple, those Greenbergs.

"Good luck to you, Ruth." Mike said sincerely, taking Linda's hand and leading her to the door.

Ruth Cohen followed them to the porch, kissed them both and waved them off, then hurried back into the house — the screen door popping and pinging and slapping three times behind her.

To wait for Jake.

Crossing the footbridge one last time, dallying to hear the water-cahtter on the rocks in the ravine, cabins shuttered and bolted, the boathouse boarded and padlocked, the empty beach... they stopped at the shuffleboard courts for a final look at Limberlost.

Time to go. Everything packed. All details arranged. Time.

"We'll be back once a month or so," he promised Linda, to salve his own pain. "You know, I once asked Jake what he thought about the beauty that speed adds to the deer and he replied: 'Only when it's running.' The proper answers are so simple. We all know them. I came to Serendipity searching for the quality that lends beauty to human life. With Anna's help... and Sam's... and the Masters... I believe I've found it. Anna taught me that the human equivalent of the deer's speed is proper thought in the midst of spiritual turmoil — from Winnie-the-Pooh to the Bible, from the horrific to the beautiful, from birth to death, from Sunday School to Seventh Heaven, from King Street to Serendipity. She taught me that all diversions are intended to slow us down so that we, as conductors, give earthbound spirits easy access to physical existence; that our earthly activity is like a hot rock to God — a cauldron inside, a hard and smooth untouchable curiosity outside. I have thought that since Serendipity must appear to be a hot rock to most. If Anna showed me the speed, Sam showed me the leap that speed allows: that instead of praying and snivelling for God to come to us, we must go to him; that the human predicament is that we say 'God' — even the most religious of us — without having the foggiest notion of God's nature — God is Love, God is the Creator and Prime Mover, God is the Father and Son and Holy Ghost (Ghost? God forbid!). We cannot approach the jump unless we understand that physical harmony is essential to God's proper thought — that a toe is a toe is a toe. And if we will not acquiesce to be one, we will simmer in a gangrene stew. The zoo is portable. And the Masters are with me to show me the true nature of my God, to poke me in the ass and time me as I run. Run with me Linda McDermott! Not through bank accounts and taxicabs and houses and children and lodges… run with me to… Linda?"

Apparently, she hadn't been listening. Or perhaps he hadn't been speaking, just thinking. He put his arm around her shoulder to take her to the car, but she gently pushed him away.

"Go on ahead," she told him. "I'll join you in a minute. Ariel has asked me to linger."

"Ariel!" Mike grumbled, repacking the last of the luggage and locking the trunk. "Why me?"

Standing by the car, waiting for Linda in the autumn stillness, he heard the loons calling on the lake, gossiping of the harlequin Muskoka show that would set the rim of Limberlost ablaze.

"Stupid loons," he mumbled, getting into the car. A fat porcupine, back from the fishing camps, rolled out from under the kitchen steps, sniffed at the empty garbage cans and rolled back again.

Mike waited ten minutes. Then he honked the horn.

THE

END